Friedrich Glauser was born i̶... referred to as the Swiss Sime... ...ged forty-two, a few days before he was due to be married. Diagnosed a schizophrenic, addicted to morphine and opium, he spent much of his life in psychiatric wards, insane asylums and, when he was arrested for forging prescriptions, in prison. He also spent two years with the Foreign Legion in North Africa, after which he worked as a coal miner and a hospital orderly. His Sergeant Studer crime novels have ensured his place as a cult figure in Europe.

Germany's most prestigious crime fiction award is called the Glauser prize.

Other Bitter Lemon books featuring Sergeant Studer

Thumbprint
In Matto's Realm

FEVER

Friedrich Glauser

Translated from the German
by Mike Mitchell

BITTER LEMON PRESS
LONDON

BITTER LEMON PRESS

First published in the United Kingdom in 2006 by
Bitter Lemon Press, 37 Arundel Gardens, London W11 2LW

www.bitterlemonpress.com

Originally published in German as *Die Fieberkurve*
in serial form in *Zürcher Illustrierte* in 1937

First published in book form in German as *Die Fieberkurve*
by Limmat Verlag, Zurich, 1996

This edition has been translated with the financial assistance of
Pro Helvetia, the Arts Council of Switzerland

German-language edition © Limmat Verlag, 1996
English translation © Mike Mitchell, 2006

A CIP record for this book is available from the British Library

ISBN 1–904738–14–1

Typeset by RefineCatch Limited, Broad Street, Bungay, Suffolk
Printed and bound by
Bookmarque, Croydon

The story of the clairvoyant corporal

"Read that," said Studer, thrusting a telegram under his friend Madelin's nose. It was dark outside the Palais de Justice, the Seine gurgled as it lapped against the *quai* and the nearest street-lamp was a few yards away.

"greetings from young jakobli to old jakob hedy." The commissaire read out the words haltingly once he was under the flickering gaslight. Although Madelin had been attached to the Sûreté in Strasbourg some years before, and therefore was not entirely ignorant of German, he still had difficulty working out what the message meant.

"What's this all about, Studère?" he asked.

"I've become a grandfather," Studer replied morosely. "My daughter's had a little boy."

"That calls for a celebration!" Madelin declared. "As it happens it fits in rather well. A man came to see me today. He's leaving tonight for Switzerland, on the half-past-ten train, and he's asked me to recommend him to a colleague there. I'm meeting him at nine in a little bistro by Les Halles. Just now it's –" keeping his woollen gloves on, Madelin unbuttoned his overcoat, its collar raised in a protective curve round his neck, and took an old silver watch out of his waistcoat pocket – "eight o'clock. We've plenty of time," he added in a self-satisfied voice. With the north wind whipping at his unshielded lips, he became philosophical. "When you get old, you always have plenty of time. Strange, isn't it? Don't you find that too, Studère?"

1

Studer muttered something. But then he looked round abruptly as a high-pitched, squeaky voice said, "And I may offer my congratulations too? Yes? To our revered inspector? My heartiest congratulations?"

Madelin, tall, lean, and Studer, equally tall only thickset, with broader shoulders, turned round. Trotting along behind them was a tiny figure. At first it was impossible to say whether it was male or female: its long coat came down to its ankles, its beret was pulled down over its eyebrows and its nose was wrapped in a woollen scarf, leaving only its eyes uncovered, and even they were hidden behind the lenses of a huge pair of horn-rimmed spectacles.

"You be careful you don't catch cold, Godofrey," said Commissaire Madelin. "I'll need you tomorrow. The Koller business is unclear, but I only got the papers this evening. You'll need to examine them tomorrow. There's something not right about Koller's papers . . ."

"Thanks, Godofrey," said Studer, "but it's *me* that's inviting you two. After all, you have to splash out a bit when you've just become a grandfather."

He sighed. Greetings from young Jakobli to old Jakob, he thought. Now you're a grandfather, that means you've lost your daughter for good. Once you're a grandfather, you're old – on the scrap heap. But it had been a stroke of genius to escape from the empty apartment in Bern and the dirty dishes in the sink, even more from the green-tiled stove in the living room that only his wife knew how to light; whenever he tried, the monster just belched out smoke like a badly rolled cigar, then went out. Here in Paris he was safe from such disasters. He was staying with Commissaire Madelin, he was treated with respect, was not addressed as "Sergeant" but as "Inspector". He could spend all day with Godofrey, ensconced in the laboratory at the top of the Palais de Justice, watching the little man analyse dust and X-ray documents. There was a soft hissing from the Bunsen burners, a somewhat louder one from the steam in the radiators, and there was a pleasant smell of chemicals and not of floor polish, as there was in police headquarters in Bern . . .

The marble tables in the bistro were square, with ribbed paper napkins on them. In the middle of the room was a black stove, the top glowing red hot. The large coffee machine on the bar was humming and it was the owner himself – he had arms as fat as a normal person's thighs – who was serving.

They began with oysters, and Commissaire Madelin's favourite pastime. Without asking Studer, he had ordered a 1926 Vouvray, three bottles at once, and he downed one glass after another. In between he quickly slurped three oysters, chewed and swallowed them. Godofrey took little sips, like a shy girl; his hands were small, white, hairless.

Studer was thinking of his wife, who had gone to Frauenfeld to be with their daughter. He was silent and let Godofrey babble on. Madelin was silent as well. Calm and unperturbed, two huge dogs – a skinny Great Dane and a shaggy Newfoundland – ignored the yapping of a tiny fox terrier . . .

The landlord put a brown terrine of tripe on the table. There followed some bitter lettuce, and another three full bottles appeared in front of them; they were suddenly empty, at the same time as the plate with the runny camembert – it stank, but it was good. Then Commissaire Madelin opened his mouth to make a speech. At least that's what it looked like, but nothing

3

came of it, for the door opened and a man entered who was so strangely dressed Studer wondered whether the Parisians had their carnival before the New Year.

The man was wearing a snow-white monk's habit and a cap on his head that looked like a huge red flowerpot made by an incompetent potter. On his feet – they were bare, totally and completely bare – he wore open sandals; his toes and instep were visible, his heel covered.

Studer could hardly believe his eyes. Commissaire Madelin, who ate priests for breakfast, stood up, went to meet the man, brought him back to the table, introduced him – "Father Matthias of the Order of the White Fathers" – and told him Studer's name, adding that this was the inspector of the Swiss criminal investigation department.

A *Père Blanc*? A White Father? The sergeant felt as if he were having one of those strange dreams that sometimes come to us after a serious illness. Light as air and full of delight, they take us back to our childhood, when we lived out fairy tales . . .

For Father Matthias looked exactly like the tailor who killed "seven at one blow" in the fairy tale. His chin was covered in a sparse grey goatee, so sparse you could count each hair of his moustache. And such a skinny face! Just the colour of his eyes, his big grey eyes, reminded you of the sea with clouds passing over it – and sometimes there is a brief flash of sunlight on the surface, which spreads its innocuous veil over unfathomable depths . . .

Three more bottles . . .

Father Matthias was hungry. He polished off one plate of tripe in silence, then a second, did not stint himself when it came to the wine, clinked glasses with the others. He spoke French with a slight accent that reminded Studer of home, and indeed, hardly had the man in the white habit eaten his fill than he said, patting the sergeant on the arm, "I'm a fellow-countryman, from Bern."

"*A bah!*" said Studer. The wine was starting to go to his head.

"But I've been abroad a long time," the tailor went on – tailor! What was he thinking? He was a monk. No, not a monk, a . . . a priest. That was it! A White Father. A father who had no children – or, rather, all people were his children. But he was a grandfather himself. Should he tell his fellow-countryman, this expatriate Swiss? No need, Commissaire Madelin was doing it for him.

"It's a celebration for our inspector. He's just had a telegram from his wife telling him he's a grandfather."

The priest seemed pleased for him. He raised his glass, toasted the sergeant, Studer clinked glasses with him. About time the coffee came. Ah, there it was, and a bottle of rum with it. And Studer, who was starting to feel a bit funny – that Vouvray, not as harmless as it seemed! – heard Madelin tell the landlord to leave the bottle on the table.

Godofrey was sitting next to Studer. Like many short people, he dressed with exaggerated elegance. But that didn't bother the sergeant. On the contrary, he found the presence of the little manikin, who was a walking encyclopedia of criminology, calming and comforting. The White Father was sitting on the other side of the table, beside Madelin.

Finally, Father Matthias had finished eating. He clasped his hands over his plate, his lips moving silently, his eyes closed. Then he opened them, pushed his chair back from the table a little and crossed his

5

right leg over his left, revealing two sinewy, hairy calves under his habit.

"I have to go to Switzerland, Inspector," he said. "I have two sisters-in-law there, one in Basel, the other in Bern. And it's quite possible I may get into difficulties and have to turn to the police for assistance. If that should happen, would you be willing to help me?"

Studer slurped his coffee, silently cursing Madelin, who had fortified the hot drink all too generously with rum. Then he looked up and replied to Father Matthias, also in French.

"The Swiss police does not usually concern itself with family matters. If I'm to help you, I have to know what it's about."

"It's a long story," said the priest, "and one I hardly dare tell. You'll all," he made a circular gesture with his hand, "laugh at me."

Godofrey protested politely in his parrot's voice. He called the priest *mon père*, which for some unknown reason struck Studer as extremely funny. His laugh was concealed by his moustache, and he was still spluttering with laughter as he raised his cup, which had been refilled, to his lips. In order not to give offence he pretended he was blowing on his hot coffee to cool it.

"Have you ever had anything to do with clairvoyance?" Father Matthias asked.

"Cartomancy? Crystal balls? Telepathy? Cryptomnesia?" Godofrey reeled off his litany of questions.

"I see you're well informed. Have you had much to do with that kind of thing?"

Godofrey nodded, Madelin shook his head and Studer muttered a curt, "Con tricks."

Father Matthias ignored him. He was gazing into the distance, though in the little bistro the distance was the bar with its shining coffee percolator. The landlord was sitting behind it, hands clasped over his belly and snoring. The four at the table were his only customers. The bistro didn't start to liven up until around two in the morning, when the first carts with hothouse vegetables arrived.

"I would like to tell you," the White Father said, "the story of a little prophet, a clairvoyant, if you prefer. It's because of that clairvoyant that I'm here, instead of visiting the little forts in the south of Morocco, reading mass for the lost sheep of the Foreign Legion.

"Do you know where Géryville is? Four hours beyond the back of beyond! In Algeria, to be precise, on a plateau 5,000 feet above sea level, as the inscription on a stone in the middle of the barracks square tells you. Ninety miles from the nearest railway station. The air is dry, which is why the Prior sent me there last September, since I've got a weak chest. Géryville's a small town with only a few French living there; most of the population is made up of Arabs and Jews. You don't get anywhere with the Arabs, they don't want to be converted. They do send their children to me – that is, they allow their little ones to come to me . . . There's a battalion of the Foreign Legion up there as well. The legionnaires came to see me sometimes. My predecessor had set up a library, so along they came – corporals, sergeants, now and then a private – and went off with books, or smoked my tobacco. Occasionally, one of my visitors felt the need to confess. Strange things go on in the souls of those men; there are moving conversions of which people who think of the Foreign Legion as the dregs of humanity have no conception.

"Well . . . One evening a corporal came to see me. He was shorter than me, with a face like a crippled child, he looked sad and old. He was called Collani, he said, paused and then started to speak in a feverish

7

rush. It wasn't a regular confession in the sense the Church understands it. More of a monologue, almost as if he were talking to himself. He spoke for quite a long time. There were lots of things he had to get off his chest which have nothing to do with my story. It was evening and the room was filled with a greenish half-light; it comes from the skies they get there in autumn, they often have strange colours . . ."

Studer was resting his cheek on his hand and was so engrossed in Father Matthias's story he didn't notice he had pushed up the skin round his left eye so that it was a slanting slit, like a Chinaman's.

The high plateau! . . . The wide-open spaces! . . . The green twilight! . . . The soldier making his confession!

It was so completely different from what you saw around you every day! The French Foreign Legion! The sergeant remembered he had once been going to enlist, when he was twenty, after an argument with his father. But he hadn't wanted to cause his mother distress, so he'd stayed in Switzerland and made a career for himself, even rising to the rank of chief inspector in the Bern city police, before that business with the bank had cost him his job. Then, too, he'd felt like dropping everything and . . . But he had a wife, a daughter, so he'd given up the idea, swallowed his pride and started at the bottom again, patiently working his way up. But deep inside there still slumbered a yearning for the wide-open spaces, the desert, the battles. And then along came a White Father and awakened it all again.

"So he spoke for quite some time, did Corporal Collani. In his pale green greatcoat he looked like a chameleon in need of a rest-cure. Then he was silent for a while and I was just about to get up and send him back to barracks with a few words of comfort when he suddenly started to speak in a completely different voice, deep and hoarse, as if there were someone else speaking from inside him. And the voice sounded strangely familiar to me:

" 'Why's Mamadou taking the sheet off the bed and hiding it under his coat? Aha, he's going to sell it in the town, the swine. And it's me who's responsible for the linen. Now he's going downstairs, across the barracks square to the railings. Of course, he's too scared to go past the guards. And Bielle's waiting for him at the railings, takes the sheet from him. Where's Bielle off to? Aha! He's going to the Jew in the alley, sells the sheet for a *duro*—' "

"A *duro*," Madelin explained, "is a silver five-franc coin."

"Thank you," said Father Matthias. He was silent for a while as he rummaged in his habit under the table. It must have had a deep pocket somewhere, for he brought out a magnifying glass, a rosary, a wallet woven out of strips of red leather and, finally, a snuff-box, from which he took a generous pinch. Then he blew his nose with a loud blast. The landlord behind the bar woke with a start, but the priest went on with his story:

"I said to him, 'Collani! Wake up, Corporal, you're dreaming!' But he went prattling on: 'I'll teach the pair of you to swipe Legion property. I'll show you tomorrow!' Then I grabbed him by the shoulder and gave him a good shaking, I was finding the whole thing pretty eerie. He woke up and gave me an astonished look. 'Do you know what you were telling me?' I asked. 'Of course,' Collani replied and repeated what he had said in his trance – that's what it's called, isn't it?"

"Certainly," Godofrey hastened to assure him.

"– in his trance. After that, he left. When I came out of the house at eight the next morning – it was a very clear September morning, you could see the *chotts*, the great salt lakes, sparkling in the distance – I ran straight into Collani with the quartermaster and the captain. Captain Pouette told me Collani had reported that sheets had been going missing and claimed he knew both the thieves and the receiver. The thieves were already locked up, now it was the turn of the receiver. Collani looked like a water-diviner without his divining rod. Though he was completely conscious, there was a fixed look in his eyes and he was pressing forward.

"I won't bore you any more. At the bottom of an orange box in a tiny shop run by a Jew who sold onions, figs and dates, we found four sheets. Mamadou was a negro in the fourth company, he admitted the theft. At first Bielle, a red-haired Belgian, denied it, but then he too confessed.

"From then on Collani was always called the clair-voyant corporal and the battalion doctor, Anatole Cantacuzène, organized seances with him: table-turning, automatic writing, in short they tried all the accursed nonsense on him that the spiritualists practise here without the least idea of the danger they're putting themselves in.

"You will be asking yourselves, gentlemen, why I have told you this long story. It was just to explain why I could not ignore Collani when, one week later, he told me things that affected *me* personally.

"It was 28 September, a Tuesday."

Father Matthias paused for a moment, put his hand over his eyes and continued:

"Collani came to me. I spoke to him, as is my duty

as a priest, imploring him to give up these satanic experiments. He remained defiant. And suddenly his eyes glazed over again, his upper lids came halfway down over his eyeballs and his lips were twisted in a disagreeable, mocking smile, revealing his broad, yellow teeth. Then he said, in a voice I knew so well, 'Hello, Matthias, how's things?' It was the voice of my brother – my brother who died fifteen years ago!"

The three men round the table in the little bistro by Les Halles listened in silence. Commissaire Madelin gave a faint smile, as you might after a weak joke. Studer's moustache quivered, though it wasn't obvious why. Only Godofrey attempted to relieve the feeling of embarrassment at the improbable story.

"Funny how life keeps forcing you to deal with ghosts . . ." It could be a profound statement.

Very quietly Father Matthias said, "This strange and yet so familiar voice was coming to me from the lips of the clairvoyant corporal . . ."

Studer's moustache stopped quivering, he leant over the table. The stress on that last sentence. It sounded false, feigned, affected. He shot a glance at Madelin. There was the hint of a grimace on the Frenchman's bony face. So the commissaire had sensed the false note too. He raised his hand and placed it gently on the table. "Let him speak. Don't interrupt." And Studer nodded. He had understood.

" 'Hello, Matthias, d'you remember me? Did you think I was dead? Alive and kicking, that's me.' That was the point at which I suddenly realized Collani was speaking German. 'You'll have to hurry, Matthias, if you want to save the old ladies. Otherwise I'll come for them. In . . .' At that point the voice, which was not Collani's voice, became a whisper, so that I couldn't understand what came next. But then it was loud and

11

clear again: 'Can you hear the hissing? That hissing noise means death. Fifteen years I've waited. First of all the one in Basel, then the one in Bern. One was clever, she saw through me, I'll save her till last. The other brought up my daughter badly, she must be punished for it.' There was a laugh, then the voice fell silent. This time Collani was in such a deep sleep, I had difficulty waking him.

"Finally his eyes opened fully and he looked at me, astonished. So I asked him, 'Do you know what you have just told me, my son?' At first he shook his head, then he replied, 'I saw a man I nursed in Fez fifteen years ago. He died, he had a nasty fever . . . in 1917, during the Great War. Then I saw two women. One had a wart by her left nostril . . . The man in Fez, what was his name now? What was his name?' Collani rubbed his forehead, he couldn't remember the name and I didn't prompt him. 'The man in Fez gave me a letter. I was to post it – fifteen years later. I sent it. On the anniversary of his death, on 20 July. The letter's gone, yes, the letter's gone!' he suddenly shouted. 'I don't want anything more to do with it. It's beyond bearing. I did!' he shouted even louder, as if he were responding to an accusation from someone invisible, 'I did keep a copy. What am I to do with the copy?' Collani wrung his hands. I tried to calm him down by telling him to bring me the copy. 'That will ease your conscience, my son. Go and bring it now, at once.' 'Yes, Father,' the clairvoyant corporal said, got up and went out. I can still hear the screech of his hobnails on the stone outside my door . . ."

"And I never saw him again. He disappeared from Géryville. They assumed he had deserted. The battalion commander instituted an inquiry, which discovered that a stranger had come by car to Géryville

12

that evening and left that same night. Perhaps he took the clairvoyant corporal with him."

Father Matthias fell silent. The only sound to be heard in the little room was the snoring of the landlord interspersed with the quiet tick-tock of the clock on the wall . . .

The White Father took his hands away from his face. His eyes were slightly reddened, but their colour still recalled the sea – though now there was a bank of mist over the water, hiding the sun. The old man who looked like the tailor from the fairy tale scrutinized his audience.

It was no easy task telling a ghost story to three seasoned members of criminal investigation departments. They let the silence drag on until finally one of them, Madelin, rapped the table with the flat of his hand. The landlord shot up.

"Four glasses," the commissaire ordered. He filled them to the brim with rum and said, in an expressionless voice, "A little something will do you good, Father." Father Matthias emptied his glass obediently. Studer took a long, slim leather cigar case out of his pocket and found to his dismay that he had only one Brissago left. He went through the ritual of lighting it, then handed his matches to Madelin, who had filled his pipe, with which he gave his Swiss colleague a sign, clearly inviting him to start the interrogation.

Now Studer pushed his chair back too, propped his elbows on his thighs, clasped his hands and, in slow, measured tones, began his questioning.

"Two women? Your brother hadn't committed bigamy by any chance?

"No," said Father Matthias. "He got a divorce from his first wife and married her sister, Josepha."

"Did he now? Got a divorce?" Studer repeated. "I thought that didn't exist in the Catholic religion?" He looked up and saw that Father Matthias was blushing. A wave of red swept down from his high forehead over his sunburnt face. When it faded, it left peculiar grey blotches on his skin.

"I converted to Catholicism when I was eighteen," said Father Matthias in a low voice. "As a result I was disowned by my family."

"What was your brother?" Studer asked.

"A geologist. He prospected for ore in the south of Morocco: lead, silver, copper. For the French government. Then he died in Fez."

"You've seen his death certificate?"

"It was sent to his second wife in Basel. My niece has seen it."

"You know your niece?"

"Yes. She lives in Paris. She had a job here with my late brother's secretary."

"Now," said Studer, taking his notebook out of his pocket – it was a new ring binder that gave off a strong scent of Russia leather, a Christmas present from his wife, who was fed up with the cheap jotters bound in oilcloth he used. He opened it.

"Would you be so good as to give me the addresses of your two sisters-in-law?"

"Josepha Cleman-Hornuss, 12 Spalenberg, Basel; Sophie Hornuss, 44 Gerechtigkeitsgasse, Bern." The priest was slightly out of breath as he spoke.

"And you really believe the two old women are in danger, Father?"

"Yes . . . really . . . as I hope to be saved, it is my belief that that is the case."

Again Studer felt like telling him to stop speaking in such an affected manner, but he couldn't do that, so he just said, "I'm staying here in Paris for the New Year's Eve celebrations, then I'll take the overnight train and be in Basel on the morning of New Year's Day. When are you going to Switzerland?"

"Today . . . tonight."

"Then," came Godofrey's parrot voice, "you've just got time to get a taxi."

"My God, you're right. But where . . .?"

Commissaire Madelin dipped a sugar lump in his rum and, sucking his *canard,* called out to the snoring landlord, who leapt up, rushed to the door, stuck two fingers in his mouth and whistled. It was so piercing Father Matthias put his hands over his ears.

Then the storyteller was gone.

Commissaire Madelin growled, "There's just one thing I'd like to know. Does the man think we're little children? I'm sorry, Studère, I thought he would have something more important to tell us. He came with a recommendation. From above. He has friends in high places – and he didn't even pay for a single round! It's him who's the child, really, a little child."

"Excuse me, *chef,*" said Godofrey, "but that's not true. Children can talk to the angels, but our White Father's certainly not on speaking terms with the angels."

"Eh?" Madelin stared, wide eyed, and Studer, too, gave the over-elegant manikin a look of astonishment.

Godofrey remained unperturbed.

"You can only talk to the angels," he said, "if you're pure in heart. Our White Father's heart is full of deviousness. You haven't heard the last of him. But now we're going to drink the health of our inspector's grandson." He waved the landlord over. "In champagne!" And he repeated the German words of the telegram, "greetings from young zhakoblee to old zhakobbe." Studer laughed until the tears ran down his cheeks, then he raised his glass to his two companions.

And it was a good thing Commissaire Madelin had his police identity card on him, otherwise the three of them would have been arrested for disturbing the peace at two in the morning. Studer had taken it into his head to teach his two friends the song of "The Farmer from Brienz" and a uniform policeman was of the opinion that a Paris boulevard was not the place for a singing lesson. He withdrew his objection, however, after he had established their profession. Thus it was that Sergeant Studer was able to continue to regale his colleagues from the Paris Sûreté with jewels of Bernese culture. He taught them "I Know a Vale So Fair and Merry" in which the word "Emmental" gave him the opportunity to expound on the difference between Emmental and Gruyère cheese. For the French subscribed to the heresy that all Swiss cheese came from the Gruyère region.

Gas

After Sergeant Studer had stowed his scuffed pigskin suitcase in a compartment of the Paris–Basel overnight express, he pulled down the corridor window to say goodbye to his friends. Grunting and groaning, Commissaire Madelin extricated a bottle wrapped in newspaper from his coat pocket. Godofrey handed a neat little package, doubtless containing a terrine of *pâté de foie gras*, up to the carriage window, whispering, "*Pour madame.*" Then the train pulled out of the Gare de l'Est and Studer returned to his third-class compartment.

A young woman had sat down opposite his corner seat. Fur jacket, grey suede gloves, grey silk stockings. She lit a cigarette, a decidedly male brand: Gauloises. She held out the blue packet to Studer and he helped himself. Then she told him she was from Basel and was going to see her mother. For the New Year. – Where did her mother live? – On Spalenberg. – Really? On Spalenberg? – Yes.

Studer let it go at that. The young woman, a girl really, was at most twenty-two or twenty-three and the sergeant found her enormously attractive. Not that there was anything more to it than that. After all, he was a grandfather, a respectable citizen . . . It was just that it was nice chatting to the girl . . .

Then Studer grew drowsy, excused his yawns by saying he had had a very busy time in Paris. The girl smiled, a slightly impudent smile, but so what? He rested his heavy head on his grey raincoat in the corner and went to sleep. When he woke up the girl was still sitting opposite him, she hardly seemed to have moved. Only the blue packet of cigarettes, which had been full in Paris, was lying, empty and screwed up, in a corner. And Studer had a headache from the blue smoke filling the compartment.

He carried his own suitcase and hers to the customs, then said goodbye and almost ran straight into a man wearing a cap that looked like a misshapen flowerpot; his skinny body was wrapped in a white monk's habit and he had open sandals on his feet – his bare feet.

If Sergeant Studer expected a hearty greeting, he was disappointed. There was a sad, apprehensive expression on the face with the sparse goatee, and his lips – how pale they were! – mumbled, "Ah, Inspector. How are you?" Then, without waiting for an answer, Father Matthias turned to the young woman who had shared Studer's compartment and took her suitcase. Outside the station the pair of them got into a taxi and drove off.

The sergeant shrugged his broad shoulders. Surely it cast serious doubt on the prophecies of the clairvoyant corporal with which a White Father had regaled three members of the police in a bistro by Les Halles in Paris? If the priest believed them, it would have been his duty to keep watch over . . . what was she called? No matter . . . over the woman living on Spalenberg, to protect her from a death that had something to do with hissing. Hissing? What things made a hissing noise? An arrow . . . a dart from a blowpipe . . . What else? A snake? They all belonged in detective stories by Conan Doyle, who had joined the spiritualists. There was one of those stories . . . What was it called? Something with speckled . . . the speckled . . . Oh yes, "The Speckled Band". In it a snake wrapped itself round a bell-pull.

Well, Conan Doyle was certainly full of imagination, but Sergeant Studer's cigar case was empty. Charming and hospitable as the French were, Brissagos were unknown to them. So the sergeant had his long, slim leather case filled at the station kiosk. But he denied himself the pleasure of lighting one straight away, instead he went to the buffet first, where he had a substantial and peaceful breakfast. Then he decided to visit a friend who lived on Missionsstrasse.

On the way there, on Freie Strasse first of all – it was still early in the morning and he was going the long way round so as not to disturb his friend at too unearthly an hour – Studer shook his head. It didn't matter, there were no people in the street to get worked up about a man shaking his head and talking to himself. So Sergeant Studer shook his head and muttered, "He's not on speaking terms with the angels." Father Matthias did seem to be a man whose heart was full of deviousness.

In the Market Square he shook his head once more and muttered, "Greetings from young Jakobli to old Jakob." A strange woman, Hedy! Getting on for fifty now, and a grandmother, but still she insisted on finding amusing ways of putting things. It used to annoy Studer, but after twenty-seven years of marriage you learn to ignore things . . . Hedy! She'd not always had an easy life. But she was a brave lass – a brave grandmother now.

A grandmother . . . Studer looked up and stopped. The road was going uphill. Of course, Spalenberg! And a house number shone out.

Then a door was flung open, a girl came dashing out and, since the sergeant was the only person in the street, she grabbed him by the arm and gasped, "Come with me, please . . . My mother . . . There's a smell of gas . . ."

And Jakob Studer, a detective sergeant with the Bern police, followed his destiny, which this time had appeared in the person of a young woman who liked strong French cigarettes and wore a fur jacket, grey suede shoes and grey silk stockings.

"Stay out on the terrace," Studer said after he had panted his way up three flights of stairs. No doubt about it, there was a definite smell of gas. No latch, no key in the door. A plain pine door and a weak lock.

Studer took six steps run-up, no more, but a plain pine door cannot withstand the impact of sixteen stone. It dutifully yielded – not the wood, the lock – and a cloud of gas poured out, enveloping Studer. Fortunately, his handkerchief was large. He tied it round his neck so it covered his nose and mouth.

"Stay outside," Studer shouted to the girl. Two steps and he was across the tiny kitchen. He pushed open a door. The living room was a whitewashed cube. The sergeant flung open the window and leant out, and his handkerchief came off like a carnival mask.

A jumble of roofs, chimneys peacefully puffing out their smoke into the cold winter air. Hoar-frost gleaming on the dark tiles. A pale winter sun was slowly creeping along the highest roof-ridge. The draught blowing in swept the poisonous gas away.

Studer turned round: a desk, a sofa, three chairs, a telephone on the wall. He strode across the room into the corridor-like kitchen. The two taps on the little portable stove were open and there was a hissing noise of gas coming out of the burners. Mechanically, Studer turned the taps off. It wasn't easy, because there was a chair in the way, upholstered in green velvet. In it an old woman was sitting. She looked strangely at peace, relaxed, as if she were sleeping. One hand was resting on the arm of the chair. Studer took it, felt for the pulse, shook his head and carefully replaced the hand on the carved wood.

The kitchen really was tiny. Six foot by five, more of a corridor. On the wall over the gas rings was a wooden shelf with enamel containers, originally white, now stained brown, chipped: "Coffee", "Flour", "Salt". Everything was shabby. And beneath the faint smell of gas that remained another was clearly discernible: camphor.

A smell of old woman, of lonely old woman.

It was a quite specific smell, with which Studer was familiar. He was familiar with it from the tiny apartments in Metzgergasse, where now and then an old woman got too bored or too lonely and turned on the gas-tap. Sometimes, though, it wasn't boredom or loneliness, it was poverty . . .

Studer went out. On the left-hand doorpost, under the white bell-push, was a nameplate:

Josepha Cleman-Hornuss
Widow

Widow! As if widow were a profession.

He called out to the girl, who was leaning against the balcony rail. It was a funny building – even though the apartment was on the third floor, the terrace led into a little garden. There was a wall round the garden with a door in it. Where would the door lead to? Presumably into a side street. He called to the girl and she came over.

Gently – of course – the sergeant led the girl to the armchair where her mother was sleeping peacefully. But as she took out her tiny handkerchief and dried her tears, something struck Studer: the old woman in the armchair was wearing a red dressing gown covered in coffee stains, but on her feet she had lace-up boots. Not slippers at all, outdoor shoes!

Then Studer looked for the gas meter. It was sitting on a shelf up on the wall by the door to the flat. With its dials it looked like a podgy, green, sneering face.

But the lever that served as the mains tap wasn't straight! It was sloping at an angle. At an angle of forty-five degrees, to be precise.

Why was it only half open? Why not fully open?

Basically the case was none of his business. He was a detective sergeant with the Bern police, it was up to the Basel police to deal with it. Anyway, it looked like suicide, suicide by gas, nothing unusual, nothing they weren't used to dealing with.

He went into the living room, which also served as a bedroom – the couch in the corner! – and looked for the telephone directory. It was on the desk, next to a pack of cards that had been laid out. As he looked up the number of the police ambulance, the sergeant vaguely wondered why someone should play patience before they committed suicide. It was unusual, to say the least. Then a sheet of paper fell out of the tele-phone directory on to the floor. Studer picked it up and placed it beside the cards on the desk – strange, the cards had been laid out in four rows and in the top left corner was the jack of spades . . . Studer dialled the number. It rang and rang. The police must have had serious New Year celebrations. Finally a croaky voice answered and Studer gave the details: 12 Spalenberg, third floor, Josepha Cleman-Hornuss. Suicide. Then he hung up.

He found he was still holding the sheet of paper that had fallen out of the telephone directory. It was yellow with age, folded up, nothing written on the outside. He opened it. A temperature chart:

HÔPITAL MILITAIRE DE FEZ

Nom: Cleman, Victor Alois *Profession*: Géologue
Nationalité: Suisse *Entrée*: 12/7/1917 *Paludisme*

When Victor Alois Cleman had been admitted to the military hospital in Fez on 12 July 1917 he had been seriously ill. *Paludisme* – that was malaria.

The temperature chart had sharp peaks. It went from 12 to 30 July, after which someone had drawn a cross with a blue pencil. So the Swiss geologist Victor Alois Cleman had died on 30 July 1917.

Cleman? . . . Cleman-Hornuss? . . . 12 Spalenberg?

Studer took out his new ring binder. There it was, on the very first page of his Christmas present! . . .

"Missy," Studer shouted. The young woman in the fur jacket did not seem particularly surprised at the form of address.

"Listen, miss," said Studer, telling her to come and sit down. He had put his notebook on the table and made notes as he questioned the girl.

It really did look as if Sergeant Studer had taken on a new case.

"Was that your father?" he asked, pointing to the name on the temperature chart.

A nod.

"What's your name?"

"Marie . . . Marie Cleman."

"Well, I'm Sergeant Studer from Bern. And the man who met you at the station this morning asked me for assistance if something should happen in Switzerland. He told me a fairy story, but there was one thing in the story that is true: your mother is dead."

Studer paused. He thought of the hissing. Not an arrow. Not a dart. Not a speckled band . . . Gas! Gas hissed when it came out of the burner. Make a note of it.

He examined the temperature chart closely. On the evening of 18 and the morning of 19 July his temperature had been 37.25. Above the line was written: *quinine sulphate 2 km.*

Since when had quinine been administered by the kilometre? A slip of the pen? It was probably an injection and instead of cm^3 – the abbreviation for cubic centimetre – some bungler, a German nurse perhaps, had written just km.

Oh well . . .

"Your father died in Morocco," Studer said. "In Fez. I was told he was prospecting for ore there. For the French government . . . By the way, who was the man who met you at the station this morning?"

"My Uncle Matthias," said Marie in surprise.

"That's right," said Studer. "I met him in Paris."

Silence. The sergeant sat at the flat-topped desk, leaning back comfortably in his chair. Marie Cleman sat facing him, playing with her handkerchief. The silence was broken by the shrill sound of the telephone ringing. Marie was going to get up, but Studer waved to her to stay seated. He picked up the receiver and said, as was his habit in his office in Bern, "Yes?"

"Is Frau Cleman there?"

An unpleasant voice, loud and shrill.

"Not at the moment, can I give her a message?" Studer asked.

"No! No! Anyway, I know Frau Cleman's dead. You'll never catch me. You're the police, I presume? Hahaha . . ." A real actor's laugh. The man had *spoken* the "ha". Then a click sounded in the receiver.

"Who was it?" Marie asked anxiously.

"Some idiot," said Studer tersely, then immediately asked – was it the voice that had suggested the idea? – "Where is your Uncle Matthias?"

"Catholic priests," she said wearily, "have to say mass every morning . . . wherever they are. Otherwise they need a dispensation, from the Pope, I think, or the bishop, I don't know." She sighed, picked up the temperature chart and started to study it intently.

"What's that?" she suddenly asked, pointing to the blue cross.

"That?" Studer stood behind the girl. "That will be the day your father died."

"No!" The word came out as a scream. Then she calmed down and went on, "My father died on 20 July. I've seen the death certificate and the letter from the general. My father died on 20 July 1917."

She fell silent and Studer did not say anything either.

After a while Marie went on: her mother had told her often enough. A telegram had arrived on 21 July, it must be among her souvenirs, in the desk there, the second drawer from the bottom. And then, about a fortnight later, the postman had brought the large yellow envelope. There wasn't much in it. Her father's passport, 4,000 francs in Algerian State Bank notes and the letter of condolence from a French general. Lyautey was his name. A very flattering letter. It said how well Herr Cleman had acted in the interests of France, how grateful the country was to Herr Cleman for unmasking two German spies . . .

"Two spies?" Studer asked. He had gone to a chair in the corner, by the open window, and sat there, elbows on his thighs, hands clasped. He was staring at the floor. "Two spies?" he repeated.

Marie closed the window. She looked out into the courtyard, her fingers drumming a monotonous march on the window-pane. Her breath made a clouded patch on the glass; drops formed and trickled down until they were stopped by the window-frame.

"Yes, two spies." Marie spoke in a monotone. "The Mannesmann brothers . . . I remember the day the letter arrived. At the time we had a large apartment, on the Rheinschanze. And one day the letter arrived. I was on holiday from school. The postman brought the big envelope, it was registered and Mother had to sign for it. Two tears fell on the postman's notebook and smudged the indelible pencil. Father didn't leave much and things were difficult after his death. Later Mother often said how surprised she was how little money was left. My aunt in Bern, she had plenty . . ."

Studer leafed through his notebook. His first wife. Hadn't the priest, the White Father, spoken of her? There it was: Sophie Hornuss, 44 Gerechtigkeitsgasse, Bern.

"Those two spies, the – what did you say they were called? Oh yes, the Mannesmann brothers. How did your father get on with them?"

"Quite well at first – I only knew about this from my mother. They were prospecting, as I told you, particularly in the south of Morocco. That is, it was my father who discovered the presence of ore. The Mannesmann brothers pretended they were Swiss, but then, during the war, they helped some Germans in the Foreign Legion to get back home. Father found out about it and told the general. The two of them were simply put before a firing squad. Soon after that Father was given an official appointment by the French government, as a reward for betr— for the information."

"So that's how it was." Studer nodded. He got up and leant over the desk again. He was fascinated by the cards that had been laid out.

"And what about these cards?"

Marie Cleman perched on the window-ledge, steadying herself with her hands; the tips of her toes touched the edge of the worn carpet. The girl had slim ankles!

"Oh, those cards! That was the worst of it, that was why I left my mother." She sighed. "It was all a big con trick and I couldn't stand it any longer. The servant girls who paid ten francs to know if their boyfriends were faithful; the businessmen who wanted advice for their speculations; the politicians who wanted Mother to tell them they'd get elected again . . . Eventually even the bank manager came, though that gentleman came because of me. And do you know, Uncle Studer, I don't think it even bothered Mother that I . . . with the bank manager . . . so one day I just took off."

Studer had jumped up. He was standing facing the girl. What had Marie called him? Uncle Studer? It took his breath away . . . but of course it meant nothing. He'd called the girl by the familiar *du*, as they did in Bern. Didn't that give Marie the right to a certain familiarity? Uncle Studer! It gave him a warm feeling . . . just like a glass of schnapps.

"If," said Studer, and his voice was a little hoarse, "you're going to call me uncle, then at least make it Cousin Jakob. Uncle! That's what the Krauts say."

Marie blushed. She looked the sergeant in the face. She had a particular way of looking at people: not quite searching, more astonished – a calmly astonished look you could call it. The look suited the girl, Studer thought, but he could imagine it would get on other people's nerves.

"All right then," said Marie, "Cousin Jakob it is," and she shook the sergeant by the hand. It was a small hand, a strong hand.

Studer cleared his throat. "So you took off . . . fine. To Paris, your uncle told me. Who with?"

"With the man who'd been my father's secretary. Koller he was called. He came to see us once and told us he'd set up on his own and was looking for someone he could trust. He asked me if I fancied going with him, as a shorthand typist. I'd been to the commercial college, so I accepted."

A fur jacket, silk stockings, suede shoes . . . Expensive. Was a typist's salary enough to buy that kind of thing? He plunged his hands into his trouser pockets. He felt a little sad, so he hunched up his shoulders and asked, "Why did you decide to come to see your mother?"

Again that strangely searching look.

"Why?" Marie repeated. "Because Koller suddenly disappeared. Overnight. Three, three and a half months ago. On 15 September to be precise. He left me with 4,000 French francs. I survived on that until the end of December, then I had just enough left for the fare to Basel."

"Why didn't you come with your uncle?"

"He wanted to travel by himself."

"Did you report Koller's disappearance?"

"Yes. To the police. They took all his papers. A Commissaire Madelin was in charge of the investigation. He questioned me once . . ."

There was something . . . What was it? Something Madelin had said, that evening, when Studer had shown him the telegram about young Jakobli. Could he bring it back to mind? What was it Madelin had said to the walking, talking encyclopedia, to Godofrey? "There's something not right about Koller's papers." That was it. Was it the same Koller?

"Where did your mother keep the souvenirs of your father?" Studer asked.

"In the desk," Marie replied, turning her back on the room again. "In the second drawer from the bottom."

28

The second drawer from the bottom . . .

It was empty. That in itself would not have struck him particularly.

What did strike him was that the burglar who had broken it open had carefully replaced a piece of wood that had splintered off. Studer shut the empty drawer and then, following the example of his predecessor, carefully fitted the splinter of wood back in its exact place. He straightened up, took out his handkerchief, bent down to the drawer again and wiped everything clean, muttering, "You never know."

"Have you found anything, Cousin Jakob?" Marie asked, without turning round.

"Your mother must have moved them to another place," Studer grunted. Louder he added, "So your father's first wife lives in Bern and she's called . . ."

Studer took out his notebook, but Marie got in first. "She's called Hornuss, Sophie Hornuss, 44 Gerechtigkeitsgasse. She was my mother's elder sister, so she's actually my aunt, if you prefer . . ."

"Funny family relationships," said Studer drily.

Marie smiled. Then the smile vanished and her eyes darkened with sadness. She'd sometimes thought that herself, she said. And Studer kicked himself because his stupid remark had clearly caused the girl pain.

There were steps approaching along the corridor. The broken door screeched on its hinges and a voice asked if someone had committed suicide here. It must be here, said a second voice, there was the nameplate on the doorpost: Cleman. "You see?" it added. "What did I tell you?"

Studer went back into the kitchen, where he bumped into a uniform policeman. It was a soft bump, since the officer was as plump, rosy and smooth as a baby. He seemed to be suppressing a yawn all the time and swamped the sergeant with a flood of questions, all plentifully studded with "Yes?" and "No?". Moreover, he gargled his "R"s as if they were mouthwash, instead of rolling them with his tongue against the hard palate, like any decent Swiss. The duty doctor was old and his moustache yellow from cigarettes.

Studer introduced himself, introduced Marie.

The dead woman in the armchair looked as if she were smiling. The sergeant had another look at her face. There was a wart beside her left nostril . . .

The body was taken away – out through the little door Studer had seen in the garden wall. It took a long time before they could get a key for the gate; there wasn't a single key to be found in the dead woman's apartment. One of the tenants, lured by the noise, supplied his.

Studer was tired. He felt no desire to tell his uniformed colleague all the odd aspects of the case: the half-open tap on the gas meter, the old woman wearing outdoor shoes with a dressing gown . . . The sergeant stood up and stared at the brass plate: Josepha Cleman-Hornuss, Widow.

Then he invited Marie to have a coffee with him. It seemed the most sensible thing to do.

The first wife

Not long after Olten it started to snow. Studer sat in the restaurant car staring out of the window. The hills gliding past were soft shapes behind the curtain of white, which was falling with such uninterrupted regularity, it looked motionless.

On the table in front of the sergeant was a blue coffee set and beside it, within easy reach, a carafe of kirsch. Studer drew his gaze away from the window and turned his attention to his new ring binder, which lay open in front of him. Holding his pencil between index and middle finger, he wrote in his tiny handwriting with the letters printed separately, as in Greek:

Cleman-Hornuss, Josepha: widow, 55. Gassed. Suicide?
Against: half-open tap on gas meter; keys to apartment door
and garden gate missing; drawer broken into on desk – and
the telephone call.

The telephone call! Sitting in the restaurant car of the Basel–Bern express, Studer heard the voice again. And, as in Josepha Cleman-Hornuss's living room, it sounded familiar. It reminded him of another voice he had heard only a few days before, in a little bistro by Les Halles in Paris – that is, the *tone* of voice was the same, the register similar.

And the voice had sounded drunk. Breathless, as if the man had just tossed down a few glasses of brandy, one after the other. Question one: what did the drunk expect to achieve with his call? And question two: where had Father Matthias of the Order of White Fathers been at that point? In which church had he celebrated his morning mass? In that cement church the Baslers had christened the "soul silo"?

Staring out of the window, lost in thought, Studer stretched out his hand, picked up the carafe of kirsch instead of the coffee pot, filled his cup, raised it to his lips and only noticed his mistake after he'd emptied it. Looking up, he saw the waiter grinning at him. He grinned back, shrugged his shoulders, picked up the carafe again, defiantly emptied the rest of the schnapps into his cup and started to write busily:

> *Cleman, Victor Alois: geologist working for Mannesmann brothers; prospecting for lead, silver, copper. His employers executed by firing squad in Casablanca, 1915, for helping a few Germans to desert from the Foreign Legion. Cleman as informer! Returns to Switzerland in 1916, but goes back to Morocco later in same year, working for the French government. Inspects the lead-smelting furnaces installed by Mannesmann brothers in the south of the country. Falls seriously ill in 1917 and flown to Fez. Dies there – according to daughter, based on telegram that has disappeared – on 20 July. Leaves very little. Married twice. First wife lives in Bern, see Father Matthias's statement. Seems to be well-off. Sister of Joespha Cleman, who died in Basel.*

. . . Herzogenbuchsee . . . It had stopped snowing. The dry heat in the train was soporific and Studer fell into a daydream.

The Foreign Legion! Morocco! Now the longing for foreign lands and exotic places, which had tugged at him shyly when Father Matthias had told his story, was swelling in Studer's breast. Yes, in his breast. It was a strange feeling, more of an ache. Unknown worlds beckoned, images appeared, he was dreaming of them yet still wide awake. The desert stretched on for ever, camels trotted over the golden sand, brown-skinned people in billowing robes strode majestically through dazzling white towns. Marie had been kidnapped by a robber band – how had Marie suddenly got into his dream? – she had been kidnapped and he was the one who freed her. "Thank you, Cousin Jakob," she said. Happiness! That was different from writing interminable reports in the police station in Bern, in the tiny office that smelt of dust and floor polish. There were different smells down there, unknown smells, foreign. And memories came back to mind: *The Song of Solomon, The Arabian Nights* . . .

Perhaps this really was his big case.

Perhaps he would be sent officially to Morocco. Perhaps . . .

In any case, it would be a good idea to go to 44 Gerechtigkeitsgasse first thing in the morning to question the geologist's divorced wife.

. . . Burgdorf . . . Studer poured the rest of the cold coffee into his cup, drank the mixture – it tasted horrible – and called out, "Bill." The waiter gave him another sly grin, but Studer no longer felt like smiling. He could not get Marie out of his mind, Marie who had gone off to Paris with Koller, her father's former secretary – fur jacket, silk stockings, suede shoes! He'd grown fond of Marie, there was no denying it. As if he'd got a daughter back. A year ago his own daughter had married a country policeman from Thurgau. Now she was a mother and the sergeant felt he had finally lost her. All these confused emotions presumably explained why he only gave the grinning waiter twenty *rappen* as a tip.

His mood did not improve once he had arrived in

Bern. His apartment in Kirchenfeld was empty and Studer could not be bothered to try to light the stove. He went to the café for a game of billiards, then to a cinema, where he got irritated at the film. Later on he had a couple of beers somewhere – and they disagreed with him too. The result was that when he went to bed at eleven o'clock he had a raging headache. It took him a long time to get to sleep.

In the darkness he was visited by the old woman with the wart by her left nostril who had sat in her green armchair beside the two-ring gas stove, so calm and relaxed . . . Marie appeared and disappeared. Then it was New Year's Eve, Commissaire Madelin and Godofrey, the encyclopedia, were there. Godofrey – with his horn-rimmed spectacles he looked like an unfledged owl – proved particularly difficult to get rid of. "*Pour madame*," said Godofrey as he handed a terrine of *pâté de foie gras* in through the carriage window. But the terrine swelled up until it was sitting there on a shelf, green and solid and sneering – it had turned into a gas meter, which was a head, a dream monster signalling with its one arm . . . vertical, horizontal, sloping at an angle . . . and Marie was arm-in-arm with Father Matthias, only it wasn't Father Matthias, it was Koller, her father's former secretary, who was the sergeant's double . . .

Still half awake, Studer heard himself say, "*Chabis!* What a load of nonsense!"

His voice echoed through the empty apartment. In desperation, Studer felt the bed beside him. But Hedy was still in Thurgau, looking after the new Jakobli. Groaning, he pulled his arm back, it was freezing. Then all at once he fell asleep.

*

Had he had a nice time in Paris? Detective Constable Murmann, who shared the office with him, asked at nine o'clock the next morning. Studer was still in a bad mood; he grunted something incomprehensible and continued to thump away at the keys of his typewriter. Inside the room it smelt of cold tobacco smoke, dust and floor polish; a chill north wind was whistling at the windows and the steam made the radiators clunk.

Murmann sat down opposite his colleague, took the *Bund* out of his pocket and started to read. His powerful biceps had formed bulges in the sleeves of his jacket.

"Hey, Köbu, listen to this" he said after a while.

"What?" said Studer impatiently. He had to write a report on a theft that had taken place in an attic apartment ages ago; the investigating magistrate had been on the telephone screaming for it.

"A woman killed herself in Basel," Murmann went on, unperturbed. "With gas."

He knew that already, was Studer's irritated reply.

Murmann was not to be put off. "Committing suicide with gas must be catching," he said. "I was called out to Gerechtigkeitsgasse at six o'clock this morning with Reinhard of the city police – there's no one else there at the moment, they're all still on holiday ... Anyway, the woman in Gerechtigkeitsgasse had killed herself with gas."

"In Gerechtigkeitsgasse? What number?" Studer asked.

"Forty-four," Murmann mumbled, chewing on his cigar. He scratched his neck, gave the *Bund* a good shake and went back to reading the editorial.

Suddenly he looked up with a start. A chair had fallen over and Studer was leaning across the desk, breathing heavily. His normally pale face was red.

"What was the woman called?"

"Köbu," said Murmann calmly, "are you hearing voices?"

No he was not, Studer growled, with a violent shake of the head at the suggestion, he just wanted to know the dead woman's name.

"A divorcee, a fortune teller – cards," said Murmann. "Hornuss, Sophie Hornuss. The body's with Forensics already."

"Is that so?" said Studer, hammered out one more sentence, ripped the sheet out of the typewriter, scribbled his signature, went over to the coat hook, put on his raincoat and slammed the door behind him.

Murmann nodded. "That's our Köbu for you," he said to no one in particular, relighting his cigar. Then he finished the editorial, a smug grin on his face. It was about the growth of the Red Peril and Murmann, being a Liberal, believed in the Red Peril . . .

Forty-four Gerechtigkeitsgasse. Beside the front door the name plate of a dance school. Wooden stairs. Very clean, not like that other house, on Spalenberg. A yellow door on the third floor was open; there was a visiting card pinned to it:

Sophie Hornuss

So this woman hadn't been a professional widow! Studer went in.

When the door had been forced open the lock had fallen off and was lying on the floor.

Silence . . .

The hall was spacious and dark. On the left was a glass door into the kitchen. Studer sniffed. A smell of

36

gas here, too; the kitchen window was open. The lamp hanging from the ceiling had a china shade covered by a square of purple silk with brown wooden balls hanging from the corners. It was swinging to and fro.

By the window was a solid gas stove with four rings, oven and grill. And beside the stove was a comfortable leather armchair, which looked rather odd in the kitchen. Who had dragged it out of the living room into the kitchen? The old woman?

Cards were laid out on the oilcloth over the kitchen table, four rows of eight cards. The first card in the top row was the jack of spades.

Hands clasped behind his back, Studer paced up and down the kitchen, opened the cupboard, closed it, took a pan down off the wall, lifted a lid . . .

In the sink was a cup with a black deposit on the bottom. Studer smelt it: a faint smell of aniseed. He tasted it.

That bitter aftertaste that stayed on the tongue! That smell! It was mere chance that Studer recognized both. Two years ago the doctor had prescribed Somnifen to help him sleep.

Somnifen! That acid taste, that smell of aniseed . . . Had the old woman suffered from insomnia?

But why the devil had she taken sleeping pills, then dragged an armchair into the kitchen and opened the taps on the gas stove? Why?

One dead woman in Basel, one dead woman in Bern. And the link between the two their husband, Victor Alois, a Swiss geologist who had died in the military hospital in Fez during the Great War. Why should Cleman's two wives commit suicide fifteen years later? One today, the other yesterday? And commit suicide in what was, to put it mildly, an odd way?

Was this perhaps the "Big Case" every detective dreamt of, even if he was only a simple sergeant?

"Simple"! The word just didn't fit the sergeant. If Studer had been "simple", then his colleagues, from the chief of police down, would not have said he had "the odd screw loose".

Part of the reason for this was the business with the bank that had cost him his comfortable job as chief inspector with the city police. He'd been forced to resign and had had to start again from the bottom with the cantonal police. He'd quickly risen to the rank of sergeant – he could speak French, Italian and German; he could read English; he'd worked with Gross in Graz and Locard in Lyon. He had good contacts in Berlin, London, Vienna and, above all, in Paris. He was usually the one who was sent to conferences on criminology. When his colleagues maintained he had the odd screw loose, what they probably meant was that he had a bit too much imagination for someone from Bern. But that wasn't quite true. It was probably just that he could see a bit further than the end of his nose, which was long, thin and pointed and didn't really go with his bulky body.

Studer remembered that he knew one of the assistant doctors at the Institute for Forensic Medicine from an earlier case. He went round the apartment looking for the telephone. It was in the sitting room – red velvet armchairs with antimacassars, ornate table, escritoire – fixed to the wall.

He lifted the receiver, dialled.

"I'd like to speak to Dr Malapelle . . . Yes? . . . Is that you, *Dottore*? Have you done the autopsy already? . . . Yes, the 'gas corpse' as you call it . . . *Senti, Dottore* . . ." And Studer continued in Italian, telling the doctor of his suspicions about Somnifen. Malapelle promised his report by the afternoon.

Then Studer leafed through the telephone directory. No, no temperature chart hidden there. The room did not look as if it had been searched. Studer tried the drawers in the escritoire. They were locked.

The bedroom . . . A huge bed and red velvet curtains. They made the room dark and Studer opened them.

Over the bed was the portrait of a man.

A lonely woman in Bern, a lonely woman in Basel. The one in Bern was a bit better off: a two-room apartment with kitchen, while Josepha in Basel used the corridor to her bedsitting room as a kitchen. But they'd both been lonely. Studer found himself using the women's Christian names: Josepha in Basel, Sophie in Bern. They'd both shuffled round their apartments in slippers, they'd probably "just popped out to the shops" in slippers too . . .

Odd that there was no picture of the late geologist in Josepha's flat in Basel. Josepha had been his wife, while Sophie was just a divorcee. But it was over her bed that the enlarged photo of Victor Alois Cleman hung in its elaborate wooden frame.

In the picture he had a dark, curly beard that covered his shirt front so completely you couldn't tell what kind of tie he was wearing. A beard! A sign of masculinity before the war.

The beard must have made him hot, the Swiss geologist, down there in Morocco digging for silver, lead and copper. He wore spectacles as well, with oval lenses that hid his eyes. Hid? No, that wasn't the right word. They just gave him a dull, uninvolved look – impersonal. They made his whole face expressionless.

A handsome man. At least what was considered a handsome man in those antediluvian times.

Studer stared at the portrait. He seemed to be hoping the man with the two wives would tell him something.

But the well-travelled geologist just looked back with the indifferent stare only scientists can achieve. Eventually the sergeant turned his back on him in irritation.

When he went back into the kitchen, the leather armchair was no longer empty.

A man was sitting in it playing a strange game. He'd taken off his hat, which looked like a flowerpot made by an incompetent potter, and hung it over the index finger of his right hand. With his left hand he kept prodding the lopsided object, making it spin round slowly.

The man, who was wearing a white monk's habit, looked up. "*Bonjour, Inspecteur,*" he said, adding in his foreign-sounding Swiss German, "A happy New Year."

"And the same to you," Studer replied. He stayed in the doorway, leaning against the jamb.

Father Matthias

"Our great cardinal, Cardinal Lavigerie, the founder of our order," Father Matthias said, as he continued to prod his misshapen flowerpot, which in Africa is called a *sheshia*, "once said, 'A true Christian is never late.' I am sure that can only be understood in a metaphorical sense, it cannot be true of our life here on earth, since in that we are dependent on human agencies such as railway trains, steamships, motor cars ... My niece, Marie, whom I saw yesterday evening, told me what had happened in Basel. I immediately hired a taxi to take me to Bern, since there were no more trains. It broke down on the way – these things happen. That is why I have only just arrived. The door had been broken open, the lock was on the floor, there was a faint smell of gas ... Then I heard footsteps in the apartment. 'Could it be,' I thought to myself, 'that nice inspector I had the honour and the pleasure of meeting in Paris? That would truly be divine providence.' And it was ..."

At first Studer hadn't listened to what the priest was saying. Instead he had concentrated on the tone of Father Matthias's little speech, comparing it with the voice that had mocked him on the telephone. The priest spoke excellent German, though just occasionally the Swiss German could be heard in the thick sound of the "ch" formed on the back of the palate. It was a real preacher's voice, deep and sonorous, which did not really go with his scrawny body. But voices could be disguised, couldn't they? In the bistro in Paris his voice had sounded slightly different, a little higher perhaps. Was it the French the priest had been speaking that had caused the difference?

Studer suddenly bent down and picked the lock up off the floor. He examined it closely, then looked up. Where was the gas meter? It wasn't in the kitchen. It was sitting on a shelf right over the door in the hall and it had exactly the same podgy, green, sneering face as its brother in Basel.

And the lever that served as the mains tap was sloping. At an angle of forty-five degrees . . .

Studer looked again at the lock in his hand. Then he heard the preacher's voice say, "If you should happen to need a magnifying glass, Inspector, I can provide one. Botany and geology are hobbies of mine, so I always carry a magnifying glass in my pocket."

The sergeant did not look up. He heard the springs of the leather armchair groan, then something was pushed into his hand. He held the magnifying glass up to his eye.

No doubt about it, there were grey fibres to be seen all round the keyhole, especially on the upper part, where it protruded. It looked as if a piece of string had rubbed against the sharp edge.

. . . And the mains tap was at an angle of forty-five degrees . . .

Crazy! Even assuming the old woman had taken a sleeping pill and dropped off in her leather armchair, wouldn't it have been easier for the presumed murderer to have opened the mains tap as he passed and then quietly slip away? Always supposing it had been murder . . . Why complicate things unnecessarily? Tie a string to the mains tap, pass it over the gas pipe above, push the end of the string through the keyhole,

42

then pull it from outside until the loop slipped off the lever and the string could be pulled out?

"Old women are light sleepers," said Father Matthias. Was he smiling? It was difficult to tell, despite the sparseness of the moustache that fell over his lips like a finely woven net curtain. Anyway, he was keeping his head bowed, spinning his red cap round and round. A ray of sun shone in through the kitchen window, making the short hairs round the tonsure on the top of his head glisten like hoar-frost.

"Thank you," said Studer, handing back the magnifying glass. The priest stowed it in the apparently bottomless pocket of his habit, produced his snuff box, took a substantial pinch and said, "In Paris, when I had the honour of making your acquaintance, I had to depart so abruptly I did not have the opportunity to give you other important details . . ." he hesitated ". . . about my brother, my brother who died in Fez."

"Important details?" Studer asked, holding a lighted straw under his Brissago.

"It all depends on your point of view." The priest fell silent, playing with his *sheshia*. Then he suddenly seemed to come to a decision. He stood up, leaving the lopsided cap on the chair, and said, "I'll make you a coffee."

"If you must," Studer muttered. He was sitting by the door on a kitchen stool that had been scrubbed so often it had gone white, his eyes almost closed. Don't let him see how surprised you are, he thought, and especially not how curious. The man was trying to confuse him. The fact was that only a few hours ago an old woman had died in this room, yet the priest seemed to be ignoring that completely. He picked up a pan, filled it with water and put it on the gas ring. Then he shooed the sergeant off his stool and climbed on to it

43

to switch on the mains tap fully, straightened up, climbed down and said absentmindedly, "Now where can the coffee be?"

In his mind's eye Studer saw the wooden shelf over the gas stove in the Basel apartment with the chipped enamel containers: "Coffee", "Salt", "Flour". There was nothing like that here, just a red paper bag in the kitchen cupboard with ground coffee.

A gentle "pop" – the priest had lit the gas under the pan. Now he started striding up and down the kitchen. The folds of his habit dissolved, then formed again and sometimes, just for a second, a sunbeam struck the white cloth, making it shine like a newly minted silver piece.

"He foresaw it all, did my clairvoyant corporal," said Father Matthias. "He knew: first the one in Basel, then the one in Bern. And neither of us was able to save the two old women. Not me, because I arrived too late both times. Nor you, Inspector, because you lacked belief."

Silence. The gas flame blew back with a strangely dull, mocking hiss; Father Matthias got it burning properly again.

"I had written to both women, warning them of the danger, telling them to be on their guard. I went to see Josepha in Basel, immediately after I arrived – the day before yesterday that was, in the morning. I was going to go and see her again in the evening, but by the time I got there it was late, eleven o'clock. I rang the bell, but the flat was dark and no one came to the door."

"Was there a smell of gas?" Studer asked. He too was speaking formal German.

"No." Father Matthias had his back to the sergeant. He was busying himself with the pan on the stove: the water boiled, Father Matthias tipped the ground coffee in, let it boil up, turned the gas off, poured a little cold water from a ladle into the mixture. Then he took out two cups, muttering, "Now where would the old woman keep her schnapps? Where else but in the bottom of the kitchen cupboard. What do you bet it's in the bottom of the kitchen cupboard, Inspector? . . . There you are, see!"

He filled the cups and bustled about – "No, don't get up, just stay where you are" – bringing the coffee, which he had generously laced with kirsch, over to the sergeant. It was eerie, Studer thought, drinking coffee at ten in the morning in the empty apartment. He felt as if the old woman – he didn't even know what she looked like – were sitting in the leather armchair saying, "Do help yourself, Sergeant, but then go and find my murderer."

So he asked, as if to flesh out his vision, "What did she look like, this Sophie Hornuss?"

Father Matthias, who had resumed his pacing up and down the kitchen, stopped. His hand disappeared into the bottomless pocket of his habit and brought out a small object made of red leather. It looked like a pocket mirror, but when he opened it Studer saw not a mirror but two photographs.

He looked at the pictures. One of them was Josepha, the wart beside her left nostril was unmistakable, only it had been taken when she was still young. There was a kindness in the eyes, round the mouth . . .

The other picture – without being aware of what he was doing, Studer cleared his throat and stared and stared. The eyes above all, that sly, piercing look. And thin lips, no more than a line in the youthful face. Youthful? You could say that. The photo showed a woman in her mid-twenties, but it was one of those faces that never seem to age – or are never young. Both applied. And there was something else the photo told him: why Victor Alois Cleman had wanted a divorce. It would be no fun living with a woman like that. A blouse buttoned up to the neck, a pointed chin resting on a stand-up collar with stiffeners . . . Studer couldn't help it, it sent a shiver down his spine.

Those eyes! They were loaded with scorn, with scornful knowledge. They screamed at you, "I know! I know a lot. But I'm not saying anything."

What was it the woman knew?

"When did your brother get his divorce?" Studer asked; his voice was slightly hoarse.

"In 1908. And he got married again the next year. Marie was born in 1910."

"And your brother died in 1917?"

"Yes."

Silence.

Father Matthias stood there, looking at the floor, then he started pacing up and down again.

"There is one strange fact I forgot to tell you. Collani, my clairvoyant corporal, was recruited in Oran in 1920; that in itself is unusual, to enlist in Africa. And according to documents in his personal file, he spent the Great War as a nurse in Morocco – in Fez. Now as you know, Inspector, it was in Fez that my brother died. I was in the country too at that time, in the Rabat area, and I had no idea Victor was dying."

So he admits he was in the country, Studer thought. And he has a beard. Not a curly beard, a straggly goatee. But the similarity to the picture over Sophie's bed is unmistakable. What's put this crazy idea in my head? The geologist and the priest one and the same person? He stared at the portraits of the two women, which were lying on his knee.

"I didn't even make it to my brother's funeral. When

I got to Fez a month later, Victor was already dead and buried. I couldn't even visit his grave. I was told he'd been dumped in a mass grave, there was a smallpox epidemic at the time . . ."

Studer took out his ring binder to add a note to the entry on "Cleman, Victor Alois". As he did so, a folded piece of paper fluttered to the floor. The priest was more nimble; he picked it up and handed it back to the sergeant, though as he did so he kept hold of it for a moment and gave it a close look.

"Thanks," said Studer, observing the White Father from beneath his eyelashes. Just at that moment he did not merit the name. His sunburnt complexion had grey blotches. The sergeant would have bet anything the man with the straggly goatee had gone pale.

Why? With an apparently casual air the sergeant stuffed the folded sheet in his breast pocket. The paper felt thick. It had not struck him in Basel when he had coolly pocketed the temperature chart under the nose of the uniformed policeman.

So Father Matthias had recognized the temperature chart? Where had he seen it before? In the room of his "clairvoyant corporal"?

And for the first time Sergeant Studer entertained the possibility that the story of the clairvoyant corporal, which he had dismissed as pure invention, might have some meaning – not an occult, metaphysical, clairvoyant meaning, no. You had to look at the story of the clairvoyant corporal as you would an apparently stupid move by a clever opponent at chess. You dismiss the move with a shrug of the shoulders but, surprise, surprise, six or seven moves later you realize you've fallen into a trap.

It would be a good idea to check everything connected with this clairvoyant corporal as thoroughly and carefully as possible. That would be difficult here in Bern. But he had good friends in Paris, didn't he? Commissaire Madelin, whom a dozen inspectors called "*patron*"? Godofrey, the walking encyclopedia? Of course, you couldn't build a theory merely on a man going pale. Anyway, theories! First and foremost he must familiarize himself with the funny relationships in the Cleman family. Yes, *familiarize* himself. Then he'd see.

And at the bottom of the entry in his notebook on Cleman, Victor Alois Studer wrote the words "mass grave" and underlined them twice.

The priest was standing at the window looking out into the courtyard.

"A smallpox epidemic," he said. "I demanded to see my brother's case notes. All the case notes for 1917 were there, even those of an anonymous negro, which said, 'Mulatto, five years old, admitted on ... died on ...' My brother's case notes had gone missing. Yes, Inspector, missing. 'We don't know ...' – 'We're sorry ...' Three months after his death his case notes couldn't be traced.

"Unlikely, don't you think?

"And fourteen years later a man with clairvoyant faculties tells me, after I've woken him from his trance, 'The dead man is going to come to fetch the women. He wants revenge. The dead man is going to come to fetch the women ...' Collani repeated that, then he described my brother, his curly beard, his spectacles. I know you can't imagine the effect it had on me, for that you'd have to know Géryville. You'd have to have seen my room, the greenish twilight, the town all around the house, the *bled*. *Bled* – it means land in Arabic, but we use the word for the plains, the endless plains with the dry esparto grass; it's never sappy, it grows as hay. And it's so silent on the high plateau. Silent! I'm used to silence, I've lived long enough in the great hush of the desert. But Géryville's different. Nearby there's the tomb of a saint, a marabout, the desert tribes go on pilgrimage to it – in silence. Even the bugle calls when the guard is changed in the barracks are swallowed up in the great silence. The drums don't boom, all the drumsticks produce is a dull murmur. And now try to imagine it: my room in the greenish light and an unknown man describing my brother, speaking with his voice . . ." Father Matthias drew out the last word and let it fade away. Suddenly he turned round. Three long strides and he was standing directly in front of the sergeant. There was urgency in his voice and he was breathing heavily as he asked:

"What do you think, Inspector? Do you think my brother's still alive? Do you think it's him behind these two dark murders? That they are murders I'm sure you won't deny now. Tell me honestly, what do you think?"

Studer sat there, forearms on his thighs, hands clasped. He made a massive figure, hard and heavy, like the boulders you find in Alpine meadows.

"Nothing." Studer had reverted to his native Swiss German.

After the priest's lengthy outpouring, the single word had the effect of a full stop.

Then the sergeant stood up. He took his empty coffee cup over to the sink, but as he deposited it there he was seized with a fit of coughing so loud it sounded as if a whole pack of mongrels had been let loose in the little kitchen. Turning away from the sink, he took out his handkerchief – and when he put it back in the side pocket of his raincoat it was wrapped round a hard object.

It was wrapped round the cup in which he had

found Somnifen mixed in with the coffee grounds on the bottom. But the cup had been rinsed out.

By whom?

It had taken him scarcely ten minutes to check the apartment – and when he had finished, Father Matthias had been sitting in the leather armchair, playing with his *sheshia*.

Ten minutes. More than enough time to rinse out a cup.

But might they perhaps be able to find fingerprints on the cup?

"Better now, Inspector?" Father Matthias asked. "You should do something about that cough."

Studer nodded. His face was red and there was a glint of tears in his eyes. He waved the priest's advice aside and seemed to be about to say something, but was saved from the necessity by a knock at the door.

The short man in the blue raincoat and the tall man

At the door was a very thin lady with a birdlike head and a page-boy hairstyle. She introduced herself as the director of the dance school that had its premises in the same building, and did so with such a pronounced English accent that the sergeant had the feeling that in this investigation – even if it was the "Big Case" every detective hoped for – his Bernese German was rather underused: one moment he was speaking French, then formal German, then listening to the Basel gargle, and now it was the turn of English. There's something highly un-Swiss about the whole affair, was the vague thought going through Studer's mind, even if all those involved are Swiss – with the exception of the clairvoyant corporal, of course, the priest never said what his nationality was . . . Un-Swiss or, to be more precise, expatriate Swiss, a rather clumsy expression, it didn't exactly trip off the tongue . . .

"I have some information," the lady said, twisting and turning her slim body – Studer found himself looking round for the Indian fakir playing the flute to charm this cobra. "I live below . . ." An arm snaked its way downwards and an index finger pointed at the floor, but then the lady suddenly broke off and stared in amazement at the priest, who was back in the leather armchair, playing with his *sheshia*.

The sergeant just stood there, like a statue, hands on hips, his raincoat pushed back. He looked like a tortoise standing on its hind legs, the way you sometimes

51

see them in picture books. His slim head and skinny neck only served to emphasize the similarity.

"Well," he asked brusquely.

"Someone rang at the door last night," the thin lady said in her strong English accent. "It was a short man wearing a blue raincoat. When he spoke it was not very clear since he was wearing a *scarf* . . . a *cache-nez*, oh, what's the German? A long woollen thing wrapped round his neck and covering the lower half of his face."

A dry cough as she cleared her throat, then, "He had pulled his hat down over his forehead. He asked for Frau Hornuss. 'The next floor,' I said. The man thanked me and left. It was quite quiet in the building, so I could hear him ring the doorbell up here."

"What time was that?"

"About . . . about eleven o'clock, perhaps a little later. I had just given a lesson, it finished at five to eleven. Then I had a shower —"

"Aha," said Father Matthias, settling even deeper in his armchair. "So you took a shower. Hm?"

"That's of no interest," Studer snapped.

The lady seemed not to notice the impoliteness of the two men, she was staring spellbound at the priest's *sheshia*, which was going round and round, now slower, now quicker.

"And then? Did you hear anything else?" Studer asked impatiently.

"Yes . . . Wait . . . So I heard him ring – our apartment is directly underneath this one. I hadn't closed the door, I wanted to see if Frau Hornuss would come to the door, perhaps she had already gone to bed . . . but she seemed to be expecting the visitor, he had hardly rung than I heard the old woman's voice. 'At last!' she said. It sounded like relief. 'Do come in.' Then the door was closed."

"Can you remember Frau . . . Frau . . ."

"Frau Tschumi."

That was all he needed, thought Studer. An English-woman with a Bernese surname!

"Well, Frau Tschumi, can you tell me how Frau Hornuss addressed this man. I mean, did she use the familiar form, or the formal *Sie*?"

"In England we only have the one word, so I imagine she said *Sie*."

"But you're not sure, Frau Tschumi?"

"Sure? My God! You must remember I was tired. Are you the police?" the thin lady suddenly asked.

"Yes . . . Sergeant Studer. And you didn't hear anything else?"

"Oh yes," said the lady with a smile, "quite a lot . . . I'm sorry, Mr . . . Herr Studer" – there was no point in trying to do anything about it: the French called him "Studère" and the English lady said something like "Styoodah", like the purring of a contented pussy-cat – "but do you think that gentleman could stop playing with his hat? It's getting on my nerves."

Father Matthias blushed like a little schoolboy caught in some misdemeanour, quickly popped his *sheshia* back on his head and stuck his arms up the sleeves of his habit.

"I heard steps in the kitchen," said the lady, writhing like a snake. "Then some heavy object being dragged right across the apartment, then the murmur of voices; it went on for a long time, a very long time, almost an hour. I said to my husband, 'What do you think is going on? The old lady has never had a visitor that late before, what can it be?' You must know, Inspector" – it came out as "Inspectah" – "we liked the old lady. She was all alone and sometimes we went to visit her and sometimes she came to our apartment. She was always sad . . ."

53

"Yes, yes," said Studer impatiently. "Get on with it."

"Suddenly it went silent in the kitchen. Someone crossed the apartment above very quietly, so quietly it sounded as if they were deliberately trying not to make any noise. We can hear what's going on upstairs very clearly, the floor must be hollow. Then the door opened . . . and I opened ours. Curiosity, you know, Inspector, curiosity! . . . I heard the key being turned in the lock of the apartment door, then it went quiet. Completely quiet, you understand, no steps going away, nothing. I said to my husband – he was standing beside me – 'What can her visitor be doing up there?' But hardly had I stopped whispering than I heard steps creeping down the stairs. They were dark, the man didn't put the light on, perhaps he didn't know where the switch was. He was creeping down the stairs in the darkness, coming towards us, when he saw the chink of light. He stopped, waiting. Then, quite suddenly, he took a few long strides and ran past – no, he didn't run . . . he jumped . . ."

Such a dramatic account! Why was it women always had to put on an act? In a matter-of-fact voice Studer asked, "Did he seem frightened?"

"Yes, very, very frightened. He dropped something. It didn't make a noise when it landed on the floor, but I could see it in the light from our door. I heard the man hurrying down the stairs in leaps and bounds. And then the front door slammed shut."

"Doesn't it get locked at ten?" Studer asked.

"No, not until eleven, because of my dancing classes, and even then it's often forgotten. There's a man on the ground floor who's always forgetting his house key. He lives alone and when he gets home too late he rings our bell. That's why we usually leave the door open . . ."

"Hmm," Studer muttered. "And what was it he dropped, madame?"

"This here," the thin lady said, holding out her hand to Studer, palm upwards. On it was a thin piece of string rolled up into a figure of eight with a knot round the middle. Studer glanced at the man with the bare, sinewy calves before he picked it up, then again when he had the string in his fingers. There was a smile playing round his lips that was difficult to interpret. Enigmatic? Mocking, perhaps? No, not mocking, the expression in his eyes ruled that out, they were wide and sad, a grey sea with clouds above – and an occasional, very occasional glint of sunlight on the smooth surface.

Studer undid the knot. There was a loop at one end. He climbed up on to the stool and placed the loop round the lever, after he had returned it to the horizontal position, then moved the stool so that he could pass the string over the gas pipe above the door, letting the end dangle down. Having threaded that end through the keyhole, he went out into the corridor and, holding the door shut with his left hand, began gently to pull on the string with his other. After a while he could feel no more resistance and the whole string came out, with the loop at the end that he had so carefully placed round the lever. Only then did he go back into the kitchen.

The mains tap on the gas meter was at an angle of forty-five degrees.

"*Quod erat demonstrandum,*" said the priest. "Do you remember? QED. That was what they put at the end of the theorems – Pythagoras's theorem, for example – in the geometry books we had at secondary school. Only the way the murder here was committed is easier to prove than Pythagoras's aforementioned theorem.

For that theorem, Inspector, is not just something for the schoolchildren . . ."

The man talks just for the sake of talking, Studer thought. Empty words. He shivered again, despite his coat. He buttoned it up and turned the collar up too. Father Matthias went chattering on. From Pythagoras's theorem he got on to the games of cops and robbers the boys played and from those childhood memories to the Moroccan *djishes*, what they called the bands of robbers on the borders of the great desert, he explained . . . he'd once been attacked by one of them . . . The words kept pouring out, like a stream cascading into a rocky pool.

"You can go," Studer broke in, turning to the lady. "Your statement was very informative. Perhaps it will help us. Thank you, madame – *Goodbye*," he added, to show that he could speak some English.

But the lady seemed to feel that was being too familiar. She wrinkled her nose and left the apartment without a word. From the floor below she could be heard going on about something in shrill tones, interrupted by calming words from a deep voice.

"It's true, you can hear what's going on in the other apartments, can't you, Father Matthias?"

The priest stood up, his *sheshia* sitting crookedly on his small head. He kept his eyes fixed on Studer's breast, as if in mute appeal to the organ that is generally regarded as the seat of our emotions. But the sergeant's heart did not respond to the silent call.

"I'll be back in a minute, then we can go," said Studer, leaving the priest standing. When he returned, accompanied by Frau Tschumi, Father Matthias was still standing in the middle of the kitchen, a long-suffering expression on his face.

Studer nodded towards the man in the white habit and asked, "Yes?"

"*Yes*," said the lady, falling back into English in her excitement. With a look of disgust on her face she waved away the drift of blue smoke from the sergeant's Brissago. "The eyes," she went on, "I think the eyes are the same."

"*Meeerci*," said Studer in a broad Swiss accent, and the lady departed.

The silence in the brightly lit kitchen was becoming oppressive, but neither of the men seemed to feel like breaking it. Studer made a business of putting his gloves on – thick, grey woollen gloves. His Brissago was dangling down from the corner of his mouth, which probably explained why the following words sounded somewhat strained:

"You do realize you're a suspect, Father? The lady thinks she recognizes you. You're the right height, she says, and your eyes, too, they . . . You'll have to prove exactly when you left Basel yesterday, when you arrived in Bern. And I'd like to see your papers, too."

Now there was a thing! Tears appeared in the old man's eyes, they ran down his cheeks, clung to his sparse beard, then more came, and a gulp that sounded like a sob, and another. His right hand dug into his deep pocket while his left clung on to the edge of his habit. A handkerchief appeared – he needed to use it – the magnifying glass, the snuff box and finally a passport.

"*Meeerci*," said Studer, with the same broad accent as before. But the emphasis was different, there was an undertone of excuse in the word.

Passeport Pass Passaporto . . . pour . . . für . . . per . . .

"What on earth does this mean?" Studer asked.

After the three prepositions came: *Koller, Max Wilhelm.*

Sergeant Studer took off his grey woollen gloves again, stuffed them in his pockets, sat down on the kitchen stool, took his new ring binder out of his breast pocket and said, without looking up as he licked his index finger and leafed through the passport with gestures you see in policemen all around the world, from Cape Town to the North Pole, from Bordeaux to San Francisco, "Sit down."

He did not look up, but he heard the creaking of the springs in the leather armchair – the armchair in which the old woman had fallen asleep for good.

But the interrogation was not to proceed uninterrupted. An elderly man appeared in the doorway asking, in a strong Bernese accent, whether there was a detective here, he had something to tell.

The elderly man did go on rather, but what he had to say could be summarized in a few sentences: When he had come home late the previous evening – he lived on the ground floor, he told them, from which it was not difficult to guess that he was the man who kept forgetting his keys – he had seen a car waiting outside the house and a tall man had been walking up and down on the pavement. He'd asked this man if he was waiting for someone, but all he had received in reply was a surly grunt. Immediately after that a man in a blue raincoat had come dashing out of the building, grabbed the tall man by the arm, pushed him into the car, slammed the door and away they'd gone. He'd thought – Rüfenacht, Ernst Rüfenacht, by the way – he'd thought the cops – sorry, the police – might be interested, the skinny cow – sorry, the dancing teacher on the first floor had suggested he should inform them of what he'd seen. Which is what he was doing . . .

"*Merci*," said Studer for the third time, rather brusquely. Since he was conscientious, however, he wrote *Rüfenacht, Ernst, 44 Gerechtigkeitsgasse* down in his notebook since, like Frau Tschumi, the man was a possible witness.

Then he just sat there on the stool at the kitchen table covered with its oilcloth, staring into space. As the ash on his Brissago grew longer and longer, the silence grew more and more oppressive. From time to time it was broken by a shy sniff. Then Studer squinted from beneath his half-closed lids at Father Matthias, whose passport called him "Max Wilhelm Koller" while he claimed to be the brother of the dead geologist. But his name had been Cleman, not Koller . . . What had Koller to do with Cleman – or Cleman with Koller, for that matter?

Two men. A short man in a blue raincoat and a tall man waiting out in the street . . . An old woman playing patience in her lonely apartment. Or had she been playing something less innocent? Had she been telling her visitor's fortune from the cards? Or her own? And her visitor? He was short, so he'd been told – like the priest. And he was afraid – like the priest! At least that was what Frau Tschumi had said.

The cup with the coffee grounds and traces of Somnifen in the bottom had been rinsed out. When? The sergeant had walked round the apartment and when he'd got back to the kitchen the priest had been sitting in the leather armchair. Strange, too, how well Father Matthias knew his way around: there's the coffee and there's the kirsch. Had he been surprised to learn there were fibres stuck to the keyhole of the lock that had been broken off? Not a bit of it. But he'd suddenly burst into tears, like a little child, when he'd been accused of the murder and asked to show his papers.

Contradictory, that was the only word for it.

At times the sergeant felt he could trust the man in

the white habit, and then at others he distrusted him. When he lectured him – about Cardinal Lavigerie or Pythagoras's theorem – there was something childlike about the way he talked; but when he was silent there was something sly, something devious in his silence. The childlike, unworldly side to him could be easily explained: it was not for nothing that he had spent years roaming the wide plains as a missionary, saying mass in distant outposts, hearing confession. And his devious side? Was devious the right word for it? Might his behaviour, his exaggerated self-assurance in a room which had, after all, been the scene of a murder, not come from something like embarrassment? Embarrassment: the improbable story of the clairvoyant corporal in Géryville . . .

And while the silence continued to hang heavily over the kitchen, Sergeant Studer wrote in his new ring binder: *Get Madelin to enquire whether Corporal Collani really disappeared.*

He cleared his throat, knocked the ash off his Brissago, found it had gone out, relit it and asked, without looking up, "Why do you have a different name from your brother?" The words echoed round the kitchen, and it was only when he had finished that Studer noticed he had used the familiar form to the priest, as if he were just an ordinary suspect.

"He was" – a sob – "my stepbrother, from . . . from my mother's first marriage."

Studer looked up and could not suppress a smile. Once more Father Matthias had his *sheshia* balanced on his right index finger and was making it spin round by prodding it with his left hand. His tears dried up without needing to be wiped away. But after that one answer his lips remained sealed and Studer gave up the interrogation.

Two hours later – by that time it was half past twelve – a sergeant of the Bern cantonal police and a priest in a white habit with open-toed sandals were walking along, much to their mutual embarrassment, through the arcades of the city of Bern. Much work had been done in those two hours, work that had borne some fruit, for which the sergeant had his good fortune to thank, and his contact with a man who, instead of postage stamps, collected fingerprints, fingerprints of all Swiss criminals. Criminals, note, old Herr Rosenzweig was not interested in lesser miscreants. The walls of his study were covered in pictures – all framed and under glass – which looked like reproductions of surrealist paintings. In fact, they were enlarged photographs of thumbs, index fingers, palms, enlarged ten, twenty times, with tiny dots among the loops, whorls and arches: the pores . . .

Before Studer left the priest in Sophie Hornuss's lonely flat, he said, "As far as I'm concerned, you can run away if you feel like it, though I don't advise it, we'd soon get you again. I have to go and see an acquaintance of mine. Since my friend Madelin recommended you to me, I don't like just to take you to the police station and lock you up there. Let me go and visit my friend, that might perhaps clear up a few things. After that I'll come back for you and then we can see what the next step is."

Sounds good, thought Studer, see what the next step is . . . But what will that next step be?

Old Herr Rosenzweig, who collected photos of fingerprints as avidly as an art lover might collect African carvings, lived on Bellevuestrasse. Studer took the bus.

The door was opened by a tall, bony man with gold-rimmed spectacles perched on the end of his nose. Clean-shaven, his hair cropped close, he had small, podgy hands.

"Ah, it's Studer." Herr Rosenzweig's welcome was hearty, and in the same breath he asked whether the police were stuck again. It was happening more and more now, he said, someone was coming to see him almost every day. Wouldn't it be simpler if the authorities were to set up their own fingerprint collection, eh?

"The crisis," said Studer apologetically, "the world economic crisis."

That set the old gentleman off on a rant. "Always the same old excuse! The crisis, the world economic crisis! The crisis is a very convenient excuse. But what have you got for me today, Sergeant?"

Studer took the cup out, very carefully, so as not to touch the sides. Herr Rosenzweig picked up one of the shakers of fingerprint powder that he always kept on his desk, as other people would a lighter or an ashtray. Herr Rosenzweig never smoked.

The cup was light coloured, so graphite powder was carefully sprinkled over it, then blown away: two clear prints.

"Thumb and index finger," said Herr Rosenzweig, taking up his magnifying glass. He examined the prints for a long time, shook his head, looked at Studer, then finally asked him, intrigued, "Where did you get this, Sergeant?"

Studer told him the whole story. The old gentleman stood up murmuring something about a scar . . . a scar, and took down a file from a shelf (Studer saw the date, 1903), leafed through the contents and thrust a sheet under the sergeant's nose.

"It's guesswork, of course," he said, "but it could be

right. To do it properly we'd have to photograph the prints on the cup. We can do that later, but *à première vue,* as our French neighbours would say, they seem to be from the same person. Have a look yourself, Sergeant."

Studer compared them. A demanding task. Finding fibres on a keyhole was simplicity itself by comparison. But there was definitely a certain similarity between the thumbprint on the cup and the thumbprint on the photograph. At the bottom of the photograph it said: *Unknown.*

"What case was that?" Studer asked.

"Nineteen hundred and three, the beginnings of fingerprinting. This is unique, Sergeant, the first photograph of a fingerprint taken in Switzerland. You won't find it anywhere else – I mean the reproduction of the fingerprint. Locard once spent a whole hour begging for it, he'd come straight from Lyon, it was Reiss in Lausanne who'd wished him on me. But I stood my ground and said no. I don't know why. When I'm dead my collection will go to the Canton of Bern – it's in my will – and the cousin of some member of the Federal Council will be appointed custodian. But he won't bother with the collection much, he'll go off and play cards instead and when a visitor happens to come along it'll be closed. Ah well . . . But I'm supposed to be telling you about this. Right, then . . ."

The first thumbprint

"Fribourg . . . You know Fribourg, Sergeant? An old town, very pretty. A girl was found murdered there on 1 July 1903. At first it was assumed it was suicide. There was a glass on the bedside table with prussic acid in it, or KCN, to be more precise, potassium cyanide.

"How had the girl managed to obtain the poison? A mystery. Her parents found her dead in her bed one morning at eight and immediately called the police. At that time the superintendent of the Fribourg police was a man who had heard something of the latest methods of detection. On the glass – it was a straight-sided glass, such as people use to keep their toothbrush in – he noticed a clear fingerprint. So he wrapped the glass up in tissue paper and, since in those days there was only one man in Switzerland who knew anything about this new science of dactyloscopy, he rang me up.

"I happened to be fairly free – in July there's nothing much for an lawyer to do – so I went to Fribourg, taking my camera with me, some powdered cerussite and powdered graphite.

"I won't bore you with details. I got a nice clean photo of the fingerprint, developed it, took the dead girl's fingerprints, her parents', the superintendent's. And then I compared them. It was a tedious business, comparing all the fingerprints, but soon I was sure that some other person had been in the girl's room and put the glass with the potassium cyanide on her bedside table. And that person had murdered her."

Herr Rosenzweig, who, despite his name, did not look at all Jewish, got a piece of cotton wool and put it in his ear.

"My teeth," he said apologetically. "They ache. What can one do, Sergeant? It's old age."

He didn't use the Bernese dialect but the standard Swiss German all educated people spoke by then . . .

"Yes, someone from outside had put the glass with potassium cyanide on the girl's bedside table. When the autopsy revealed that she was pregnant, it seemed clear the girl had been murdered – and by a very cunning killer, since the only clue he had left was a thumbprint on the glass.

"You must remember, Sergeant, in those days criminals were not as well informed as they are today; they didn't know that a fingerprint could give them away. They didn't go about their business in surgeon's gloves. And it was chance, pure chance that the superintendent in Fribourg thought of me and rang up. Chance, too, that I had time . . .

"That's how I came to have this photograph. I've looked at it a lot – I enlarged it, but the enlargements weren't a success. I compare it with every new fingerprint I get for my collection, in the hope I'll eventually find the man with that thumbprint.

"To complete the story I was telling you, the 1903 investigation got nowhere and fizzled out. The girl was allowed a lot of freedom, by the standards of the time. She came to Bern twice a week – she had piano lessons here – and sometimes she stayed overnight. With a girlfriend, she said.

"The superintendent in Fribourg contacted the Bern police and they established that the girl had stayed in the Hotel zum Wilden Mann several times, each time accompanied by a young man. But the young man could not be found. The police, as the saying goes, were baffled. The hotel porter did give a description of him, but it was so sketchy it was no use.

"A student? Someone studying in Bern? Chemistry? Medicine?

"That left the mystery as to why he had travelled to Fribourg. He could just as well have given the girl the potassium cyanide tablet and told her it was very good for headaches. But no, he'd gone to Fribourg, got into the girl's room, dissolved the poison in water and got her to drink it. It wasn't too difficult. Ulrike – the girl was called Ulrike Neumann – had an attic room and the front door stayed open until ten o'clock. There were three families living in the building . . . Who could check all the comings and goings?

"And now, Sergeant, you turn up with my long-sought-after fingerprint! At least I think it is the same. I couldn't swear to it, of course, just see how yellowed the photo is, despite all my care. But that scar . . . You can see the scar, can't you? The cut across the skin, slicing through the loops? Where did you find the print?"

Studer cleared his throat; he wasn't used to staying silent for so long. Then he told Herr Rosenzweig about the two dead women, the cup in the sink, how it had been rinsed out while he was looking round the apartment.

"It sounds like my man," said Herr Rosenzweig. "Twenty years on, but the same modus operandi, I'd say. You haven't taken the priest's fingerprints?" Studer shook his head. "Pity."

Silence. Then Herr Rosenzweig stood up and said, "Leave the cup with me, Sergeant, I'll make an enlargement of the print." He looked at his watch. "If you want, you can have a copy at four o'clock."

Studer stood up as well. His hand automatically went to his breast pocket. Automatically because he intended to light a Brissago the moment he was out of Herr Rosenzweig's sanctum. So he put his hand in his pocket, and as he did he felt something rustle. When he took out the piece of paper, the long, slim cigar case was completely forgotten, for what he had in his hand was the temperature chart.

The temperature chart. He unfolded it and looked at it, knitting his brows with concentration. Suddenly he was far away: the whitewashed room that still smelt of gas, the gables with hoar-frost on them and a pale winter sun edging over the roof ridge opposite . . .

But Marie was standing at the window. She was wearing an expensive fur jacket, her breath was making a cloudy patch on the glass, drops were forming . . .

"What's that treasure you have there, Sergeant?"

"A temperature chart . . ." And Studer told him about the document.

"Leave it with me," said Herr Rosenzweig. "I'll treat it with iodine vapour, perhaps I'll be able to get a fingerprint from it. Whether I'm successful or not, I'll certainly be able to tell you where it was sent from. You know that the impression of a postmark through the envelope can still be made out years later."

Studer thanked him and promised he'd be back around four.

"No need," said Herr Rosenzweig, "no need at all. I'm coming into town anyway, we can meet somewhere, if you like. How about a game of billiards?"

"I don't know if I'll have the time," said Studer. "*Merci* all the same."

*

Father Matthias was sitting in the leather armchair reading a little book in a black binding. He had a bent pair of steel-rimmed spectacles on his nose and his lips moved silently.

After a curt greeting Studer demanded to see the priest's thumbs. They were smooth, no scar cutting through the loops.

That meant? That meant that in the few minutes Studer had been out of the kitchen someone apart from the priest must have come in and rinsed out the cup. Which seemed highly unlikely. More likely was the alternative theory, namely that the thumbprint Studer's retired lawyer friend had found on the cup had been left there by the murderer the previous evening. And Father Matthias had, for reasons that were as yet unclear, rinsed the cup out and thus helped the murderer. Why? Everything pointed to Father Matthias knowing who the murderer was and yet wanting to cover up for him ... Suddenly the sun burst in through the window and Studer came to a halt, dazzled, in the middle of the kitchen.

Koller ... He knew that name. He'd heard it before ... connected with a Christian name that sounded like his ... Yes, "greetings from young jakobli to old jakob". But ...

The secretary! The late geologist's former secretary, the secretary who had taken Marie Cleman to Paris, bought her a fur jacket and silk stockings, the secretary who had disappeared three months ago and whose disappearance was being investigated by Commissaire Madelin of the French Sûreté. The man was called Koller.

Koller was a fairly common name, true, but still ...

Sergeant Studer stood there, in the middle of the kitchen where the divorced Sophie Hornuss had died, with such a faraway look in his eyes that they looked like those of an ox chewing the cud.

And again the silence in the little kitchen grew oppressive, until Studer took his watch out of his waistcoat pocket and pointed out that it was half past one. What did Herr Koller intend to do now? "Herr Koller!" the sergeant said.

"May I accompany you, Inspector?" Father Matthias asked shyly. He seemed to be afraid of being alone.

"If you like."

Contradictory. That wasn't an explanation, it was simply the way the White Father was. And it was to get closer to an explanation for this contradictory character that a police sergeant put up with the embarrassment of walking through the town alongside a man in a white habit.

"Come on then," he said. "We can go and eat somewhere. But first I have to go to my apartment, there may be a message from my wife. You know," he added suddenly reverting to the polite "*Sie*", "that I've just become a grandfather."

They had reached the street and were walking slowly along through the arcades.

"A grandfather," the priest said in a choked voice, so that the sergeant was afraid the skinny man was about to burst into tears again.

He quickly carried on. "Yes, it's a strange feeling, as if you've lost a daughter. She married a country policeman in Thurgau – my wife sent me a telegram to Paris to say they were both doing fine. But I've already told you that."

"Congratulations . . . Once more, heartiest congratulations."

"Why congratulate me?" Studer asked in irritation. "I've nothing to do with it. It's my daughter who's had the child, I'm just the grandfather ... Congratulations!" He shrugged his broad shoulders. A foreign fashion, these kind of compliments.

The sergeant was so irritated he stopped abruptly and asked, "Now listen, Herr Koller, are you related to your brother's former secretary who disappeared a few months ago and is now being sought by the Paris police?"

"I ... What do you mean, related? Related to whom?"

"To a certain Jakob Koller who went to Morocco with your stepbrother Victor Cleman. Afterwards he started up a business in Paris and took on Marie ... as his secretary ... his secretary!"

Silence. It seemed as if the sergeant had expected no other answer to his question. The priest was taking long, ranging strides; his chin was down on his chest and his hands tucked well into his sleeves, like a muff.

A wintry sun shone down. The hoar-frost on the pavements looked like a thin layer of glittering dust. The two unequal figures were crossing Kirchenfeld Bridge when the priest suddenly stopped, leant over the balustrade and stared for a long time down at the Aare. Its waters were pale, almost colourless. The north wind was blowing.

"Everything is so different here," said Father Matthias. "Beautiful too, of course, but I long for the red hills and the wide plains." He spoke very calmly. Studer rested his elbows on the balustrade and looked down. Then the priest turned round. Studer heard a car drive past and then, hardly had the hum of the engine passed, an exclamation from his companion. "Inspector! Look!"

Studer looked round, but all he saw was the rear of a car and its number, which he automatically read: BS 3437 – a Basel number ...

"What is it?" he asked.

"If I didn't know it was impossible ..." said the priest, rubbing his eyes.

"If what was impossible?"

"I think Collani was in the car, with my niece Marie."

"Marie? Marie Cleman? *Chabis!*" Studer was beginning to lose his temper. Was this spindleshanks having him on? Marie together with the clairvoyant corporal? In a car with a Basel number plate?

"He was wearing a blue raincoat," said the priest, more to himself.

Studer said nothing. What would be the point of asking questions? He felt as if he were being sucked down into a whirlpool: he could not longer tell what was truth, what lies. At times the man in the white habit struck him as sinister, at times as ridiculous. What he really ought to do would be to cross-examine the priest: Why did you rinse out the cup with the remains of the Somnifen? Why did you come to Switzerland? Why did you leave Marie in Basel? ... Above all, he ought to check whether the man really was a priest. Didn't Catholic priests have to say mass every morning? thought Studer, remembering what Marie had told him.

"When precisely did you arrive in Bern?" Studer asked. He'd already asked the question once, but he asked it again – not actually expecting to get a reply. He was right. The priest said, "I had dinner with my niece, then I set off."

"By train?"

"I've already told you I took a taxi."

"And where are you staying? Where've you left your luggage?"

"In the Hotel zum Wilden Mann."

"Where?" Studer almost screamed. He halted in the middle of the pavement.

"In the Hotel zum Wilden Mann . . ." said Father Matthias, and a helpless, tormented look appeared in his eyes, as it had before, a look that could all too easily dissolve into tears.

"The Hotel zum Wilden Mann!" Studer repeated, setting off again. "Zum Wilden Mann!"

"Why does that surprise you, Inspector?" the priest asked shyly. His voice was strangely hoarse. "It was strongly recommended. Has it got a dubious reputation?"

"Recommended, was it? By whom?"

"I . . . I can't remember. By someone on the ship, I think."

"You didn't know the hotel before?"

"Before? Before what? I've been in Morocco for over twenty years."

"Twenty years? And before that?"

"Before I went to Morocco I was in the Order's house, it's near Oran, in Algeria. I entered the Order when I was eighteen."

"And you've never heard of a girl called Ulrike Neumann? Eh? A girl who used to stay at the Hotel zum Wilden Mann?"

Studer was just in time to catch the priest as he fell – God, was the man skinny! – and stood there holding the slim figure in his arms, looking at a face that had gone green while the hairs of the sparse goatee literally stood on end.

"Hey-up," said the sergeant. It was a call he had used while herding the cattle as a boy. "Hey-up," he repeated. "Steady on. Are you ill?" he asked, adding, "I've been stupid, Father Matthias, you must forgive me, I never thought . . ."

"It's all right," said the White Father. Fortunately he could say that without moving his lips much, for they were stiff and white.

Cries could be heard: "'S'e ill?" – "What's up?" – "Poor old soul!" – " 'E must be frozen stiff with them bare feet." – " 'E's used to it, blockhead."

Angrily, Studer told the well-meaning onlookers to go to the devil, he could see to the old man himself. He lived nearby and . . .

"Let's get on, Inspector," said Father Matthias in a loud, clear voice. "And forgive me all this fuss. I can manage if you just support me a little. And when we get to your place I can warm myself up, can't I?"

Just at that moment Studer would have done anything for the skinny little man. Even lit the stove in the living room, the monster he could never get to draw properly. Still, who would have thought the name of Ulrike Neumann would have such a devastating effect on the priest – a name the sergeant had heard for the first time that morning? Had the man become a priest to . . . what was the word? . . . to . . . atone, yes, that was it, to atone for the murder of the young girl?

But the thumb in Herr Rosenzweig's photograph had had a scar, and the priest's thumbs were smooth.

Cleman – Koller . . . Koller – Cleman . . . A son from his mother's first marriage. What was it the sergeant had said in Basel? Funny family relationships. You could say that again. The relationships in the Koller family – or should it be the Cleman family? – were more than just funny, they were strange, remarkable, complicated – clear as mud.

And the north wind was whipping across the bridge. It was hardly better when they turned into Thunstrasse. Studer supported Father Matthias. They were not just walking through the streets of Bern side by side, no, they were arm in arm. But the sergeant had no time to be embarrassed at the idea of acquaintances seeing them.

When they reached the door to his apartment, Studer sniffed the air. Fried onions! Hedy was back! The sergeant was delighted. Things were back to normal and the green monster in the living room would be sure to be giving off heat.

Frau Studer was already there when the sergeant opened the door. She showed no surprise at the visitor he'd brought along, just waited patiently for an explanation, her hands loosely clasped over her starched white apron. When she saw that the odd little man in the white habit with his bare feet sticking out from under it was clinging on to the sergeant so as not to fall down, she hurried up to them and asked, in a soothing, motherly voice, "Is he ill? Can I do anything to help?"

Not waiting for an answer, she grasped the priest under the arms, helped him into the living room and laid him on the couch. In no time at all blankets appeared, a pillow in a fresh pillowcase, a hot-water bottle and a stool beside the couch with a steaming cup of limeflower tea. Next to each other on the floor were the sandals; the straps were thin and worn, the soles curved up at the front.

"You can see they've been a few miles, can't you, *Vatti*?"

Studer muttered something. He hated it when his wife called him *Vatti* in front of strangers. Father! It made him sound old. Still, she immediately made up for it when she went on, "You know, Köbu, I rang the office twice yesterday evening and once this morning, but they couldn't find you anywhere."

He'd had a lot to do, Studer said, and finally found time to give her a kiss on the forehead. A forehead that was high and smooth. The hair above it, divided by a parting and tied in a bun at the back, was brown and shone like chestnuts that had just popped out of the

74

shell. No one, thought Studer, would take her for a grandmother.

The *sheshia*, the misshapen red flowerpot, lay beside the sick man. Absentmindedly, Frau Studer picked it up, put it over her right index finger and prodded with her left hand until it started to spin round. When she looked up, she saw a shy smile on the priest's lips. Studer couldn't help laughing.

"You see, Inspector," said Father Matthias, "it really is the only thing a cap like that's any use for. That thin English lady was quite wrong to let it get on her nerves. You must forgive me, Inspector, forgive me, madame, for putting you to all this trouble. I was taken with a fever out in the street, the change of climate probably, the cold." And the little face with the shining, feverish eyes appeared to confirm that version of events.

"A fever. Huh!" muttered Studer once his wife had left the room. "A fever's a good excuse. Why should a name —"

"Please, Inspector, no more just now," said Father Matthias, and he spoke with vigour, like a man who knows what he wants. "It's unchristian to torment a sick man – and perhaps I haven't entirely forfeited your trust, perhaps you still believe I'm not just putting on an act . . ."

"Hmm," Studer growled, still not entirely won over, not entirely convinced. But an appeal to his humanity was never without effect. "Here in Switzerland," he said softly, "we have not yet introduced the methods employed by neighbouring states. Do you want to go into hospital, Herr Koll— . . . er . . . Father Matthias?"

"No, no, it'll pass. Just a minute, I must have some quinine powder somewhere . . . Or did I leave it in the hotel? . . . No, here it is." He took a round tin, the kind usually containing cough sweets, out of another of his deep pockets, tipped a little of the brown powder into the herb tea, stirred it and drank it down. Suddenly there was a loud clatter as he put the cup down and stared at a small sewing table by the window. There was fear in his eyes.

Frau Studer's voice came from the kitchen, telling the sergeant there was a letter for him, on the little table by the window.

Father Matthias followed the sergeant's every movement with his eyes as Studer picked up the letter and examined it. A women's handwriting, unknown. The postmark: "Transit". Posted at the station, or handed in directly to the mail train.

He tore open the envelope.

A single sheet:

Dear Cousin Jakob,

I enclose my find. I think it will interest you. You didn't look through the telephone book carefully enough. As you will see, the empty envelope I'm sending came from Algeria. It was posted on 20 July last year in Géryville. On 20 July! The anniversary of my father's death – even if the temperature chart says something different. I've heard of the death of my aunt in Bern. How? That I cannot tell you. I'm afraid, and that's why I'm going to disappear for a while. Don't come looking for me, Cousin Jakob, there's no point, I've already told you everything I may tell you. Now it's up to you to solve the case. I'm sure you don't believe they were both suicides either. I know you will see my Uncle Matthias; give him my best wishes. If it's of any interest, he had dinner with me in the second-class station buffet and set off for Bern around twelve in a taxi. I wish you luck.

Yours
Marie Cleman

The envelope accompanying the letter was fairly crumpled. It was addressed to *Madame Veuve Cleman-Hornuss, 12 Spalenberg, Bâle.* On the back was the address of the sender: *Caporal Collani, 1er Régiment Étranger, 2ème Bataillon, Géryville, Algérie.* And the postmark was indeed dated 20 July.

When Studer looked up his eyes met the priest's apprehensive expression. And his voice was apprehensive too, when he asked, "Is it my niece who's written to you?"

Studer just nodded silently. He sat by the window, in his favourite position, legs apart, elbows resting on his thighs, hands clasped. If this really is the "Big Case" I've been dreaming of all these years, he thought, it's a real mess. A mess? There's a jinx on it. But we'll crack it somehow, even if we have to go to Algeria or Morocco. Just like kings and other crowned heads, when Studer talked to himself he didn't think of himself as "I", he used the royal "we".

Frau Studer came in with a tureen of soup.

"It won't bother you if we have our lunch, Friar?"

Father Matthias smiled and Studer informed his wife that he wasn't a monk, but a priest. Frau Studer apologized, then sat down opposite her husband and ladled out the soup. Just as the sergeant was about to take his first spoonful, he heard murmuring from the couch. Surprised, he looked up. Father Matthias had put his hands together and was murmuring a Latin prayer. "*Benedicite . . .*"

The man and woman at the table were so embarrassed, they clumsily folded their hands by their soup plates.

The will

At two o'clock in the afternoon Studer entered the office of the chief inspector of the Bern city police. He knew it well; it had been his own office for fifteen years before the business with the bank had driven him out. But Studer had managed to remain on friendly terms with his successor.

Chief Inspector Werner Gisler consisted of a bald head, which looked as it if were polished with emery paper every morning, on top of a squat body clothed in suits of peasant cloth. His feet were large and the corresponding lace-up boots made to measure, for Gisler had flat feet. He was always telling people how delicate his feet were, an inexhaustible topic with him since he was convinced that having delicate feet was proof of his aristocratic ancestry. Nothing wrong in that: some people have a thing about their stomach, others their digestion or their circulation – and with the superintendent it was his feet.

As Studer entered his office, Gisler was tying his bootlaces. Tying his bootlaces with much grunting and groaning, since his pot belly got in the way. He greeted the sergeant, then said, "If only you knew how difficult it is, Studer. You put your boots on in the morning, you're in a hurry, you're not really paying attention, and before you know it, the tongue's got a crease in it. You didn't smooth it out properly, so now you've got a crease that's pinching your foot, and it keeps pinching all day. You're always concentrating on getting the top of the boot right and that takes so much time you never get round to smoothing out the tongue. It's uncomfortable, but you put up with it, you assume you'll have a minute or two sometime during the day to smooth it out. You can't get down to your work properly, you keep getting distracted by the crease in the tongue of your boot. Now I've got a moment to myself and what happens? You come breezing in! You'll have to wait a minute . . . I have such difficult feet, you know."

Studer offered his deepest commiseration. He was adept at letting other people's – colleagues', friends', prisoners' – complaints about their afflictions wash over him. People needed to talk, to unload their troubles; once they'd got things off their chest he found he could talk to them about more serious matters.

"I'm here," he said, sitting down, "about that business in Gerechtigkeitsgasse."

"Gerechtig . . . keits . . . gasse," groaned Gisler as he struggled with his bootlaces. His bald head had gone purple and there were little beads of sweat glistening on it.

"Yes," said Studer patiently – you have to be patient with people, especially if they're fat and have to do their bootlaces up. "Forty-four Gerechtigkeitsgasse. Sophie Hornuss . . . Gas . . . I've been to the apartment myself. I must apologize for starting an investigation off my own bat."

"Puuf . . . ahh . . . puuf," groaned the inspector, then straightened up at last, subjected his boots to a suspicious scrutiny, waggled his toes and finally said, "I think that'll do – as long as the sock hasn't got any wrinkles."

It didn't seem to have since Gisler placed his flat feet

on the floor, looked around innocently out of his pale blue eyes, said, "To be sure," and nodded meaningfully. "Forty-four Gerechtigkeitsgasse. Sophie Hornuss. Yes . . . yes . . ." So the sergeant had been in the apartment already, had conducted a private investigation, as you might say – hahaha. No one was going to take that amiss, he'd been quite right to go ahead, and it showed a true spirit of cooperation that he had come to see him, Chief Inspector Gisler of the city police, to inform him of the result of his investigation. Which was?

"That it is a case of murder."

"Aha," sighed Gisler, "murder. Reinhard said something similar . . . Indeed . . . And so you think . . . that is . . . you think it's . . . er . . . murder, Studer?"

Yes, said Studer, that was what he thought.

"So perhaps we should call Reinhard in? Or not?"

"Yes, we could call Reinhard in. And perhaps Murmann, too. He was there when the body was found."

"Oh, that's right, yes, Murmann."

So Inspector Gisler picked up the receiver, summoned Detective Constable Murmann of the cantonal police and Detective Corporal Reinhard of the city police, replaced the receiver and wiped the beads of sweat from his bald pate.

A council of war . . . Strangely enough, no one laughed Studer out of court, probably because little Reinhard supported him from the very beginning. At first Murmann did try to ridicule the suggestion, saying it was just another of Köbu's crazy ideas, but all he got for that was a tongue-lashing from Reinhard. He too, he said, had had the feeling there was something not quite right about the Hornuss case. And he'd noted all the odd features in his report: the cards laid out on the table, the leather armchair in the kitchen, the half-open lever on the gas meter . . .

Who was it had reported it to the police? Studer wanted to know, and Reinhard, taking a long drag on his Parisienne, explained that a labourer who sublet from Sophie Hornuss – a furnished attic – had noticed the smell of gas as he passed and had rung the police, so the two of them – he and Murmann – had gone to Gerechtigkeitsgasse.

Here Murmann interrupted him to tell them how excited the sergeant had been, that morning, when – But Murmann was talking far too slowly for the lively Reinhard and felt the rough edge of his tongue again, telling him to shut up and let the sergeant do the talking. The inspector agreed with Reinhard. He had lit his pipe and was sitting at his desk, casting the occasional worried glance at his boots.

And Studer told them the whole story, told them about Cleman, the geologist who had worked for the Mannesmann brothers in Morocco and then betrayed his employers; he told them about Cleman's second wife, who had been killed in similar fashion in Basel, about the Somnifen in the bottom of the cup in the sink and about Herr Rosenzweig's strange conjectures about the thumbprint. He told them how he had met Father Matthias, who in reality was called Koller, and he didn't forget to mention the story of the clairvoyant corporal either, though just as an aside, to indicate that the case had ramifications that spread to distant countries. Then he got back on to Basel and told them he hadn't said anything there. After all, he was a detective with the Bern force and the Basel police should realize —

"That they can't see further than the nose on their face," little Reinhard broke in.

"Exactly," agreed the inspector and, "Goes without saying," muttered Murmann.

They were all agreed that this was the "Big Case". And they were all agreed that the Old Man, that is the chief of police for the Canton of Bern, had to be prodded into action. Bern mustn't miss out on this! Hahaha . . . the very idea . . . ridiculous! And, anyway, those Baslers . . .

There was no holding Chief Inspector Gisler. He rang the bar next door and ordered four bottles of beer.

"Cheers, Studer."

"Köbu's the man!"

Balm to the soul!

They all agreed unreservedly that Studer was the man to solve the case. Who had the knowledge of foreign languages, the connections with the French authorities? Who could call a *commissaire* of the Police Judiciaire his friend?

Köbu Studer.

There you are!

"What?" said the massive figure of Murmann. "An unusual murder's been committed in Bern and we should hand over the case to Basel? Who just sent a uniform along instead of an experienced detective?"

But how could they convince the Old Man?

For what was clear as cow piss, said Reinhard, was that it would be an extensive investigation. They'd have to make enquiries in Basel, ring Paris . . . perhaps it would even prove necessary to go to Géryville to check up on a certain clairvoyant corporal . . . maybe even as far as Morocco?

And it was still within the bounds of possibility that Father Matthias, the monk, the White Priest, Chief Inspector Gisler added, getting into a slight muddle, was the murderer. But if he wasn't, and the Bern police arrested him, what fools they'd look – they all had a healthy respect for the Old Man's outbursts of fury. And the good people of Lucerne and Schwyz would take the opportunity to drag Bern through the mud, there'd be vitriolic editorials in the *Vaterland*.

No, there was only one possible course of action: Studer had to take the case on. He'd put the priest up in his flat, left him in his wife's care, and the priest was at the centre of it all, he was – the Chief Inspector had completed high school – the *nervus rerum*, the crux of the matter.

Immediate instructions were given to the young policeman in the outside office to get changed into plain clothes as quickly as possible and go and guard the sergeant's flat in Thunstrasse.

They still had to convince the Old Man. But how?

The air in the room was thick with blue smoke, but none of the men thought of opening a window. They stared into space, trying to work out how they could get Studer some room to manoeuvre.

What they had heard was enough for them – but only for them, for the three men Studer had convinced. Three men who did not carry much weight: a chief inspector in the city police, a corporal and a constable. Not men whose voices counted for much in the counsels of the mighty; modest professionals, intelligent, true, experienced in their work ... But that was all.

It was Herr Rosenzweig who solved their problem. He came into the office and immediately drew back.

"Spring is here, let in the air," he sang, until he was forced to stop by a fit of coughing. Since none of the men showed any intention of moving, he had to carry out his melodious suggestion himself, and a wave of dusty city air cleared the atmosphere.

One minute later Chief Inspector Gisler, whose delicate feet could not stand the cold, was demanding that the status quo be restored, and Reinhard closed the window.

"I rang your apartment, Sergeant," said Herr Rosenzweig in his best standard Swiss German, "but I was told you weren't there, you'd probably be at the city police. I've got something remarkable to show you, very, very remarkable."

Murmann grunted and said it would be sure to be something very special, but Rosenzweig ignored him. He took two sheets of paper out of his pocket and placed them gently on Studer's thighs.

"What do you say to that?" he asked, leaning against the wall since there was nowhere left to sit. Studer picked up the two pieces of paper – one thick, one thin – and examined them. The thicker piece was the temperature chart. The other was covered in writing and signed. In the top corner was a stamp. Studer glanced through the document. Then, holding it up close to his eyes, he read it a second time, more attentively, and it was some time before he had finished reading it.

The air in the office was clear, transparent. From outside came the honking of horns from passing cars, interrupted from time to time by the slow clip-clop of horses' hooves on the tarmac. Otherwise all was quiet. Inspector Gisler was busying himself with the cover of a file, little Reinhard had lit another Parisienne, and Murmann was taking his time filling his pipe.

But all three heads shot up when a strange sound came from where Studer was sitting. It was something between a sigh, a clearing of the throat and suppressed swearing.

"What's wrong?" asked Gisler, looking at him in surprise.

Old Rosenzweig, who was leaning against the wall, grinned, revealing a set of sparkling teeth with many gold fillings. After a time he switched off his beaming smile and started asking questions, though only rhetorical ones, to which he clearly didn't expect an answer:

"You didn't suspect that, did you, eh, Sergeant? Sensational, isn't it, eh? Even puts my unique photograph in the shade, eh?"

He fell silent, enjoying keeping the policemen in suspense. But when none of the four said anything – they were from Bern, they were very good at hiding their excitement behind a show of indifference – he chattered on.

"Of course, you'll be wondering how I came by the document, Sergeant. It's quite simple. You asked me to see if I could find any fingerprints on the temperature chart. Now there are two methods: iodine vapour and ultraviolet rays. I tried it out on my latest machine – and what did I see? Not just two fingerprints – they were also similar to the print with which I started my collection, by the way – no, I saw something else. Writing appeared! Handwriting!"

Herr Rosenzweig paused, obviously expecting a flicker of curiosity from at least one of his audience. But none of them showed any response. Murmann was balancing on the corner of the desk, Reinhard was staring at the glowing tip of his cigarette, Studer was making heavy weather of relighting his Brissago and Inspector Gisler was busy annotating the margin of a file. There was a note of disappointment in the retired lawyer's voice as he continued.

"Handwriting! Where could the writing be? On one side of the sheet was the temperature chart, the other side was blank. I felt the edge with my finger: two documents had been stuck together. Apply steam, dry them out and you can read the will."

That brought the four policemen to life.

"The will?" Gisler asked.

"*Chabis!*" said Murmann.

"That couldn't ..." said Reinhard, but he didn't finish the sentence.

Studer handed the document to Chief Inspector Gisler. One head appeared on the left, one on the right, three heads in all bent over the piece of paper, and, though it was hardly necessary, Gisler insisted on reading it out in a low voice:

My Last Will and Testament

I the undersigned, Victor Alois Cleman, geologist, from Frutigen, Canton of Bern, make the following disposition: my estate, consisting of eight hectares of land around the village of Gourama in the south of Morocco, I leave jointly and equally to my daughter, Marie Cleman, born 12. 2. 1907 in Basel, and to the Canton of Bern. By accepting this bequest, the Canton of Bern commits itself to ensuring that half of any proceeds that may accrue from the sale of the aforementioned property be transferred to my daughter named above for her free disposal.

The purchase of the aforementioned land has been certified according both to French law and to the Islamic law in force in Gourama. I have established the presence of oil on this piece of land, the boundaries of which are defined in the relevant documents; I estimate that the value of the land in fifteen years time will be some two or three million francs. The documents confirming my right to the land have been buried in an iron chest in a place which can easily be found with the help of the attached document. I have given instructions that this document, together with my last will and testament, shall be sent to my wife, Frau Josepha Cleman-Hornuss, 12 Rheinschanze, Basel, fifteen years after my death. If by that

time my wife should have died, I have made arrangements for
the documents to be given into the possession of my daughter.
    Signed: Victor Alois Cleman
    Fez, 18 July 1917

Chief Inspector Gisler leant back and started to tap his teeth with his pencil; Murmann straightened up and crossed his arms over his chest; little Reinhard took a bright yellow packet out of his trouser pocket and, deep in thought, tamped the cigarette on his thumbnail.

The silence was broken by Rosenzweig saying, "I don't know if you gentlemen are aware of it" – gentlemen, he said! – "but both Shell and Standard Oil are engaged in a struggle for new oilfields, a struggle as desperate as that between God and the devil for souls in the Middle Ages. Consequently a rough estimate would suggest that the oilfields purchased by Herr Cleman are probably worth three or four times what he forecast, not two millions but six or eight – and Swiss francs. That would mean three to four million for Bern, and since the canton is named as executor, the sum would be increased by the fees it could claim. Four and a half million. Not bad, eh?"

"And is the will valid?" Gisler asked.

"As valid as can be in French law. It's a holograph – in the testator's own hand, signed and dated. And since from the point of view of international law it is the attitude of the French that will carry most weight, I don't think we need worry. I imagine the canton could do with the money."

"You can say that again," said Murmann dryly and lit his pipe.

That document, Reinhard said, would make the Old Man see reason.

Studer said nothing. Various vague thoughts were going through his mind: Marie, who would now be rich; an old proverb about a donkey going dancing on the ice when things went too well – and he saw himself as the donkey; the business with the bank that had cost him his job: wouldn't it be nice to get his revenge by securing a small fortune for Bern? That would stop the malicious tongues wagging and guarantee his promotion to inspector. But a lot of water would have to flow under the bridge over the Aare before that happened. It wasn't straightforward . . .

A sharp knock at the door startled him out of his musing. The young policeman was reporting back. He had been to Studer's flat, he said, and Frau Studer had told him Father Matthias had left at half past two. His fever had gone.

As he made his report, the young policeman stood to attention with perfect posture, heels together and the middle fingers of his hands pressed against the blue piping of his uniform trousers.

Gisler just said, "Dismiss," but Studer stood up. At the door he said, "You sort things out with the Old Man, Gisler. Tell him I'd like to speak to him tomorrow morning, I've still got lots more to do today. Then see that your superintendent lets me have his office and his telephone at six o'clock, I've got an hour's telephoning to do. You get on well with him."

Then the door closed. The chief inspector of the city police stared at his feet, turning what the sergeant had just said over and over in his mind. It was the first time the sergeant had used the familiar *du* to him and Gisler was wondering whether to take it as a compliment or an insult. He decided on the former. Sergeant Studer's familiarity was surely a token of recognition for his diplomatic skills. But, still, the fact that the hero of the "Big Case" should address him as an old friend filled Gisler's heart with pride, displacing for five minutes his other pride, his pride in his delicate aristocratic feet.

Clearing the decks

"*Sicuro,*" said Dr Malapelle of the Institute for Forensic Medicine. "Barbituric acid. No doubt about it. A massive dose. Somnifen. The stomach contents seemed to have a strong smell of aniseed and since I don't know of any sedative derived from barbituric acid with an aniseed smell apart from Somnifen, I think we can conclude that's what it was. The woman didn't have long to live, anyway. Terminal endocarditis. Or, to put it more plainly for the lay mind, Inspector, the old lady had a weak heart, a very weak heart. Too much excitement – *e poi* . . . Yes . . . Could she have taken it of her own accord? Perhaps. Probably. One really cannot exclude the possibility of suicide. But you think it murder? You're an old romantic, but if that's what you enjoy . . ."

So Studer told him about the string and the traces of fibres on the edge of the keyhole.

"*Fantasmagoria!*" said Dr Malapelle irritatedly. "You have a vivid imagination and you're letting it run away with you. Pull yourself together."

Then Studer took out the temperature chart – he'd left the will with Gisler – and showed it to the doctor. Malapelle frowned and said, "What's this? Either the diagnosis is wrong, or . . . That isn't a malarial chart. Neither tertiary nor . . . And then – *vedi, ispettore,* either the nurse didn't take the temperature properly or . . . Instead of giving it in tenths of a degree, she's marked it in quarter, half or whole degrees. See for yourself:

36.75, 39.5, 38.0. Impossible! Even taking into account the fact that this chart comes from a colonial hospital, and one run by French doctors at that . . . And anyway . . . It's odd, *singolare*, it's no more work recording the temperature in tenths of a degree . . ."

A furtive smile played around the corners of the sergeant's mouth.

"Thank you, *dottore*," he said, "*mille grazie* . . . Could I see the body of Sophie Hornuss?"

A wrinkled face, with a look of horror on it. It was puffy – and there was no wart beside the left nostril.

At the Hotel zum Wilden Mann Studer asked at the desk if he could speak to Father Matthias. His Reverence had not come back yet, he was told. It just went to show how polite hotel receptionists were. Of course! A priest was "Your Reverence". But Hedy had simply called him "Friar"!

Could he have a look at the priest's room, Studer asked. He took out his warrant card, which proved to be unnecessary. He was known there. The *chef de réception*, who was busy doing nothing in the lobby, had no objection to Studer taking a look at Father Matthias's room.

First floor, second floor, third floor . . . lifts were certainly convenient. You didn't have to waste energy and breath climbing the stairs.

Room 63. The lift boy came with him and waited when Studer really wanted to be alone. But a two-franc piece worked wonders. The little lad vanished in a trice.

There was a lonely toothbrush in the tumbler on the glass shelf over the wash-basin. Beside it a cake of cheap soap. One of the towels had been used. And on a chair was a fairly large, brown vulcanite suitcase.

When Studer opened it, he found in it, carefully folded: one blue raincoat; an ordinary grey off-the-peg suit; a white shirt, worn; a cheap tie and a pair of black shoes.

Spread out on the bed was a pair of blue pyjamas, the kind you could get for five francs in any chain store.

Studer whistled softly to himself, the Bern March. Then he left, but as he went out he glanced back and noticed something, something brown that was sticking out from between the arm and the seat of the armchair. He went over. It was firmly wedged in and took some effort to pull out.

A small bottle. Somnifen. Empty. He popped it in his coat pocket.

"When did Father Matthias arrive?"

The receptionist could not tell him. Probably during the night, his colleague would know, but at the moment he was sleeping. Couldn't it wait?

Studer nodded and left the hotel, ushered out by the solicitous *chef de réception* beseeching him to keep things quiet should the hotel be involved in any criminal affair. He would be very grateful, said the *chef de réception*, who gave off a strong scent of brilliantine, the sergeant must understand how damaging something like that could be to the hotel . . .

Studer cut short the flow of words by turning back and demanding to see the hotel register.

Koller, Max Wilhelm, b. 13 March 1876, missionary.

Missionary . . . Studer stood there, his raincoat pushed back, hands on hips, staring at the name he had already seen that day, in a passport.

Father Matthias, alias Max Wilhelm Koller, had had a brother, Victor Alois Cleman, who had been active as a geologist and informer; he was Swiss as well, and he'd died in Fez of an acute tropical fever and been buried in a mass grave. And, according to his brother, this Cleman was now active as a ghost, speaking through the mouth of a clairvoyant corporal, threatening, three months in advance, to kill his two wives and going through with the murders. Hissing murders, if you could put it like that. The gas hissed as it came out of the burners and the mains tap was half open, sloping at an angle of forty-five degrees.

One old woman in Basel, one old woman in Bern. Sophie had been well off. Why had the geologist given his ex more money than his lawful wedded wife? Why had his wife had to live in poverty with her daughter in a bedsitter with a tiny kitchen that wasn't really a kitchen, more of a corridor, while the ex lived in comfort: two-room apartment, ornate furniture, gas stove with grill and oven?

All there had been in Basel was a little portable stove with two rings and above it a lopsided shelf with old chipped enamel containers: "Salt", "Coffee", "Flour". Good-natured people had a hard time of it down here on earth, they always got the worst deal, while the others, the ones with the thin lips, the mocking eyes, exploited their knowledge.

Josepha had never nagged her husband, of that he was sure. But Sophie? Why the divorce after only a year? Knowledge was not only power, as the popular saying had it, knowledge could also bring in the money. Knowledge was the basis for a cleverly planned piece of blackmail. *Could* be the basis . . .

Every action could be explained, and if the explanation was not in the conscious mind, then you had to look for it in the unconscious. The simple detective sergeant from Bern had learnt that in the course of a case he had had to investigate in a lunatic asylum. A psychiatrist had taken it upon himself to hammer home the difference between the conscious and the unconscious mind in rather graphic detail.

The *chef de réception* did not know what to make of the silent detective who seemed hypnotized by the hotel register.

Koller, Max Wilhelm, b. 13 March 1876, Fribourg, missionary, arriving from Paris, returning to Paris . . .

Born 13 March 1876. That meant he was fifty-six. He looked older, did Father Matthias with his sparse goatee. On 13 March. Unlucky thirteen. At the age of eighteen he'd joined the Order of the White Fathers, an order founded by Cardinal Lavigerie to convert the Mohammedans. A hopeless task, as the priest himself had admitted. In 1917 he had been forty-one. And he came from Fribourg . . .

Fribourg . . . Ulrike Neumann had lived in Fribourg. The Ulrike Neumann who had had an affair with an unknown man in Bern and had died after taking KCN, potassium cyanide. And she'd met her lover in the Hotel zum Wilden Mann . . .

The *chef de réception* with the perfectly groomed hair, which smelt so strongly of brilliantine, started when the silent man suddenly opened his mouth and ordered, in a slightly hoarse voice, "Call the manager."

"I'm not sure whether just at the moment the manager is —"

"Call the manager!" It was a tone that brooked no argument.

"I'll just go and see whether —"

"I expect to see him in three minutes. Take me to his office." The order was delivered in formal German. The receptionist disappeared and Studer marched over to a door, the upper half of which consisted of a pane of frosted glass on which was written in black letters: MANAGER.

Two minutes thirty seconds. A little man with bandy legs and a pot belly appeared before him, continually rubbing his hands.

"I would like," said Studer, returning his friendly greeting with an absent-minded nod, "to see the hotel registers for the years 1902 and 1903."

"I don't know whether that will be possible," the pot belly replied. "I only took over the hotel in 1920, so it will —"

That was as far as he got.

"If the required books are not here on this table in fifteen minutes," said Studer, patting the red velvet cloth covering the table in the middle of the manager's office, "I'll telephone the city police and they'll send six detectives to carry out the search. I guarantee my men *will* find the books, only they'll make a bit of a fuss and it will be impossible to keep it from the hotel guests that the police are searching the premises. I leave it to you," he went on, "to decide whether that will enhance or harm your reputation. Perhaps it will be excellent publicity for your hotel . . ."

The bandy-legged little man's lamentations would have melted a heart of stone, but Studer just placed his fat silver pocket watch on the table. After a while he said, "Ten minutes left." The little man started to swear and curse and threaten Studer with city councillors and federal councillors and members of the national council and members of the upper house.

"Seven minutes," Studer said. The glass door was slammed shut as the bandy-legged little man disappeared.

Five minutes later three dusty tomes were on the table in front of Studer. He pulled up a chair and started to leaf through them. January 1902 – nothing. February – nothing. March – nothing on the first, second, third . . . On the tenth: *Neumann, Ulrike, b. 21 June 1883, Fribourg . . . one night.* No man's name to go with it.

And in April the name Ulrike Neumann appeared again, in May, June, July . . . Always alone.

At last! Underneath the entry for Ulrike Neumann on 23 September 1902 was a man's name: *Koller, Victor Alois, b. 27 July 1880, Fribourg, philosophy student . . .*

The same for October, and for November. In December there were three names between those of Ulrike Neumann and Victor Alois Koller. The same handwriting appeared in January 1903.

But in the following months the man's name was missing. It did not appear again. Nor his handwriting, a rather individual style with curling flourishes. It was absent for the rest of 1903. But the name Ulrike Neumann continued to appear regularly, every two weeks. For the last time on 27 June.

Victor Alois Koller. You didn't have to be a graphologist to see that the man who had written his name in the hotel register was the same as the man who had written the will – the will that left several millions jointly to the Canton of Bern and Marie Cleman . . .

But – and this was the most remarkable thing about it – neither the handwriting on the will nor the handwriting in the register bore the least resemblance to the writing on the letter addressed to Madame Josepha Cleman-Hornuss, 12 Spalenberg, Bâle.

The individual script with the self-proclaiming flourishes was closer to the hand that had written in the register: *Koller, Max Wilhelm, b. 13 March 1876, Fribourg, arriving from Paris, returning to Paris.*

Father Matthias's handwriting!

In addition to the similarity of the handwriting, there was the brown vulcanite suitcase containing: one blue raincoat; one cheap, grey, off-the-peg suit; one white shirt, worn; one tasteless tie; one pair of socks; one pair of black shoes . . .

Father Matthias, alias Max Wilhelm Koller, had disappeared. He had got over his bout of fever and vanished into thin air.

The sergeant's fat silver pocket watch was still on the red velvet tablecloth. It said half past four. On the desk by the window was a telephone. And in a corner of the room, silent, cowed, was the manager of the Hotel zum Wilden Mann.

"May I?" Studer asked, went over to the desk and dialled.

"Now listen, Fridu," Studer said, speaking in his broad Bernese dialect again. After a pause he went on. "Has a monk in a white habit been seen at the station? . . . Yes? . . . When? . . . The three twenty-two to Geneva? . . . Aha . . . Exactly . . . No luggage? . . . Just a haversack . . . Thanks, Fridu." The head of the police unit at Bern railway station must have made a joke, since Studer laughed. It was a forced laugh, it didn't come from the heart. Then the sergeant replaced the receiver. He turned round and in an impassive voice informed the manager that one of his guests had left in a hurry. Yes, the missionary. He hadn't paid his bill? . . . Not to worry, the sum would arrive in the next few days, probably by postal order, and with a tip included. Father Matthias hadn't looked like a man who would leave without paying, had he? . . . No, no, definitely not, he'd probably just received a telegram . . . No telegram for him had been delivered to the hotel? That didn't mean anything, he'd probably collected it at a private address . . .

Studer grinned to himself at the reaction of the bandy-legged little man. Rubbing his hands, he trotted to and fro, circling the desk and coming closer and closer to the chair concealed behind the bulky figure of the sergeant. Finally . . . finally the little man slipped under Studer's arm and flopped down in the seat with a sigh of relief.

"I think," the manager said, taking a fountain pen out of the elaborate stand on the desk, "that I have sufficiently demonstrated my willingness to cooperate with the authorities. Might I ask you to leave my office now, Sergeant?"

Studer snorted. A real little office Napoleon, this manager. The revolving desk-chair was his throne, once on it the pot belly suddenly became inviolable – ruler, dictator, emperor – a little emperor. It was the chair that gave him his dignity, his sense of security.

"Of course, sir." Studer made an exaggeratedly low bow. Then all at once he was gone. The manager had not even heard him shut the rattling glass door.

The superintendent had gone home, which suited him well. It meant he could use not only the telephone, but also the white blotting pad on the desk. You can't make proper telephone calls without being able to doodle at the same time.

Studer drove the long-distance operator to despair, and he was so immersed in his occupation he was completely deaf to anything else going on around him; he heard neither the north wind whistling at the windows nor his colleagues hammering at the door. Let them knock on the door of their superintendent's holy of holies till their knuckles were raw, let the wind blow the tiles off all the roofs in the federal capital – Sergeant Studer's left hand was holding the receiver clamped to his ear, while his right hand was sketching out marvellous dream landscapes on the blotting paper. Palm trees . . . palm trees and fantastic animals, which might have been meant to be camels but were more like hunchbacked pigs, and beside them people in flowing robes with misshapen flowerpots on their heads . . .

Along the corridors of police headquarters went the whisper: "Köbu's really gone round the bend this time."

"Basel city police? . . . It's urgent . . . Car registration number BS 3437 . . . Find out who the owner is or who it's been rented out to – Just a minute, Fräulein, we're still speaking – find out which hotel Father Matthias stayed in – in his passport he's Max Wilhelm Koller . . . Yes, and what day he left . . . Enquire of taxi drivers and garages whether a car was hired to take a man with the following description to Bern: short, white monk's habit, red cap, sandals, greying goatee beard . . . Please reply by telephone to the cantonal police in Bern . . . Yes, Fräulein, I've finished with Basel, now listen" – he fell back into his Bernese dialect – "Paris Sûreté, priority . . . You'll ring back? . . . That's great . . . *Merci*."

The medical directory . . . And while he was leafing through the list of doctors he was thinking about the car with the number BS 3437. He'd seen the car and the priest had told him Marie and the clairvoyant corporal were in it . . . Had the priest been lying?

The medical directory: the area round Gerechtigkeitsgasse, Junkerngasse, Metzgergasse . . . Dr Schneider . . . Dr Wüst . . . Dr Imboden."

"Dr Schneider? Not in? *Merci*." – "Dr Imboden? Cantonal police. Is Frau Hornuss, 44 Gerechtigkeitsgasse, a patient of yours? . . . Yes? . . . Insomnia, depression . . . What did you prescribe? . . . Somnifen? . . . *Merci*, Herr Doktor. The date of the last prescription? . . . 30 December? Now there's a thing . . . Yes, the woman who committed suicide . . . You foresaw it? . . . *Merci*, Herr Doktor. Goodbye."

"Is that the Catholic presbytery? A question. Is it the case that an ordained priest, even if he belongs to an order, is obliged to say mass every morning? . . . He is? Then has a certain Father Matthias of the Order of the White Fathers been to see you? . . . This morning? . . . Aha . . . And at what time? . . . Six o'clock? *Merci*, Father. Sorry to have bothered you."

"Your call to Paris is through."

"*Merci*, Fräulein. And don't interrupt us, it might last up to half an hour."

Studer pressed an invisible lever and switched over to French. A grumpy voice at the other end of the line asked what it was about. – Would Commissaire Madelin come to the telephone? – Braying laughter in Paris. Madelin? Who was that speaking from Bern? – The laughter sent Studer wild. He bellowed into the mouthpiece. That worked. They would transfer the call to the Commissaire's office. Studer didn't even bother to say thank you.

A pause . . . There was something missing. His Brissago! But lighting it turned out to be a problem. To free his hand, he had to press the receiver to his ear with his left shoulder, but then he managed it. It had been an effort all the same, two drops of sweat fell on to the blotting pad, forming circles. And during the conversation that followed the circles became two eyes in a face. It only took a few strokes of the pencil. But the odd thing was, the face that appeared resembled Godofrey, the walking, talking encyclopedia. And when Studer realized that, he sighed. He felt the need to see the little man and resolved to get the temperature chart examined by his friend as soon as possible.

Madelin!

". . . Fine, thanks . . . Listen, I need a date. When was the disappearance of Jakob Koller reported? Koller, yes . . . K for Krishnamurti, O for Orsay, L for Lutetia, E for Ernest, R for Rome . . . A stockbroker, yes . . . The middle of September . . . A certain Marie Cleman . . . Was Koller's secretary. By the way, did you know your Father Matthias is also called Koller? . . . Yes, exactly the same as the vanished stockbroker. You've got the dates? Good, I'll take them down."

Studer took his wife's Christmas present out of his breast pocket and started to write, mumbling to himself as he did so, "Speculation in the shares of North African mining companies, losses when the Banque Algérienne collapsed in July . . . Yes, yes, I can follow. Go on . . . Bankrupt on 2 August . . . documents seized . . . Statement by Marie Cleman, 2 September: My boss was depressed, several times said he couldn't carry on any more, gave me my notice from 1 October . . . Left the apartment we shared on 13 September . . . Shared apartment? Aha . . . Aaah! . . . No, no, sorry, I just burnt myself on my cigar. Carry on. So: left our shared apartment . . . Good. Luggage? . . . No luggage! . . . Left me some money . . . How much . . . 4,000 francs . . . Aha, and you seized the papers? And Godofrey is examining them? . . . No, no, not necessary. I'll probably have to come to Paris. Have you a description of Jakob Koller? . . . You have? . . . I'll write it down: 6'2″, sallow complexion, clean-shaven, fair hair . . . No photo? . . . Pity . . . No dead bodies the description would fit? . . . That's it, then. No, just a minute. Can you enquire as to the present whereabouts of a Corporal Collani, 1st Regiment, Foreign Legion, 2nd Battalion. Collani, like Koller only with a C at the beginning, two Ls, A for Alphonse, N for Nana, I for Isidore . . . Through Bel-Abbès? You'll know better than I do . . . Of course, if you can. Radio telegraph would certainly be quicker. I'd like to know whether

Collani is still counted as a deserter, then anything that's known about him: date of enlistment, career, etc. . . . No, not by telephone, a telegram to my home address, if you think you can get an answer tonight. Oh, and another thing. How did you get to know Father Matthias? . . . Came with a recommendation from the War Ministry? . . . And from the Minister for the Colonies? Hmm. You remember what he told us in the bistro? Well it wasn't a fairy story, both the women are dead. A remarkable case . . . Gas, yes. And it looks very much like a double murder . . . The priest's been behaving oddly. He's taken himself off to Geneva, by the way . . . No, no, don't worry, I'll get him when I need to, but for the moment I'll leave him be. D'you think I want to get into an argument with the Pope? When am I coming? I don't know yet. My boss has to give it his blessing first . . . Haha . . . The Vouvray was good and my wife was delighted to get the *pâté de foie gras*, you can pass that on to Godofrey . . . Yes, Fräulein, we have finished. Now will you get me the Basel city police again . . ."

"Yes? . . . I'll write it down . . . Registration number BS 3437, Buick, the Agence Américaine Garage . . . Male, short, skinny, sallow complexion, blue raincoat, woollen scarf . . . Six p.m., 1 January, returned it today at three p.m. . . . Accompanied by a lady . . . Thank you . . . What? . . . Aha . . . Taxi driver, name of Adrian, states he was hired last night at the railway station by a priest in a white habit to take him to Bern . . . At nine o'clock. Luggage? . . . A haversack . . . The taxi driver says he was surprised a man who didn't even wear socks had so much money on him . . . In the haversack, right . . . Several 100-franc notes . . . No, nothing special. But I would suggest you have an autopsy done on the body of Josepha Cleman-Hornuss, 12 Spalenberg. Get the chemist to analyse the stomach contents, to check for barbituric acid . . . Yes, barbituric – a sedative, if you like. How did you manage to find all this out so quickly? . . . Haha, very funny, the old jokes are the best, aren't they? Perhaps one day we Bernese will show you Baslers that we're sharper-eyed, even if we do take our time, eh? . . . The Spalenberg flat? . . . Why put a guard on it? . . . Do what you think fit . . . The rent was paid up to 1 April, was it? . . . Thanks."

Studer rested his cheek on his hand and stared at the blotting pad. Without realizing it, he had drawn some mountains, and the mountains looked like a temperature chart. He'd made rather a mess of the blotting pad, but the bottom corner was still clear and in that empty space the sergeant began to draw stick figures: a circle for the head, a vertical line for the body, two horizontal lines for the arms and two sloping ones for the legs.

Josepha Cleman
Sophie Hornuss
Jakob Koller stockbroker (disappeared)
Victor Alois Cleman
Clairvoyant corporal
Father Matthias (Max Wilh. Koller)
Marie
tall man by taxi
BS 3437
short man in blue raincoat

He stared at his drawing for a long time, pondering. Then he muttered, "Meaning?"

And the stick figures started to dance, shadows dancing across the blotting paper, shadows in time, shadows in space . . .

Koller or Cleman? Cleman or Koller? The stick man on the blotting paper comes trotting along, bows, then stands up straight: a beard, steel-rimmed glasses, a hammer in one hand, a spade in the other. He drops them, then falls down himself, Koller the philosophy student, Cleman the PhD . . . Falls down and into a hospital bed. Takes the temperature chart hanging over his bed and starts to draw on it. Then he writes, writes for a long time: ". . . buried in an iron chest in a place that can easily be found with the help of the attached document . . ." His eyeballs roll up . . . A mass grave! – But no, there he is sitting in a kitchen, shuffling the cards, laying them out . . . The first card in the top row is the jack of spades! The stick man bows, lies down, flattens out and creeps into the blotting paper.

Stand up, Jakob Koller . . . Shops, elegant shops . . . a fur coat is selected, suede shoes bought, silk stockings – Stop! It's not your turn yet. It's no use. Marie has stood up. She walks along with Jakob Koller, lives in the same apartment with him . . . What about him? Fair hair, clean-shaven . . . Oh, now he's alone, thank God. Standing inside a large building, people shouting all round him, and Jakob Koller is shouting the loudest: "796 – I'm buying . . . 800 – buying." Shouting, shouting. It quietens down. Jakob Koller lies down and the blotting pad swallows him up too.

Mist, mist, mist. Figures in the mist. A short man, a tall man. A car, number BS 3437, drives over the table, only it isn't the table, it's the Kornhaus Bridge. Should Marie stand up too? No, she's sitting in the car. Mist, mist, mist.

Is that another one getting up? A white habit waving, a goatee fluttering in the breeze . . . Studer raises his hand and lets it fall flat on the blotting pad.

The apparitions vanish.

Not yet. Not quite. Marie has stood up. There is a man facing her, broad-shouldered, bulky, with a thin face and a pointed nose sticking out. His mouth is covered by a thick moustache that already has many, far too many grey hairs. The broad-shouldered man bows to Marie, produces his wallet and takes out a piece of paper. There is a number on the piece of paper that has so many noughts it makes the man dizzy – 15,000,000. Fifteen million! "That belongs to you, Marie," the man says. "*Merci*, Cousin Jakob." – "You're welcome, Marie."

The flat of his hand comes down again. Studer rubs his eyes.

"No," said Studer out loud, "the solution's not in Bern. Millions!" He could feel the word filling his mouth.

The lamp on the desk had a flat green shade, the steam clunked in the radiators and the north wind whistled outside. But the sergeant was far away. He saw plains stretching as far as the horizon, and then came the sea. The plains were grey, no houses, no shacks, no tents. Suddenly derricks shot up out of the ground, up and up, higher and higher, and at the top they fluttered like black flags lashed by the wind.

Millions . . . oil . . . a rise in salary for the cantonal police. And who was it who did it all? Sergeant Studer, Cousin Jakob, Köbu, who's got a screw loose . . .

The telephone rang. Studer picked up the receiver.

"Cousin Jakob," a voice said. "Help me, Cousin Jakob. Please, you must help me." A click. The sergeant jiggled the telephone cradle feverishly. No reply. He dialled the exchange. "Where did the last call to police headquarters come from?" – "One moment

. . . Are you still there? . . . From Basel, a telephone booth at the station." Studer was too preoccupied to say thank you.

He stood up and stretched. Then he sloshed some water over his hands from a tin hanging from the wall in the corner of the room, dried them slowly and thoroughly, and stared for a long time at the doodles on the sheet of blotting paper. Finally he tore it out of the pad, folded it up and put it in his pocket. The corridors were empty. Faint light dribbled down from dim carbon-filament lamps.

He went to have dinner at an inn; he didn't feel like going home to see Hedy. He drank four large beers, but there was a memory he couldn't get out of his mind:

He's in his parents' bedroom. There's a thermometer on the wall. Studer is six, and he climbs on to a chair to look at the thermometer close up. Eventually he's holding it in his hand – and he drops it. Tiny globules of mercury roll across the floor. The little boy jumps down and chases the little gleaming balls, but he can't catch them. If he pushes a sheet of paper under them they refuse to stay on it, they join together, split up again . . .

Just like the people in the case of "the clairvoyant corporal and the temperature chart", as Studer has christened it. They were elastic, slippery, and the light bounced off them, just as it did off the globules of mercury. Starting with Father Matthias, who fainted when he heard the name of a long-dead girl mentioned, who hired a taxi at eleven o'clock at night in Basel, took a room in the Hotel zum Wilden Mann, then left his suitcase there, contents: blue raincoat, grey off-the-peg suit, white shirt. And as well as a worn-down toothbrush, there was a bottle of Somnifen in the room where the priest had been staying ... Did he suffer from insomnia too? And the other man, the man in the blue raincoat who had hired a Buick from the Agence Américaine in Basel, wasn't he a globule of mercury as well? Impossible to get a grip on, impossible to pin down. At six the man hires the Buick, at nine the priest hires a taxi ... How did the blue raincoat come to be in the priest's hotel room?

"Coffee and a kirsch," said Studer in a loud voice, as the waitress was hovering round his table.

"Certainly, Sergeant."

Marie! ... Why had the girl lived together with that Koller man? Hmm?

The waitress just caught him as he was going out. "That's three-twenty, Sergeant, if you don't mind: dinner, plus four b—"

"Yes, yes, there you are." And Studer slammed the door shut with such force it was a miracle the panes of glass didn't shatter.

Eleven o'clock. The sergeant was crossing the deserted Kirchenfeld Bridge. He walked slowly, his raincoat open, his hands clasped behind his back.

He had been back to the Hotel zum Wilden Mann, where he had learnt that at eight o'clock that morning a lady answering the description of Marie Cleman had taken room 64, the room next to the priest's. She had left the hotel at three in the afternoon, accompanied by a man wearing a blue raincoat, his face concealed behind a woollen scarf.

When had Father Matthias appeared in Sophie Hornuss's apartment? At nine. When had he left Studer's apartment? At two. And at three a man had come to fetch ...

Thunstrasse. Studer buttoned up his raincoat since the wind was blowing straight at him now.

At five in the afternoon the Buick had been returned to the Agence Américaine in Basel. By a man in a blue raincoat. Two blue raincoats? There had been a blue raincoat in Father Matthias's hotel room, but Father Matthias had boarded the train to Geneva at a quarter past three.

At a quarter past three . . .

Muggers in Bern and a sensible wife

Sergeant Studer was walking slowly up Thunstrasse. He kept his head down so that the broad brim of his hat blocked the view ahead.

But a drunk came along towards him, singing. This was striking in a town like Bern, where the authorities have the habit of shutting even moderate drinkers away in labour camps. Still, this man was singing, so Studer looked up and he could see the man was staggering. The drunk was tall, an imposing figure, insofar as one could use the word imposing, given his state. All at once – only three seconds before he had been ten yards away – he was standing right in front of Studer and sticking his fist under his nose. In a voice that sounded remarkably sober – and he wasn't swaying any more either – he said, "Just you wait, you bloody cop."

The movement Studer suddenly made could only be described as a reflex action, but it was an action that proved he was not yet ripe for retirement. He kicked out behind him with his left leg, like a young foal, while at the same time his fist, which was fairly large, struck the drunk on the jaw, just below his left ear. The drunk slumped to the pavement without a sound, but behind him Studer heard a shrill cry. He turned round. Doubled up on the ground clasping his stomach was a little man; there was a cosh beside his right hand. Studer nodded. Not a bad idea: the tall drunk to keep him occupied with his insults and swearing, giving his mate time to use the cosh. What the pair of them did not know was that a detective who is worth his salt has eyes in the back of his head.

"Muggers in Bern!" There was genuine regret in Studer's voice. "What do you think you're doing, Blaser? You were only released from the Big Moss in December." By "the Big Moss" he meant Witzwil Labour Camp. He knew the little man. A petty thief.

"What's all this about, Blaser? Didn't I treat you right the last time? Didn't I buy you a drink? Eh? Where's your manners? And as for your friend here . . ." He bent down over the tall drunk. "Schlotterbeck! That really is the limit!"

Schlotterbeck: chronic alcoholic, St Johansen Clinic, Witzwil Labour Camp. The last time he'd got two years in Thorberg Prison for grievous bodily harm. Who on earth had hired this pair?

"Right, then," said Studer. Schlotterbeck laboriously levered himself up onto his backside and stared at the sergeant uncomprehendingly. "Why did you attack me?" The sergeant grasped Blaser round the back of the neck with one hand, lifted him up and stood him unceremoniously on his feet. "Now talk."

It was a strange story the two had to relate. They told it as a duet, Blaser's hoarse voice complementing the alcoholic's narrative, delivered in a voice vibrant with injured innocence.

At lunchtime, they said, a man had appeared in the Witzwil Waiting Room – that was the name of a dive in the town centre – sat down with them and bought them a round. Then he'd asked whether they had the guts for a tricky little job. They'd said yes, so the man had told them Sergeant Studer had a valuable document in his wallet. Did they think they could get it? Five hundred each, 100 in advance.

110

"We followed you, Sergeant, but you never took a tram, so we tried it here."

"When did you meet this man?"

"At half past twelve."

"Was he wearing a blue raincoat?"

The astonished Blaser nodded vigorously.

"Where were you to take the document?"

"He gave us an address . . ." Blaser rummaged in his trouser pocket, brought out a crumpled piece of paper and handed it to the sergeant.

Studer read it out as he deciphered the crinkled script: "30–7 Poste restante, Port-Vendres."

Port-Vendres? Where was Port-Vendres? A port somewhere, but there were plenty of them, on the Mediterranean as well as on the Atlantic coast . . .

Apprehensively, the two would-be muggers stood before the sergeant. He looked at them. They had no overcoats on and their hands were blue with cold. Studer was not a man to bear grudges; really, he felt like inviting them home for a hot toddy. But that was out of the question. What would Hedy say?

So he just told the pair of them to get the hell out of there.

As he strode on, he grinned to himself. There were two things about the attack that pleased him. Firstly, it meant that the temperature chart really was of some value. Secondly, two authentic Bernese had finally appeared in this mess of a case. That they both had records and had tried to knock him out did nothing to lessen his pleasure.

"And what did you think of the priest, Hedy?" Studer asked his wife. He was sitting in a comfortable armchair beside the green tiled stove, wearing his grey pyjamas and felt slippers on his feet.

"A nice man," said Frau Studer, who was knitting a tiny pair of rompers. "But I have the feeling he's afraid of something. I was watching him the whole time. I think there was something he'd have liked to tell you but didn't have the courage to."

"Yes," said Studer, lighting his fourteenth Brissago of the day. He was wide awake and had decided to stay up all night. Not that he expected to solve the case, there were certain key facts he lacked for that. But in the first place he wanted to wait for Madelin's telegram and in the second he intended to talk – or, to be more precise, to hold a monologue – to his wife about the case.

"Did you see him again?" she asked.

"No."

"Why not? Didn't he come to see you?"

"He got the train to Geneva, at half past three." Studer wasn't looking at his wife. The temperature chart was on his knees. He muttered, "15 July, morning: 36.5, evening: 38.25; 16 July, morning: 38.75, evening: 37. That would mean we're starting off with the numbers 3653825387537. Could the 3 have some special meaning?"

'What're you doing, Köbu?" Frau Studer asked.

"Nothing," Studer growled, and he went on muttering to himself. "You could write it out as fractions: $\frac{361}{2}$, $\frac{381}{4}$, $\frac{383}{4}$ ... Jesus ..."

"Language, Köbu," said Frau Studer mildly.

But Studer bridled at that. He'd swear in his own home if he felt like it. No one was going to tell him —

"Jakobli's a really clever little boy," his wife said, changing the subject. "He'll be just like his granddad."

Studer looked up. Hedy was nobody's fool. Was she having a dig at him? His wife was sitting at the table, her hair shining in the lamplight . . . She looked so young . . .

"Listen, old girl," said Studer, clearing his throat, "did I tell you about Marie Cleman?"

Frau Studer bent lower over her knitting. She didn't want her husband to see the smile she could not repress. That was the third time Jakob had asked that question, the third time in an hour. Her husband seemed pretty concerned about this Marie Cleman. But that was Jakob all over. Only last year there'd been another case involving a girl, a girl who'd been engaged to a man who'd been in prison. And Jakob had got pleurisy because he'd driven a motorbike with the girl in the pouring rain. Not to mention the car accident that had closed the case. And why had Jakob put his health, his life even, at risk? To prove the innocence of the ex-convict. It was just the way he was, there was nothing you could do about it. And that business with the bank? And the case in the lunatic asylum? Hadn't women been the decisive factor in those too? It sometimes seemed to Frau Hedwig Studer as if her husband's bulky frame concealed the soul of a medieval knight fighting against dragons, death and the devil to protect the innocent. Without looking for any thanks. And now this Marie Cleman had come along.

"No, *Vatti*," said Frau Studer softly. "What's the problem with this Marie?"

Studer flew off the handle. Would she stop calling him *Vatti*! He was overwrought. He'd had a long day and a lot had happened, it was understandable if he lost his temper – and Frau Studer understood.

"The problem is," said Studer, tapping the temperature chart with the straw sticking out of his Brissago, "that Marie doesn't fit into the case. She ran off to

113

Paris with her late father's secretary – are you with me, Hedy? – because her mother told fortunes with the cards. And now this Koller's gone bankrupt. Koller! Everyone involved in this business's called Koller!" He paused and crossed his legs; the temperature chart fluttered to the floor beside Frau Studer's chair. Hedy picked it up.

So Studer told her the story. And as he told it, it seemed as if the chaos began to sort itself out. The various Kollers took shape: Father Matthias and the other one, the philosophy student who had met Ulrike Neumann in the Hotel zum Wilden Mann in 1903 . . . And the third Koller, Jakob Koller, who had gone to Morocco with the geologist, as his secretary. It was quite understandable that the second Koller – Victor Alois – had changed his name. He had been afraid of being found out; did he not have the death of Ulrike Neumann on his conscience?

Studer's brain was functioning effortlessly. Father Matthias had admitted that the geologist was his brother, his stepbrother, he'd said. Stepbrother or not, Father Matthias had admitted they were related.

That left the question: were the clairvoyant corporal and the geologist one and the same? Various factors spoke against that assumption. What reason would the geologist have had to change his name again and assume the identity of the medical orderly Collani? And why had the geologist with the curly beard waited fifteen years before sending word to his wife in Basel?

If, on the other hand, one were to assume that Father Matthias was the late geologist Victor Alois Cleman, alias Victor Alois Koller, and a guest in the Hotel zum Wilden Mann, then the whole thing looked more reasonable. A young philosophy student kills his lover. In order to frustrate the police investigation, he changes his name and his nationality, then reacquires Swiss citizenship under the new name of Cleman. And it is under that name that he gets married, first of all to Sophie in Bern. But the death of Ulrike Neumann weighs on his mind and he talks to his wife about it . . . Sophie's not stupid. Now she knows something, she uses her knowledge to exploit her husband.

"Can you imagine it, Hedy?" Studer asked when his conjectures had reached that point. "The marriage? The wife knows her husband's a murderer. She demands money – Koller-Cleman's on a good salary and she has her own bank account. And the nights? Can you imagine their nights together? You haven't seen the apartment in Gerechtigkeitsgasse. An old house with mould on the walls. And the mould gradually gets into their souls, poisons them. Victor Alois can't say a thing; as soon as he opens his mouth it's 'Shut up, murderer.' How long can a man put up with a marriage like that? One year? Two years? During the time of the marriage there are the trips to Morocco, contact with the Mannesmann brothers. His travels are the only reason they didn't get divorced sooner. You should have seen the two sisters – their pictures, I mean. When I saw him in the Gerechtigkeitsgasse apartment this morning, the monk showed me pictures of the two women when they were young. Sophie – you know the kind of woman: blouse buttoned up to the neck, a pointed chin resting on a stand-up collar with stiffeners. And her eyes! They gave me the shivers, and I'm not particularly sensitive."

Studer paused. His wife sat in silence at the table with a sheet of paper on it in front of her – the temperature chart. She had long since stopped knitting, she just nodded now and then as her husband told his story.

A church clock rang out, four high notes and one low rumble – one o'clock. Other churches joined in, among them the nearby school with its hurried, perfunctory jingle, like a schoolboy parroting a verse. And all the notes bounced on the window-panes and came quite close before fading away somewhere far off in the dark sky, leaving the room in even deeper silence.

"Divorce . . ." said Studer softly. "The man can't stand the marriage any longer. He sees his wife's sister, compares them. It does happen, doesn't it, Hedy? Two sisters who are completely different? One sometimes seems to have kept all the goodness for herself, the other all the nastiness. Josepha's good-natured. Koller-Cleman marries Josepha. He's happy. The other woman accepts it. Did she make sure she was paid off? . . . And then the war comes. The geologist loves his daughter, but he has to earn money. He probably still has to pay for Sophie's silence, he can't afford the carefree life he would like to give his second wife and little daughter. Suddenly there's an opportunity to set up on his own. The Mannesmann brothers are guilty of treason and Koller-Cleman denounces them. Now he can prospect on his own account. And he does. He identifies deposits of petroleum. He hears about a gigantic project: a line is to be built across the desert from Oran to the French colonies in Equatorial Africa. They'll need fuel for the line. He speculates, he invests all his savings. Then he falls ill, is taken to the hospital in Fez."

A match flared up. Studer was relighting his Brissago, which had gone out.

"Two alternatives," he said. "Either Koller-Cleman managed to get hold of Collani's papers during the smallpox epidemic in Fez. That would mean Collani's dead and the geologist is serving in the Foreign Legion.

116

Or, delirious with fever, the geologist told Collani his story and gave him the temperature chart, which is supposed to say where the iron chest has been buried. That leads to two further alternatives: Collani is the executor of Koller-Cleman's will, or Koller-Cleman is still alive. In which case he must be —"

"The monk!"

"The monk, the priest. Quite right, old girl."

Frau Studer got up and went over to her sewing table by the window. After having rummaged around in it for a while, she went back to the dinner table with a piece of paper and a pencil. She put them down, went over to the bookshelves in the corner of the room and got a couple of illustrated magazines. Then she sat down again.

Studer went on.

"Let's assume Collani really is Collani, a former medical orderly. That's our first alternative. He's been told to wait fifteen years. Why fifteen years? Because after fifteen years the statute of limitations comes into force. Cleman-Koller wanted to be absolutely sure. The murder of Ulrike Neumann – if it really was murder, that's all supposition – happened in 1903. Perhaps he thought that after thirty years he was in the clear. Remember, he was a geologist, not a lawyer. If it's assumed he's dead, then he can be sure his estate will finally go to his daughter. For he loved his daughter. And after thirty years Sophie, who knows about the murder, knows about his past, can't do anything about it. In this version – always assuming the monk wasn't having me on – Koller-Cleman is dead. But someone who knew about it is still alive, the other Koller, the one with the same first name as me, Jakob Koller, his secretary. He knows something about purchases of land, buried treasure. That Koller disappears from

Paris in September and a few days later a foreigner appears in Géryville, an Algerian hamlet in the back of beyond. Why would the foreigner go there? To talk to Collani. And Collani, the clairvoyant corporal, disappears. The pair of them go looking for the temperature chart. Collani had posted it off to Basel. So they go to Basel. And an old woman dies. But they don't find the temperature chart. The chart is found by a detective sergeant who has a reputation for having the odd screw loose. So what do the two of them do? They hire a Buick and drive to Bern. Perhaps Josepha sent the chart to her sister? That's another well-known fact: if there are two sisters and one's nasty, while the other's good-natured, the good-natured one will always be tyrannized by the nasty one. And Bern is a repeat of Basel . . .

"But there are still a few things I can't explain. Why use such a complicated method for the two murders – if that's what they were? And why in each case did I find a pack of cards laid out with the jack of spades in the top left-hand corner? Why did the priest rinse out the cup with the traces of Somnifen in the coffee grounds? And, above all, how did the first thumbprint in Herr Rosenzweig's collection come to be on the cup? A thumbprint with a scar? When the priest's thumb has no scar?

"Now I know you're going to object, old girl," – Frau Studer had no thought of raising any objections at all – "that at the time when Rosenzweig photographed a thumbprint on a tumbler in Fribourg, the study of fingerprints was in its infancy. True. But a scar is a scar, and the monk's thumb bore no resemblance whatsoever to the one on Rosenzweig's photo, nor to the one on the cup.

"So what now? What is needed is some on-the-spot

investigation. So far I only know what I've been told. The monk may be a reliable witness, but who's to say he isn't Koller-Cleman after all? That thumbprint bothers you, doesn't it, Hedy?"

Frau Studer shook her head. She was busy writing letters on the sheet of paper, dictating them to herself, "U, I, L, N, T, L, F . . ."

"What's that you're you doing, Hedy?" Studer asked. His wife waved his question aside impatiently. So Studer got up, went across to the table and leant over his wife's shoulder. She had put the sheet of white paper on the table and fixed the temperature chart to it with four drawing pins in such a way that the narrow side was at the bottom and the lines representing temperatures were vertical. Then, using a ruler, she had continued each of the lines onto the paper above the chart and written a letter at the top of each of them. At the end of the line for 35.5° was the letter A; B was in the space between 35.5° and 36°, while 36° was C. Now she started to translate the morning and evening temperatures recorded for Victor Alois Cleman into letters. On 12 July his morning temperature had been 36.5° – Frau Studer wrote E; for the evening 38.25° had been recorded – Frau Studer wrote M. On 13 July, 38.75° – Frau Studer wrote O. The result was the following series:

U I L N T L F I Z N Z P H Z I H H V X L I P L Z P I L X P I V W
N Z M

Studer stared at the row of letters. There was something about it that struck him as familiar. His elbow was on his wife's shoulder.

"Jakob," Frau Studer groaned, "you're squashing me flat."

But Studer was deaf to her complaint. That . . . that was . . . surely that was the most primitive of secret codes – the inverted alphabet.

"Get up," he ordered. With a smile, Frau Studer gave up her chair to him.

Underneath his wife's large, slightly clumsy letters, Studer wrote in his tiny handwriting, which bore some similarity to Greek:

F R O M G O U R A M A K S A R S S E C O R K O A K R O C K
R E D M A N

He read it out in a low voice: "From Gourama *ksar* SSE cork-oak rock red man."

Silence. Frau Studer had her forearm resting on her husband's shoulder. She read the words on the paper and asked, "SSE? What's that?"

"South-south-east. The direction. And *ksar*? It must be the name of a village. Or the Arabic word for village."

Of course. A clever lad was our Köbu.

Studer looked up. Was that more mockery? But this time he didn't rise to it, merely replied that his wife's cleverness must have rubbed off on him. For once, Hedy blushed.

Then Sergeant Studer went back to his armchair beside the green-tiled stove, the damn monster that refused to draw properly for him. He held the temperature chart and its transliteration up in front of him and couldn't take his eyes off them. With typical male self-centredness, he immediately forgot the part his wife had played in deciphering the cryptogram.

"Have I already told you about Marie Cleman?" he asked. At that his wife laughed until the tears ran down her cheeks. She didn't even calm down when Studer asked irritatedly, "What's up now?"

"Nothing . . . nothing," she gasped. "Give me a cigarette," she said, when she had got her breath back. Like Marie Cleman, Hedy drew the smoke deep into her lungs.

"She's like you," Studer said.

"Is she now?" And was he sweet on her? Frau Studer wanted to know.

Sweet on her? *Chabis*! Studer had gone red. No, he wasn't in love. He liked Marie Cleman, certainly, but like a daughter, and he was worried about her safety. Why had she rung up that evening? From the station in Basel? Was she going somewhere?

In the Studers' apartment the telephone was in the bedroom. That was necessary because of his work. How often had it rung during the night! And he'd had to get up and spend hours out in the cold keeping a house under surveillance . . . Studer went into the bedroom and looked up Cleman-Hornuss, Josepha in the telephone directory. There she was, 12 Spalenberg.

It took a good five minutes before he had the connection. Then he heard the monotonous buzz, rising, fading away, starting again. In his mind's eye Studer could see the empty apartment, the tiny kitchen, which was basically a passageway, and the yellowing enamel containers on the lopsided shelf: "Flour", "Salt", "Coffee".

Slowly he replaced the receiver, pulled his handkerchief out from under the pillow and blew his nose. It echoed round the apartment. Then the doorbell in the hall rang.

Telegram:
Sûreté Paris Inspector Studer Thunstrasse Bern stop Giovanni Collani enlisted 20 Casablanca stop Training Bel-Abbès stop hospital orderly 21 to 23 stop 24 corporal 25 sergeant stop

downgraded to corporal 28 away 5 days without leave stop 29
quartermaster Géryville stop August 32 volunteered for
mounted infantry Gourama Morocco stop deserted 28
September 32 stop disappeared without trace.
  Madelin

"Disappeared without trace," Studer repeated, with a look at his wife. "And the priest claims he saw Collani here in Bern, together with Marie Cleman in a car number BS 3437. The car was a Buick, from the Agence Américaine in Basel, where it had been hired by —"

Frau Studer put her hands over her ears. "Stop," she begged. "It's enough to drive a person up the wall."

But Studer carried on regardless, as if he were repeating a lesson he'd learnt off by heart, "by a man with a sallow complexion and a woollen scarf covering the lower part of his face. According to Ernst Rüfenacht's statement, the car was parked outside 44 Gerechtigkeitsgasse and a tall man was standing lookout beside it. And Madelin told me on the phone today that Jakob Koller, the stockbroker who took Marie to Paris and has since disappeared, was 6'2". That's tall, isn't it, Hedy?"

"It certainly is."

"Perhaps," said Studer, scratching his forehead, "perhaps it was Jakob Koller laughing at me over the telephone in Basel. But what's Marie doing in all this? She doesn't fit into the case at all. I keep thinking she must be married to Koller ... or perhaps she's distantly related to him? She lived in the same apartment with him in Paris. So what? Say what you like, but she's a nice girl is Marie, a nice girl," Studer insisted.

He fell silent. Frau Studer was sitting in her chair under the lamp again. She kept her head bowed so that the sergeant could not see the little smile playing round the corners of her mouth.

"If the girl was living together with Koller, Jakob Koller, I mean, then she'll have had a good reason. She may smoke, but that doesn't mean anything. You sometimes smoke too, Hedy ..." he said, and it sounded like an accusation. He didn't drop his voice, but drew out the words, as if he were expecting her to protest.

But there was no protest, just a quiet enquiry. Frau Studer asked if the sergeant was sad he couldn't get his sweetheart on the telephone

"*Chabis!*" said Studer. But he couldn't stop himself blushing. He stood there, his big hands in the tiny pockets of his pyjamas, rocking on the balls of his feet, his Brissago jutting up like an aggressive gesture. "What, me? A grandfather?"

A strange noise came from the table. To his astonishment, Studer saw his wife's shoulders shaking. Had Hedy taken the matter so much to heart? he wondered, full of concern. Was she perhaps crying because she sensed her husband was about to go away, a long way away, exposing himself to dangers that . . .? Studer went over to the table, placed a comforting hand on her quivering shoulders and told her there was no cause to be sad. Millions, he said, millions were at stake, and he couldn't leave Marie on her own.

At that Frau Studer looked up and the sergeant realized, much to his annoyance, that Hedy was laughing again. She was laughing so unreservedly that it was only with great difficulty that she managed to get out the words, which struck the sergeant like a slap in the face.

"Oh Köbu," she cried, as she got her breath back, "you are stupid."

She wrapped up the romper suit in tissue paper. Her shoulders were still twitching as she explained in a matter-of-fact voice: "So you want to go and look for Collani, to see if the clairvoyant corporal is Cleman-Koller, the geologist. That's right, isn't it? You hope you might find Marie while you're at it – but only after you've secured the millions. You know now where they are: Gourama SSE cork-oak rock red man. And I'll tell you something else for free: the treasure is two kilometres south-south-east of Gourama. And you've asked to see the Old Man about it, haven't you? Should I pack your suitcase? If you're going tomorrow afternoon, you can come back for lunch beforehand. I'll make you grilled sausage with potato salad and some onion soup. You like that."

Studer muttered something incomprehensible. He was happy with the proposed menu, but it rankled that his wife did not take him seriously, so he maintained a dignified silence and withdrew to the bedroom.

"Good night, *Vatti*," Frau Studer called out.

Vatti! That was too much!

His felt slippers flew into two different corners of the room. Then Studer turned out the light. Let the woman see how she managed in the dark . . .

Commissaire Madelin goes to ground

The chief of police was a quiet man who did not look at all like a man who spent his time indoors. His face was tanned because he went climbing in the mountains summer and winter. He also bred dogs, and that morning he was in a good mood because one of his bitches, Mayfair III, had had a litter of four pups. Studer had to listen in reverent silence for a quarter of an hour to the chief discoursing on the difference between various pedigrees.

Then the sergeant told him his clairvoyant story.

In every public organization there is at least one man whom one might call the salt of the whole organization. He's looked on as a bit of an outsider and not too much routine work is demanded of him; the humdrum, everyday business is kept away from him, or, rather, he sees to it himself that it's kept away from him. This man only comes into his own – and this is his value – when there's something out of the ordinary to be done. Then he is needed, then he's indispensable. When things are slack and he lounges around or goes for a stroll, his bosses turn a blind eye, since they know that the time will come when the man will be indispensable: he'll find ways of unravelling a tangled situation, he'll know how to put another organization, that has got a bit above itself, in its place; in a couple of hours this outsider will clear up a piece of urgent business a plodding pen-pusher would not be able to sort out in two weeks.

Sergeant Studer was the salt of the Bern cantonal police, and that was presumably one of the reasons why the chief of police raised no objection to the his planned trip. The other was not difficult to guess: Chief Inspector Gisler of the city police had prepared the ground. For a moment Studer had the feeling he could read the thoughts making their sluggish way through his boss's mind. Millions! was one of them. Another was: Studer's always been a bit round the bend. If he finds the money, I'll get the glory; if he doesn't, we can always pension him off. And the third: it makes no difference whether Studer's lounging around here or goes off on holiday and makes the Basel force look fools. But not one *rappen* expenses.

It was this final thought Studer took up when, after he had finished explaining the case, he said, "There's nothing more I can do here. I could have stopped the priest leaving, but then I'd have had to lock him up, and I didn't want to do that." He repeated his joke about the Vatican, that he didn't want to get into an argument with the Pope. "The others I don't know. I can't sort things out over the phone, I have to go to Paris, perhaps even further. I need to find the geologist's secretary, Koller, and the clairvoyant corporal. As you yourself well know, Herr Direktor, you can only solve this kind of thing on the spot. I know where the millions are buried – if those millions really exist."

"On the one hand there's the millions . . ." said the chief of police. He liked saying "On the one hand – on the other hand". Studer grinned to himself because he could see the desperate efforts his superior was making to find the second part of the sentence. Finally it came: ". . . on the other the Basel police. We'll show them what we Bernese are made of." He cleared his throat with a dry cough.

"Exactly, Herr Direktor. Basel, the force that sends a defective instead of a detective."

"Right, then, Studer," said the chief of police, getting up. "All the best. You can go – but at your own expense. If it's a success, you'll be reimbursed. If you make a fool of yourself, it'll just have to come out of your own pocket. Agreed?"

Studer nodded. "Agreed." The proposal was not unexpected. During the night he'd worked out that his savings would just about cover the trip.

"Fine," said the chief of police, gently propelling Studer towards the door. "And if you should happen across a new breed of dogs – perhaps the Kabyle have mountain sheepdogs – bring me a couple of pups. Pedigree pups, of course!"

Moroccan sheepdogs! Studer thought. With a pedigree! But he did not protest, he merely said goodbye to the chief of police, who, in Studer's humble opinion, was also one pup short of a full litter.

Studer had decided not to stay with Madelin this time. He needed some elbow room, so he went to a small hotel with the poetic name of Au Bouquet de Montmartre. It was close to Pigalle station.

Then he took the Métro. As ever when, after even a short absence, he breathed in the air with its smell of dust, hot metal and disinfectant, his heart beat faster. There was always something stimulating about Paris, even when you knew you were not interested in the kind of stimulation respectable citizens associated with Paris.

At the Police Judiciaire Commissaire Madelin greeted his Swiss colleague with, "Hey, it's you!" and "How's things?" and "Playing truant?", immediately sending the office boy to a nearby café for a bottle of Vouvray – it was half past eight in the morning. Then he asked Studer what all this business with telephones and telegrams and trips to Paris was about.

Studer had to tell him the whole story. He did this with such a guileless air that it never even occurred to Madelin that he might be concealing something from him. The simple sergeant from Bern told him about Father Matthias, who had run off, about Marie Cleman, about the two old women who had been gassed, just as the clairvoyant corporal had prophesied. But he did not tell him about the temperature chart he had found and deciphered. Careful, he told himself, careful. Otherwise the French will snatch the treasure from under your nose.

Madelin listened, occasionally interrupting with exclamations such as, "That's not possible!" – in imitation of Grock, the clown – and "You don't say!" And when Studer told him of the foiled attack on him, Madelin nodded his gaunt head in appreciation: "Bravo, Studère. Quiet little Switzerland! Perhaps it'll eventually reach international level – as far as crime is concerned, I mean. You've obviously made a start."

Very amusing, very amiable, very condescending of Madelin, the divisional head whom the dozen or so inspectors at his beck and call addressed, with respectful familiarity, as *patron*. For he was a power in the land, was Commissaire Madelin, tall and lean and grey, like a stone statue on the portal of a Gothic cathedral – a statue that drank Vouvray for preference.

"And what can I do for you?" he asked. Studer thought for a moment. All sorts of things occurred to him, but they were not the kind of thing that could be easily translated into precise questions. Before he left he had checked at the registry office in Bern, more out of conscientiousness than in the hope of discovering anything new. The marriage between Cleman, Victor Alois and Hornuss, Sophie had been duly recorded. The geologist had given Frutigen in the Bernese Oberland as his place of residence. When Studer telephoned the council offices in Frutigen, the clerk told him Cleman had settled there in 1905 and made the usual arrangements with the tax authorities; he had produced Belgian papers. There was no record of a brother . . .

"What I wanted to ask," said Studer, "was how do you get on with the War Ministry?"

"Hm," said Madelin, as he rolled himself a cigarette, a skill Studer much admired. "No *too* badly. I've got a few friends there who tip me the wink if anything's going on. You know the kind of thing. Politics change often enough round here, one moment the wind's blowing from the left, the next it's from the right, one moment you have to learn Marx off by heart and arrest all the royalists, the next you're keeping the communists in order with rubber truncheons and going to church. Between times the king of the chimpanzees and other gorillas comes to Paris and we have problems with his retinue. You have to make sure you're covered. You know what I mean? Still, I think I can say I get on well with the War Ministry."

"It's something," said Studer in measured tones, "from a long way back. In 1915, as far as I know, that is during the war, two Germans were executed by firing squad in Fez. The Mannesmann brothers, Louis and Adolf. Could you get a look at the files and tell me if there is any mention of a geologist called Cleman?"

"Of course. I know the man in charge of the archives very well, he'll lend me the files. I'll pop across to the ministry at eleven and we can meet this evening. At eight, say. At my place? That would be best; I could take the files home with me and you could have a look at them there. But now I've got things to do. See you."

"Hey! Just a minute. You were in charge of the investigation into the disappearance of Koller, the stockbroker, weren't you? We talked about it on the phone yesterday. Have you found out anything more about the man?"

"Oh yes," said Madelin, and his expression suddenly became serious. "You mean the man who was reported missing by his secretary. Secretary!" Madelin put a particular emphasis on the word as he repeated it.

That almost led to an argument between the two friends, for Sergeant Studer was ridiculously touchy where Marie was concerned.

"She *was* his secretary," he said in a loud voice, rapping his knuckles on Madelin's desk. "She's a decent girl, I tell you. Do you need proof? There, look." He pulled Marie's letter out of his breast pocket. "Listen to the way she writes to me. I'll translate it."

There was a mocking smile playing round Madelin's lips, but Studer did not notice it, he was too occupied with the feminine handwriting. The letters were dancing before his eyes, but eventually they stopped and he completed his translation without too much difficulty.

"All right, all right," said Madelin in placatory tones, "the girl's a paragon of virtue. But it wasn't the girl I was going to tell you about, but her former employer, Jacques Koller, the man who's disappeared. I think we've got a lead. This morning I had a telephone call from the recruiting office in Strasbourg. The doctor who conducts the medical examinations happened to have read the description we circulated of the missing man: 6'2" tall, sallow complexion, clean-shaven, fair hair. The doctor says a man corresponding to that description registered at the recruiting office yesterday, that is 4 January. The doctor felt it was his duty to inform the Sûreté. The surname the man gave was 'Despine'. He was sent on with a travel pass to Marseilles, where he will report on 5 January, today that is. We cannot demand the Foreign Legion hand him over to us; they only do that in cases involving murder or a theft of over 100,000 francs. Now, Godofrey has examined Koller's papers, but he could find no evidence of fraud. The bankruptcy was the result of incompetence, not of dishonesty. What should we do now, Studère? Let Koller go?"

Studer sat there, forearms on thighs, hands clasped. The Foreign Legion! he thought. So I will see the Foreign Legion in my old age. After a pause he said earnestly, "Yes, leave the man where he is, I'll . . ." But he did not complete the sentence. Was it a presentiment? He suddenly had the feeling it might be an indiscretion to inform a divisional head of the Paris Sûreté that he intended travelling to Africa. He stood up.

"This evening, then, at your place." He shook Madelin's hand. "By the way, where did Koller live in Paris?"

Madelin rummaged with both hands in a mound of documents. Finally he lit on a tiny scrap of paper: "Rue Daguerre, number eighteen. That's right up in Montparnasse. Go up the boulevard St Michel, keep going till you come to the lion and the rue Daguerre's quite near. *Au revoir, mon vieux*, see you this evening."

That evening at eight everything was dark in Madelin's apartment. Studer rang and rang. No one came. Assuming he had misunderstood the Commissaire, he went to Les Halles, to the little bistro where he'd first met the priest. The landlord was still standing behind the bar with his sleeves rolled up and his upper arms were still as fat as a normal man's thigh. Studer waited and waited. At midnight he gave up.

Back in his hotel room, he tried to get to sleep, but in vain. Over the white glass lampshade was a square of purple silk with brown wooden balls at the corners. It reminded him of Sophie Hornuss's kitchen in Bern. He lay there, hands clasped behind his head, staring at the light. As he did so, he was struck by the second remarkable aspect of the case – the first had been its un-Swiss, or rather, expatriate Swiss aspect: he was wrestling with shadows. The man who had mocked him on the telephone was a shadow, the clairvoyant corporal was a shadow, Victor Alois Cleman was a shadow, the geologist, who perhaps – it wasn't proven – was one and the same as Koller the philosophy student from Fribourg. Shadows, too, were the two old women who had died in such a strange way.

The things he had to deal with were shadowy as well: the millions, buried in Gourama, the cards laid out with the jack of spades, the letters, both the yellow envelope in which Corporal Collani had sent the temperature chart and Marie's note. And the Buick, BS 3437, was shadowy, as was the tall man standing lookout by it, at night, outside the house in Gerechtigkeitsgasse. From the lampshade in his hotel room Studer's thoughts floated off to the chipped enamel tins . . . Two kitchens . . . And Studer dreamt of those kitchens.

It was a terrible dream, troubled and laden with fear. Studer was in an isolated oasis, but he knew it wasn't empty. There was something living in it, neither human nor animal, that pounced onto the backs of those who strayed there and rode them into the grave.

132

The sergeant crept, apprehensive and keeping low, through the virulent green of the feathery-leaved palms. All at once the thing was on his shoulders, its scrawny shanks round his neck, throttling him. And Studer groaned. Father Matthias appeared. He was brandishing a cross and crying, "*Apage, Satanas.*" But the thing was not in the least bothered by this attempted exorcism, it continued to ride on Studer's shoulders and forced him into a trot. He was thirsty. Father Matthias had disappeared, but suddenly the two old women who had died were there, one with a wart by her left nostril, the other's thin lips twisted in a mocking smile. They were dancing a horrible dance, like witches ... Studer collapsed, but it wasn't earth he fell on to, no, it was tiles. And when he looked up he was in Sophie's kitchen. Everything was there: the brown leather armchair, the gas stove, the kitchen table with the oilcloth over it. But it was Marie sitting in the chair beside the stove, and she was asleep. A man with a curly beard was leaning over her, saying in a hollow voice, "I'll come for them all, I'll come to fetch them." The man, who could be none other than Cleman the geologist, passed his lean hands in circles round the girl's head, making her blond hair stand on end. Then it wasn't Marie any more, a wart grew beside her left nostril, the kitchen shrank until it was just a passageway and the two gas burners on the little portable stove were hissing in three-four time and the tins on the shelf – "Flour", "Salt", "Coffee" – clattered as they danced a lumbering waltz. And in his dream it occurred to Studer that it was the dancing that had chipped their enamel. Studer, still lying on the floor, said out loud, "Victor Alois Cleman, I arrest you on suspicion of murder." But the kitchen was empty, or at least so it seemed. A shadow danced along the wall and

Studer pursued it with the shadow of his own hand. The shadow started to laugh, louder and louder, a booming laugh . . .

Studer sat up. The windows of his hotel room were rattling and the wall gleamed in the cold light of an arc lamp as a late bus rumbled past down in the street.

No, Commissaire Madelin was not in, said the desk clerk the next day. An investigation meant he had had to go to Angers.

Had he left anything for Inspector Studer?

No, nothing at all.

OK, these things happened. A policeman, even a commissaire, couldn't always do just as he liked. But Madelin could at least have left a note, thought Studer as he strolled along beside the Seine, buffeted by a belated morning breeze. It's not very nice of Madelin, he knows I'm waiting . . . Well, at least it would give him time for a little excursion to Montparnasse to have a look at the house where Marie lived.

Rue Daguerre was a small street branching off the avenue d'Orléans. Potin, the well-known grocery chain, had a branch on the corner with a window display full of geese, rabbits, vegetables. Beside the shop a flower-seller had shivering mimosas for sale. No. 18 was a courtyard with a one-storey building huddled at the back.

Oh yes, the baker whose shop was in the building opposite No. 18 remembered the Kollers well. *Les Kollère*, stressed on the last syllable, of course, as the French always did.

"Such a charming woman, Madame Kollère, always polite, always cheerful, never losing heart, even when her husband suddenly disappeared. And *monsieur*!

Such a cultured man. Lots of friends came to see him. He was interested in philosophy, you know, the last things."

"The last things?" Studer asked in astonishment.

The fat baker, whose sparse hair was the colour of carrots, blew out his cheeks. "Oh yes, the last things. Monsieur Kollère could see into the future, the dead obeyed him."

"The dead?"

"Yes! They came and spoke to him and told him things. I was present myself once. It was fascinating. You could talk to the dead, they rapped on the table, sometimes they spoke through Monsieur Kollère. Yes, there are strange things between heaven and earth."

Poor Marie! So she'd lived with a spiritualist. And here they called him a philosopher!

But what the woman who looked after the house at No. 18 had to tell him was more agreeable. Marie never took part in the spiritualist seances that her husband – Her husband! "*Son mari,*" the concierge said! – organized. Instead she took refuge with the concierge. "I'm so afraid, madame," she would say.

Marie afraid? *Chabis!* was Studer's irritated reaction.

He left the voluble woman and set off with his long strides through the chattering crowds of pedestrians. It was close on midday. Studer felt alone, lonely, still vaguely troubled by the previous night's dream. Perhaps that was what was causing the unpleasant sensation he had on the back of his neck and between his shoulder blades. For a moment he had the feeling he was being followed, but when he turned round all he could see were normal pedestrians, housemaids, women, men, workers . . .

He continued on his way. On the boulevard St Michel the feeling was back again. The sergeant stopped to

135

look at a window display and checked the street ...
Nothing ... Or perhaps ... A man in a bowler hat was
strolling along the pavement opposite and stopped to
look at a shop window. Studer went on, there was a
Chinese restaurant he knew in a little side street. He
had his lunch there, drank lots of cups of thin, refresh-
ing tea, enjoyed fried bean sprouts and a pork stew
that was in such a hot curry sauce it burnt his tongue.
When he came out, the man in the bowler hat was
on the other side of the street looking straight at the
sergeant. Studer ignored him.

As he was crossing the Seine to enquire at the Palais
de Justice whether Madelin had returned yet, he felt
the uncomfortable sensation in his back again. He
turned round.

Without bothering to conceal himself, the man in
the bowler hat was walking ten paces behind him.
When he saw Studer's questioning look, he gave an
impudent grin.

And Commissaire Madelin had not returned from
Angers yet.

Studer spent the evening in the little bistro by Les
Halles. He wrote a picture postcard to his wife and for
ten minutes he didn't feel alone any more. But then
the loneliness returned with double the force. He felt
as if the other customers in the bistro were mocking
him and even the landlord was laughing at him.

But outside, in the street, clearly visible through the
high window, the man was patrolling up and down, the
man in the bowler hat.

That night Sergeant Studer tried to get drunk. You
need to do that from time to time, when you're tired,
nervous, irritated and annoyed. But it didn't work.

The effect of the alcohol was only superficial; the relaxation of drunkenness did not reach the deeper levels of Studer's mind. There everything was in chaos, and beneath it all lurked cold despair. The lonely sergeant had the impression someone was playing a game with him – a cruel game, cruel because he did not know the rules.

He woke up late the next morning, with a fairly clear head, strangely enough. And since Commissaire Madelin was still unavailable, Studer decided to go and see Godofrey. When he made his request, the desk clerk became confused.

"Yes . . . perhaps . . . I'm not sure . . ." Then whispering behind a closed door. His request seemed to have caught them unprepared.

"Room 138, right at the top."

"*Merci*," said Studer, not pronouncing the word with the drawn-out vowel, as was usual in the Bernese dialect.

Long corridors, stairs covered in dust, another long corridor. Now he was on the very top floor. It was dark, there were no lights on. In the flickering flame of a match Studer finally found the number.

Godofrey's welcome was touching. He was wearing an old lab coat, which had once, a long, long time ago, been white. Now it was brightly coloured with red, blue, yellow. And his laboratory stank, but the stench was pleasanter than the smell of dust and floor polish.

"Ah, Inspector Studère! How nice to see you in Paris again. I keep asking after you – but," said Godofrey, fluttering around like a colourful bird, "since the day before yesterday the *patron*'s furious with you."

Yes, Studer replied, he'd noticed. Madelin had suddenly made himself scarce. What was going on?

"Politics!" whispered Godofrey in an urgent voice, adding that Studer had only himself to blame.

"Me?" the sergeant asked. "Whatever for?"

"They suspect you're a German spy."

That made the Swiss detective laugh, though it wasn't a hearty laugh. This was degenerating into farce! It explained the man in the bowler hat. Madelin had put a tail on him – on him, Sergeant Studer! It was beyond belief!

Godofrey tiptoed over to the door, listened, then flung it open – just like in a film! He came back into the room, closed the door behind him and waved Studer over like a conspirator. Studer put his ear close to the little man's lips and Godofrey whispered, "You've been asking about the Mannesmann brothers. That was enough, more than enough, that was all it took. The War Ministry asked Madelin what he thought he was doing. The Mannesmann files? Out of the question. Why was he asking? they wanted to know, yes, him, Commissaire Divisionnaire Madelin? . . . Aha, for a friend? A Swiss policeman? From Bern? *Un Boche, bien sûr*! Impossible – Yes, the War Ministry sent the *patron* off with a flea in his ear."

Silence. I've stirred up a hornet's nest there, Studer thought. An awkward business.

Little Godofrey chattered on. "Sit down, Inspector. You've been rash. Why didn't you come to Godofrey? Godofrey knows everything. Godofrey's a walking encyclopedia. Godofrey knows all the cases, French and foreign, from the Landru case to the Riedel-Guala case. And it didn't occur to you that he'd know about the Mannesmann case? Why did you bother the *patron* with the matter?"

Studer lit himself a Brissago – and it tasted good. The most sensible thing would be to sit there quietly and let the little man do the talking.

Godofrey continued: a year ago he'd been working

in the War Ministry on an espionage case, and – purely by chance – the Mannesmann files had come into his hands. "The name struck me because in my profession I use Mannesmann tubes. That's what they call containers – as I presume you're already aware – in which you can store gases at high pressure. I wondered whether they were related to *that* Mannesmann, so I had a look at the files. Yes, at first I just leafed through them, but then I read them carefully. Two brothers, supposedly Swiss."

"Yes, I know all that," Studer broke in. "They were prospecting for lead, silver and copper, and they were shot, for high treason."

"That's right," said Godofrey. "But what you don't know is the following: the two of them wanted to buy land and always carried a lot of gold and silver coins around with them. The Arabs down there don't trust paper money. When they were arrested and shot, their luggage was searched. There was no sign of the money."

Godofrey paused for effect.

"They didn't have an account with the Banque Algérienne, so the assumption was that they'd hidden the money somewhere. An officer of the Deuxième Bureau – you know the Deuxième Bureau, it's our intelligence service – disguised himself as an Arab and set off to make contact with the geologist, Cleman, since he'd worked for the Mannesmann brothers and was also the one who had informed on them. Lyautey, the resident general governing the protectorate, was furious, he needed money for his colony. Why weren't they interrogated? he roared. But it was too late.

"It took the officer of the Deuxième Bureau two months to find Cleman – you know that he was a fellow-countryman of yours, Inspector? Yes? . . . Good. He approached Cleman but got nothing out of him. At that time the geologist was working in the area round Gourama, looking for oil and coal. There were also a couple of lead-smelting furnaces in operation there that the Mannesmann brothers had built. We couldn't do anything about Cleman, he had a Swiss passport and Belgian papers as well. The Belgians were our allies. Cleman said he'd taken residence in Switzerland so that he could get a Swiss passport in order to be able to travel to Germany freely. He claimed he could only get the machines he needed in Germany. Since he had unmasked the Mannesmann brothers, the officer believed everything he told him. Moreover Cleman was well liked by the Berbers of that district. The Deuxième Bureau officer returned without having got anywhere.

"Cleman spent a further year in Gourama, returned to Switzerland, then was recalled by Lyautey and sent back to Gourama. He'd managed to get into the general's good books. When he fell ill, Lyautey had him flown to Fez. Cleman died there, of malaria, during a smallpox epidemic. Cleman's secretary, a certain Jacques Koller, settled in Paris and set up as a stockbroker. As his assistant – his secretary, if you like – he employed the daughter of his late boss, the geologist Victor Cleman.

"And now? Now the affair, which has lain dormant for years in the vaults of the War Ministry, seems to have been reactivated: the secretary, Koller, disappears; Cleman's second wife dies in a strange manner in Basel. You told Madelin that, and he told me. And then you, Inspector, suddenly turn up in Paris asking to see the Mannesmann files. Is that not enough to arouse suspicion? Can you blame the French government for assuming you've come to look for the

Mannesmann brothers' lost hoard? It was 200,000 francs after all – and in pre-war currency. All in silver and gold coins. Perhaps Cleman buried the money. So now people are assuming you've come to play the treasure hunter and they intend to stop you. Aren't they right?"

Studer was sitting on a table, head bowed, among test tubes, flasks, Bunsen burners and bottles, sparse light trickling down from a skylight onto his back. Godofrey was walking up and down, with short, stiff steps, and when he stopped and gazed at Studer he looked like a wise old owl.

"My wife sends her warmest thanks for the *pâté de foie gras*," said Studer, with apparent irrelevance.

The little man seemed delighted: he pursed his lips and whistled, very softly. With his stiff owl's gait he came closer, bent down to Studer's ear and whispered, "Please pass on my respect, my profound respect to your wife." He grinned. "But I, Godofrey, will help you. The pair of us will play a trick on the *patron*, and I know that he will not take it amiss. In fact, he's not angry with you at all, it's the War Ministry he's cursing. You'll have to disappear, Inspector. If you try to go to Morocco, they'll arrest you under some pretext in Marseilles and deport you as an undesirable alien. It can take a long time, the deportation I mean, you could very well rot away while you're waiting, in some damp dungeon . . . No, we'll do it differently. You'll be able to shake off your shadow, won't you?"

Godofrey was looking at the sergeant in his guileless manner and could not understand why his friend should start at the word "shadow". Shadows! The case was full of shadows! Studer shook his head in irritation.

Godofrey went on. "Sergeant Beugnot, who has

been instructed to follow your every step, is not the brightest . . ." He fell silent and took to pacing up and down again.

Studer was sitting hunched up on the table, staring at his dangling feet as if they were objects of the greatest interest. Could he really trust this Godofrey, whom he did not really know, apart from their police work together? Perhaps . . . After all, he had not got to the ripe old age of fifty-nine without acquiring some ability to judge character. Godofrey's type was not unknown to him. The little man had become a forensic scientist, of this he was sure, in order to escape boredom. Godofrey needed to be busy. He was one of those people who pray, "Give us this day our daily problem." It was a type that was to be found not only among policemen, but also among philosophers, psychologists, doctors, lawyers. A not unattractive type if a little wearying, perhaps, when you had to deal with them all the time. Studer decided to risk it. His voice was gentle, caressing, as he said, "So you want to help me, Godofrey, old friend?"

The little man actually had tears in his eyes. The poor chap must be all alone, Studer thought; no one has a friendly word for him, his *patron* just swears at him or orders him about.

"I have here," said Godofrey with an odd quaver in his voice, "the passport of a friend of mine. He looked like you, Monsieur Studère. We worked together in Lyons, but he was shot a year ago during a police raid. He was an inspector in the Sûreté there. You can have his passport – you'll just have to shave off your moustache. Then you must buy a dark coat with a velvet collar and wear a starched collar. And you mustn't forget that from now on you have the same name as the *Emperor's* minister of police . . ."

"The emperor's? The Kaiser's?"

"I was certainly not referring to Wilhelm II," said Godofrey, with a note of rebuke in his voice. 'There is only one Emperor, *le petit caporal*, Napoleon I. His minister was called – surely you're not going to tell me you've never heard of that man of genius?"

History was the one lesson Studer had always slept through at school. He shrugged his shoulders and gave Godofrey a questioning look.

"His Excellency Joseph Fouché from Nantes, Duke of Otranto."

"What? I'm to be a duke," said Studer, horrified.

"You're making fun of poor old Godofrey, Inspector. From now on you are Joseph Fouché, Inspecteur de la Sûreté. All we have to do is put the finishing touches to your passport."

Godofrey went to a wall cupboard, took out a rather grubby-looking slim booklet and then started searching for something among the clutter on his desk. Finally he found it, a bottle of green ink with which he drew bureaucratic hieroglyphs on the penultimate page of the booklet. Then he took a smoothly polished stone from the same cupboard, greased the surface, pressed it on a document he had beside him, carefully lifted off the stone and applied the stamp he had thus created to the penultimate page of the passport. After that the green ink was required again. Holding the pen, Godofrey's hand performed elegant circles in the air before plunging, like a hawk that has spotted a chicken, down onto the paper. Then the little man waved the passport in the air, blew on the still damp ink and finally . . . finally held out the specimen of his skill for the sergeant to see.

Travelling on special orders from the War Ministry, it said. The signature was illegible, as any genuine signature should be, and a stamp added the final touch.

"Marvellous!" said Studer. "Fantastic!"

"If we in the police can't even forge a document," said Godofrey modestly, "then they might as well tie a bundle of files round our necks and throw us in the Seine."

"I'm really grateful to you, Godofrey, that's all I can say. But if *you* ever need help, you know where to get hold of me."

"Don't mention it, Inspector," the little man said. "If we can help somebody . . ."

Studer took the open passport and leafed through it until he found the photograph at the front. The man in the picture – it was a half-length portrait – was broad-shouldered, with a lean face from which protruded a narrow pointed nose. His mouth? Studer had not seen his own mouth since he had grown his walrus moustache.

"And you think he looks like me?" Studer asked.

"He could be your twin brother. You just have to shave off your moustache, put on a homburg and you're ready to go."

As Studer put the passport into his breast pocket a rustling reminded him – as it had done once before – of the presence of the temperature chart.

"Here, Godofrey," he said, holding it out to the little man. "Can you decipher that?"

Godofrey grabbed the sheet of paper eagerly and pushed his horn-rimmed glasses up onto his forehead, revealing a pair of watery blue eyes, blinking at the unaccustomed exposure. He brought the sheet up to within a hand's breadth of them, turning it this way and that until he finally held it so that the horizontal axis of the graph was vertical. All accompanied by little exclamations: "Childish! . . . Childishly simple! . . . Amateur! . . . The Freemason's code . . . You can read it straight off."

He skipped over to the table, sat down and started: "U I L N T L F..."

"That's enough, Godofrey, enough!" Studer cried. He suddenly started to get a little worried. The little man was to be trusted, certainly, but after all, he was French.

Godofrey ignored him and continued to read out the string of letters and write them down. Then he paused.

"The reversed alphabet," he said slowly. "Probably German. I don't want to intrude on your little secrets. You managed to decipher it yourself?"

"Er, no," said Studer, slightly embarrassed. "My wife did."

"Ah, Madame Studère! Doesn't surprise me, doesn't surprise me at all. A man like you, Inspector, is lucky in everything, even if you don't deserve it. A man like you is bound to have an intelligent wife, a shrewd wife, one only has to look at you to see that. Madame Studère ..." he repeated. "Will I ever have the privilege of presenting my profound respect to her?"

"I think," said Studer drily, "that my wife prefers *pâté de foie gras* to respect, however profound."

"You're a materialist, Inspector Fouché," said Godofrey, entering into the joke, "but I'll remember the pâté. And now, best of luck. Be careful. Here is a French police identity badge ..."

Studer in the Foreign Legion

Godofrey had been right. Sergeant Beugnot, who had been given the task of keeping the detective from Bern under surveillance, was not the brightest of officers. Or, and this was the alternative explanation for his behaviour, he considered the Swiss stupid and Sergeant Studer a particularly harmless specimen.

The same Sergeant Beugnot was waiting at the gate of the Palais de Justice. He followed Studer to the Métro, got out with him at Pigalle station, went into the hotel with him, stood behind him while he paid his bill, then followed his charge to the Gare de l'Est – putting the French government to the expense of a taxi – and waited on the platform until the Basel train left the station. Studer was in a good mood. He waved out of the window with his broad-brimmed hat and had to laugh when Sergeant Beugnot, to whom he was waving, automatically waved back. As he did so the expression of astonishment on the French policeman's face made him look even more stupid than regulations required.

He had to be careful, Studer told himself as he sat in his window seat watching the leprous houses of the suburbs judder past. Careful! How different had his journey of a week ago been! Then there had been a girl sitting opposite him: grey suede shoes, silk stockings, fur jacket . . . The sergeant forced himself back to the present. He had to take care. But what did that mean in practical terms? He couldn't go back to Switzerland. Swiss passport control would let him through with no problem, but how was he to leave the country again? Go through French passport control with false papers? Risky. Dangerous!

The thing to do was to follow the example of some of the other participants in this messy case and disappear. It pained Studer that he would not even be able to tell his wife, but this time he must avoid the least carelessness, and it would certainly be careless to entrust a letter to the French postal service.

He got out at the little town of Belfort and spent the night in a hotel there – in the centre, not by the station. He bought a new suitcase, a homburg, a dark coat and a pair of light brown boots with strong soles. Then he went to a barber to have his moustache shaved off and his hair dyed black. It was going alarmingly grey at the temples. The police badge worked wonders. The barber was flattered and gave him a conspiratorial smile, the hotel owner immediately took the registration form back uncompleted. Studer had said two words: "Political assignment", and placed his index finger to his lips. "I understand, I understand perfectly," the hotel owner had replied in the same conspiratorial tones.

Then the Swiss sergeant, who had suddenly become a French inspector, continued his journey to Bourg. There he changed trains and took a branch line to Bellegarde. In Bellegarde he waited for the overnight train from Geneva via Grenoble to Port-Bou on the Spanish border. A few stops before Port-Bou was Port-Vendres, where the unknown man had told the Bern muggers to contact him.

And while he was waiting for the express in Bellegarde Sergeant Studer said farewell to his loyal travelling companion, his scuffed pigskin suitcase. It

147

was a silent but emotional farewell. Things often have more heart than human beings: every wrinkle that years of use had etched into its leather puckered up – but it didn't cry. Suitcases don't cry, suitcases content themselves with a woebegone, reproachful look.

Port-Vendres . . . On one side of the harbour, which is nothing more than a large, foul-smelling basin, is a huge hotel, which is usually empty. Here, too, the identity badge worked wonders, but it was nothing compared with its effect on the young woman in the post office.

Studer went to the counter, said, in a tone of voice he had picked up from Madelin, "Police!" – perhaps we ought to mention here that Studer spoke French without a German accent, his mother came from Nyon – and flashed the badge at her in the palm of his hand.

The timid girl nodded with alacrity, half getting up from her chair; she remained in that semi-upright posture – knees slightly bent, body tilted forward – all the time.

"What can . . . how can . . . how can I help *monsieur l'inspecteur*?"

"I would like to examine any items of mail that have arrived poste restante in the past few weeks," said Studer, quaking just as much as the girl. "I mean, my dear girl, items that have not been collected."

The "dear girl" flushed, which was something of a disaster since the natural red of her cheeks simply did not match the artificial red of her lips.

"The . . . the . . . poste-restante letters? Certain . . . certainly, *monsieur l'inspecteur*."

Five letters. *Forget-me-not 28, Mimosa 914, Lonely violet in the spring air, Rudolf Valentino 69* and – at last! – *Port-Vendres 30–7*. The handwriting!

"I need this letter." Studer tried to speak firmly, but

in vain, his voice quavered, but the girl did not notice. "Shall I give you a receipt?"

"A . . . a . . . receipt? If you would be . . . would be so good . . . *monsieur l'inspecteur.*"

The wind was coming off the sea, bringing with it damp air and a faint smell of seaweed and fish. Studer breathed in deeply. Then he opened the letter.

Dear Cousin Jakob,

I know you'll get this letter because you're a clever man. He's furious that the attack on you didn't succeed, but I just laughed. The panic's over – when I rang you up, I'd lost my head for a moment. Now I've found it again, it wasn't difficult, it's big enough – my head, that is. I'm very glad you've decided to make the long journey, I can't manage the whole business all on my own. And Father Matthias can't help me at all. Why? You'll find out soon enough. It's essential you go via Géryville – if you can find any transport to get you there – and I'll meet you in Gourama. It's a date! I can't manage without you, so make sure you get there. But not before 25 January. And don't worry if you don't see me, I'll appear when I have to. In the meantime you can pass the time with the man in charge of the fort there. He's called Lartigue and comes from the Jura. Perhaps you'll find another to make up a threesome for a game of Jass – but don't play higher than ten French centimes a point. So far you've followed your nose and it's not let you down. Keep it up, you're doing an excellent job!

With warmest greetings from your adoptive niece
Marie

"Little hussy!" Studer growled, then immediately looked round in alarm. No, no one could have heard his exclamation. The quayside was empty, thank God. He read the letter again, then carefully stowed it away in his breast pocket to keep the temperature chart company. But straight away a gust of wind put a damper on his satisfaction and pleasure at receiving the letter. It swept the homburg off his head and into the waters of the basin. Swear and curse as he might, there was nothing for it but to get a replacement. So Studer bought himself a beret. As he left the shop, he examined his reflection in the window. With his lean, clean-shaven face and his massive body tightly buttoned up in the dark overcoat, which was cut to fit neatly at the waist, he didn't look Swiss at all, and the beret added a rakish touch. He was very pleased with his appearance, was Sergeant Studer, pleased at having transformed himself into a different person. What he did not know was that this faint quiver of pleasure was to be his last for some considerable time. For three weeks, to be precise . . . Though three weeks can seem to go on for just as many years.

A boat leaves Port-Vendres twice a week for Oran and one was due to sail the following day. Studer was glad about that as the miniature harbour was getting on his nerves, particularly its foul stench of tanbark and Spanish nuts. The sea was filthy and the waves were like fat old women with not-quite-clean lace headscarves on their greasy grey hair – the scarves fluttered in the air as the women rolled laboriously on.

So the sea was a disappointment, and the boat did nothing to improve matters. As commonly happens in the Golfe du Lion, a storm made its presence felt, with an admixture now of hail, now of snow. Studer was not seasick, but he wasn't happy either. As a French police inspector he couldn't smoke his Brissagos. The French are unacquainted with that inspired invention, they smoke cigarettes, at most a pipe. Studer had bought himself a pipe. On board he practised not letting it go out. It was difficult. But then all at once he got a taste for it and enjoyed it so much he threw one of his last Brissagos, which he had been surreptitiously lighting up in his cabin, out of the porthole. The perfidious thing had suddenly started to taste of glue.

As there was nothing for him in Oran, he travelled straight on to Bel-Abbès, where he was plunged into a world so foreign it made his head ache.

The arrival at the little railway station to start with: a dozen men were standing to attention, dressed in green greatcoats tied at the waist with greyish-white flannel cummerbunds, the bayonets on their rifles shining with a blackish gleam. Men in uniform, but without rifles, poured out of the carriage behind the engine. They were lined up in rows of four, surrounded by the men with bayonets, then marched off.

Studer followed them. A long road between fields with stunted tree trunks. They were grapevines, but they grew them differently here than at home in Vaud. In the sky was an improbably white moon, which was vainly trying to wipe away the clouds that kept floating past its flat nose.

A town gate, the pillars and arch of red brick . . . A broad street . . . Railings, and outside the railings a sentry, also in a pale green greatcoat, guarding the entrance . . . And behind the railings a barracks square surrounded by dreary buildings; with their leprous plaster they reminded him of the houses he had rumbled past in the Paris suburbs.

Studer went up to the sentry and demanded to see the colonel. The sentry listened to his request impassively, then indicated the direction with a backwards jerk of the head. Studer was beginning to lose patience. Where should he report, he snapped.

"Guardroom," the man said, letting his rifle drop

from his shoulder with a crash. Studer jumped back in alarm. But the sentry had caught it with his left hand, which had suddenly come up to the horizontal – only then did Studer realize the sentry was presenting arms. An officer went past, being taken for a stroll by his wife, and flapped a salute at him.

"What?" Studer asked, when the rifle was back at the slope on the sentry's shoulder.

"You have to report to the guardroom," the legionnaire repeated. The words were as hard as flint. But the intonation of his French? The timbre? Yes, there was no doubt about it, the sentry spoke French with a Bernese German accent. Studer looked at him and was immediately reminded of the song about the soldier "on lonely watch in midnight dark", thinking of the girl he left behind. But the familiar sounds only made the whole thing more eerie. And there was a cold wind blowing that tasted of soil and sand . . .

The sergeant commanding the guard was a Russian, a well-mannered man who made an effort not to let his dislike of the police become too apparent. But his expression spoke volumes. "Just let me catch you down a dark alley," it seemed to say. Detectives were not popular with the Foreign Legion.

Colonel Boulet-Ducarreau, he informed Studer, was in his quarters, but he would advise *monsieur l'inspecteur* Fouché to come back the next day.

Studer departed with a sigh. One more day! But he had time, plenty of time. As long as he was in Gourama on 25 January. Today was the eleventh. He had his dinner in a brightly lit restaurant, no worse than in Paris. He drank a very acceptable white wine, which, however, turned out to have a sting in its tail. At one point – he was just about to put a forkful of food in his mouth and it gave him such a shock he stabbed his lip – he felt a hand grasp his ankle. Had he been unmasked? Was he about to be clapped in irons? Trembling, he lifted the tablecloth. A tiny Arab boy grinned up at him with two rows of snow-white teeth. A shoeshine boy.

The best way to imagine Colonel Boulet-Ducarreau was as an Edam cheese balanced on a huge balloon of blue cloth. The cheese was his head, the blue balloon his trunk, without his legs, which he kept concealed under the table.

"Enlisted in Strasbourg?" he wheezed. "Despine? Yes, I know, I know. Took the money and deserted. When? Just a moment. Saturday today, isn't it? They get their pay on Thursday. Two hundred and fifty francs. By the evening Despine had vanished. Haven't been able to find him yet, you'll have to look for him yourself. One thing we do know, he didn't take a ship in Oran. Perhaps my secretary has more details. Vanagass," he squawked.

Vanagass was a sergeant and had bandy legs like the manager of the Hotel zum Wilden Mann.

"Go with Inspector Fouché, he has authorization from the War Ministry and he's looking for Despine. You did tell me Despine had deserted, didn't you?"

"Deserted, sir. Yessir."

"Right, then. Off you go. Dismiss! Dismiss, both of you. I've got things to do. Where would I be if I had to waste a quarter of an hour on every deserter? I'm a busy man, Inspector, tell that to the Minister of War when you next see him . . . Though perhaps you won't recognize him, our good Minister of War?" A cold shiver ran down Studer's spine. Had the colonel seen through his disguise? Ah, no, the fat colonel –

Boulet-Ducarreau, translated it would come out as "Cannonball-of-Diamonds" – was just making a joke. He went on. "France changes its ministers of war as often as I do razor blades. *Adieu.*"

Vanagass did not seem to share the Legion's general dislike of policemen. It turned out he was a kind of colleague, chief of police in Kiev under the Czars. At least that was what he told Studer as they crossed the barracks square. His extreme politeness was evidence of either an excellent upbringing or a career as a confidence trickster. Studer just didn't know what to make of the man. He seemed to know something about this Despine, but to be unwilling to come out with it. Finally, after the fourth glass of anisette – that's what they called the stuff, though actually it was undiluted absinthe – Sergeant Vanagass began to thaw a little.

Despine had struck him straight away when he arrived on Wednesday with the draft from Strasbourg, he said. Twelve years with the force gave you an eye for faces, didn't it? Despine? He'd stood out from the grey mass of his comrades like a sore thumb. Yes, like a sore thumb . . . In what way? Quite simple: he looked like a guilty conscience personified. He looked like a man who had something serious to answer for, something very serious. His bet, Vanagass went on, was on murder: the shifty look, the trembling hands, the sudden start whenever he was addressed. A bad lot. No wonder he'd deserted. The Legion didn't hand people over, at least when the crime wasn't too serious. But murder, that was a different matter. It was murder they were talking about, wasn't it? Vanagass asked casually, hoping Studer might give something away. But the sergeant was on his guard. Still, he couldn't repress a minor feeling of triumph.

154

"A double murder!" he said in a deep voice. And Sergeant Vanagass, former chief of police in Kiev – if that was true! – pursed his lips and emitted a quiet, long-drawn-out whistle.

"*Tchortovayamatch!*" he swore.

"Sorry?" said Studer.

"Nothing, nothing." And Sergeant Vanagass insisted on buying a round himself, though really it was only to change the 100-franc note Studer had slipped him under the table. Then he stood up, took two steps towards the door, slapped himself demonstratively on the forehead – and turned back. He pulled his chair up close to Studer's and even put his hand over his mouth as he whispered, "I hear a lot of things, Inspector. You couldn't have found anyone who knows what's what here better than me. Have the people in Paris been talking about the disappearance of a certain Corporal Collani? Yes, Collani. Was with the Second Battalion in Géryville. Supposed to be a clairvoyant. And vanished in September. Or was abducted, rather. By a stranger. In a car." Vanagass's speech had become disjointed. He seemed to be getting worked up about the matter. "We were given a good description of the stranger. From the owner of the hotel in Géryville and from a mulatto Collani used to visit. And the owner of the garage in Oran confirmed it, the description, that is. However, each time we were too late, unfortunately. No, that's not quite right. The car was deposited in Tunis and returned to its rightful owner in Oran. But of the stranger, or of Corporal Collani – no trace. What I was going to say was . . . Another vermouth? No? No need to stand on ceremony. *Patron!* Two Cinzanos. . . . What I was going to say was . . . Your good health, Inspector. Yes, now what I —"

"Was going to say," Studer broke in. "Well, get on

and say it. Do you think I've all the time in the world?" Studer spoke sharply, exaggerating his annoyance.

"Yessir!" said Sergeant Vanagass, whose eyes had narrowed to little slits. "*Daite mne papirossu.* Give me a cigarette." There was no doubt that Colonel Boulet-Ducarreau's secretary was drunk. But when Studer handed him his tobacco pouch, he quickly rolled himself a cigarette. Then he spoke, everything pouring out at once: "The description of the stranger in Géryville matches the description of Despine, go to Géryville, Inspector, yessir, your servant, sir, goodbye."

With that he marched across to the door, arms outstretched, palms upward, like a tightrope walker carrying an invisible pole.

"So that's the Foreign Legion," Studer muttered. Then he had lunch. In the afternoon he travelled back to Oran, where he spent the night and took the Oran–Béchar train next morning. Bouk-Toub, the station from which it is easiest to reach Géryville, is on that line. A car would have cost a fortune. It is only private detectives in novels who can afford cars. A detective sergeant from Bern had to count every centime.

The village of Bouk-Toub consisted of exactly twenty-five houses. Studer counted them while he was looking for some means of transport to take him to Géryville. A dreary place. It was not obvious why twenty-five hearths had been lit in that lunar landscape.

Studer had a deep-seated mistrust of horses, and even more of the bizarre saddle he was offered: a plank at the front, a plank at the back, short straps with stirrups as long and wide as his slippers propped up against the green-tiled stove in his apartment in Bern. Bern was a long way away, as was his café with its green billiards table . . . What would Hedy be doing just now?

156

Laughing? Crying? And Münch, the lawyer he played billiards with?

Finally Sergeant Studer found a mule. But then there were endless negotiations, in which neither his police identity badge nor the warrant from the Minister of War were any help, before Inspector Joseph Fouché could mount the beast. A saddle was also eventually found, plus a pair of leather gaiters that were so old he had to buy four leather straps as well, since the coverings that were intended to protect his calves were rotten.

The mule was a real wag. When it rolled its lips back, it looked as if it had just told an excellent joke and was only waiting for the others to laugh before joining in itself. Its lips were grey, with a black patch the size of a large coin, and as soft as the finest silk muslin. Studer immediately felt he could trust the animal, and to win its favour he popped three sugar lumps in its mouth. The mule grinned.

"After thirty-five miles," said the owner, "you'll come to a farm. It's exactly halfway. You can spend the night there. Then you'll be in Géryville by the next evening."

So the following morning Studer left the twenty-five houses of Bouk-Toub behind him. At first everything went well. The mule behaved itself, trotting along with a clatter of hooves, wheezing from time to time and shaking its head, as if to clear it of dubious thoughts. But after twenty miles Studer was saddle-sore. He bravely held on for another fifteen miles and even found the farm, which lay in a shallow depression.

That evening he soothed his chafed limbs with talcum powder and his melancholy soul with red wine. The wine was sour and gave him heartburn, but the mutton stew he was given stung his tongue just like the stew in the Chinese restaurant in Paris. The twilight was bottle green, then night came, and with it an alien

157

sky: its blackness was transparent and only later, much later was there a twinkle of stars. Studer lay in the kitchen on a bed of esparto grass, sheep baaed and the liquid mewling of a lamb sounded like a baby crying ... "Greetings from young Jakobli to old Jakob" ... Was Hedy still knitting the white romper suit? Presumably she had a cigarette before she went to sleep and she'd be asking herself what old Jakob, the Jakob who had a screw loose, was doing ...

The trot of a mule can have a soporific effect, but when it's cold and keeps getting colder the closer you come to the high plateau, your sleepiness evaporates like dew at the hay-harvest. And your thoughts start to lurch and sway, which is unpleasant – it makes you feel dizzy. The road is a monotonous yellow ribbon with the dry esparto grass rustling along the sides; the black clouds in the sky make you think of death and mourning ... Is it any wonder, then, that the old women in their armchairs come to mind, the old women who died? And you ride on through the alien light.

The priest ... the clairvoyant corporal ... the geologist ... the secretary. The priest – the geologist. Two brothers. What was there to stop Koller, the stockbroker who had enlisted in the Foreign Legion as Despine, from being a brother to both of the others? Three Brothers: Father Matthias, Victor Alois Cleman-Koller and Jakob Koller-Despine? And two sisters, Sophie and Josepha, both of whom told fortunes with the cards ... Just a minute! There was also a clairvoyant corporal by the name of Collani, who put on spiritualist seances. And there was a stockbroker who went in for the same nonsense as well. What was it the baker in rue Daguerre had said? The baker with the carroty hair? "He was interested in the last things." Koller had opened an employment exchange for the departed.

They rapped tables. Steady on now, don't mock. The fact remained that this was a case with lots of brothers and sisters: the Mannesmann brothers, the Koller brothers, the Hornuss sisters. Where the hell did Collani, the clairvoyant corporal, fit in? Was he the fourth Koller brother? If that were so, then it would all work out with no loose ends.

Chabis! What was the word Dr Malapelle of the Institute for Forensic Medicine had used? *Fantasmagoria.* And what did Murmann at police headquarters in Bern say, together with all his colleagues from the superintendent down to the lowliest policeman on the beat? "Köbu's got a screw loose."

And the chief of police wanted him to bring back a pair of Moroccan mountain sheepdogs – pedigree dogs, of course. The chief of police would take a different tack if he knew that Sergeant Studer had suddenly been promoted to Inspector Fouché. But it fitted in with the case. The people involved in it kept having different names from the ones you thought they had. Cleman was called Koller and Koller was called Despine – assuming he hadn't taken a saint's name and was calling himself Father Matthias. He could imagine the look on the chief's face if he arrived back with two male or two female sheepdogs. That would fit in with the case, too. Pairs of brothers and sisters, heheheh . . .

Laughing was difficult in the cold, it tore at your lips, which were already cracked anyway. As was his habit, Studer tried to stroke the soft hair of his moustache. The skin was bare.

"Aaaargh!" Studer cried and the mule stopped. It was midday, so he dismounted to have something to eat. He sat down on a stone by the side of the road and looked round as he chewed on the tough, cold mutton.

The plateau, flat, flat, flat – and then, in the far distance, mountains, white snowy mountains. They didn't remind him of Switzerland at all. At the bottom of the snowy mountains there they had hotels with central heating and warm water. Even the mountain huts were heated! Here there was nothing. Not a tree, not a house as far as the eye could see. At the end of the flat plateau was the gleam of the salt lakes, poisonous, like chemicals in glass dishes.

Pairs of brothers and sisters . . . Weren't there stars that appeared in the sky in pairs? That would make Marie a comet. No, that wasn't right. Marie wasn't a comet. Comets were the vagabonds of the starry sky, and Marie was no vagrant, no gypsy . . . He was sure she'd been married to Koller, the stockbroker who'd burnt his fingers on black gold . . .

Studer turned to the mule. "Come on then, Fridu" – he'd decided to call it Freddie, Fridu as they said at home – "come on then." But the mule refused to budge and just went on eating, tugging occasionally at the reins, one end of which was looped round Studer's wrist. So the sergeant took a couple of sugar lumps out of his pocket. "Here." The mule came closer, stretched out its neck, blew its warm breath over Studer's hand – that was nice – picked up the sugar lumps elegantly with its soft lips, chewed solemnly, rolled its eyes demurely, then let out a sound that literally went right through every bone in the sergeant's body. It was a mongrel sound, a cross between a donkey's bray and a horse's whinny, but the poor beast couldn't help it, it could only sing with the voice God gave it.

Studer got up. His muscles were aching and he felt homesick for his office with its smell of floor polish

160

and dust, the clunk of the steam in the radiators – where it was warm, *warm*.

"Come on then, Fridu," Studer said again. "That Marie . . . Quite . . . No! Don't eat the grass, it's not good for you . . . here, I'll give you a piece of bread. You know, Marie . . . If . . . That's just it, *if* . . . then Marie'll say, 'Thanks, Cousin Jakob', and everything'll be all right. Come on now, Fridu, there's a good chap, let's be going."

The pipe was lit, the beret pulled down over his ears and he was back in the saddle. Strapped to the back was a rolled-up sleeping bag, contents: one pair of pyjamas, two shirts, two pairs of socks, washing kit. He might be fifty-nine, but anything the legionnaires could do . . .

A snowstorm started, but only – thank God! – when Géryville was in sight. The mule obviously knew its business. The gallop it broke into was as smooth as a ride on a roller-coaster and it came to a halt outside a building that was clearly the Géryville hotel. Studer climbed off the mule, looking like a snowy Father Christmas who had shaved off his beard by accident. He almost fell asleep over dinner. A glass of wine brought him back to semi-consciousness, but then a ringing started in his ears. The hotel owner seemed to be used to guests like that. He helped the large man up to a room on the top floor, took off his wet coat and tucked him in.

When Studer woke up next morning, fully dressed, he decided that the hotel owner had been very considerate. The bedbugs had only been able to get at his hands to bite them, and his forehead, a little bit.

The clairvoyant corporal begins to take shape

It was strange but true: all the senior officers of the French Foreign Legion seemed to be endowed with ample paunches. The only thing that Major Borotra, commandant of the Second Battalion of the First Regiment, who had four bands of gold braid round his kepi, had in common with the tennis champion was his name. He was an easygoing tub of lard with a sparse blond moustache.

"Collani?" he asked. "You're looking for Collani? How come a policemen from Lyons is interested in my corporal? My clairvoyant corporal?"

Studer put on an inscrutable expression and pointed to the forged signature of the Minister of War. Borotra flushed. The signature had magic powers.

"Go and see our doctor," the fat commandant said. "Dr Cantacuzène will be able to tell you what you need to know. Then I hope you'll give us the pleasure of your company at lunch in the officers' mess. We are of course –" he cleared his throat – "always ready to be of service to, er –" even more clearing of the throat – "to the Minister of War, as far as is in our power, and we trust that, in your report to His Excellency, you will not forget to –" the clearing of his throat seemed to go on for ever.

"Goes without saying," said Studer loftily, feeling like a marshall of the Great Emperor promising a prefect the Legion of Honour. Hadn't Joseph Fouché been Duke of Otranto? Studer could play the duke.

Sometimes a democracy can be the best school for aristocratic behaviour.

Dr Cantacuzène looked like a sly newspaper editor who would have difficulty convincing certain authorities of his Aryan descent. He wore a pince-nez with thick lenses which kept slipping off the bridge of his nose and which he kept catching, like a juggler, once on his finger, once on the back of his hand and once, even, on the toe of his boot.

"An hysteric," said Dr Cantacuzène, who was of Greek origin, as he immediately emphasized. "Your Collani was a typical case of male hysteria. Which doesn't exclude the possibility that he did perhaps possess certain occult gifts. Almost all the experiments I conducted with him could have a perfectly natural explanation, still –" he raised his right knee just in time to let his pince-nez rest there precariously for a moment – "what is beyond doubt is that the man had a very murky past. And in that past there was definitely *one* incident that was a great burden on Collani's mind. He never discussed it with me, but for a while he was close to a certain priest. For my part, I refused to get mixed up in confessional secrets . . ." The pince-nez fell to the floor.

"He smoked *kif*," the doctor went on, "and that wasn't good for his health, since he didn't have a very strong constitution. You know what *kif* is? Hashish. *Cannabis indica*. To many people here it looks as if Collani was abducted by a stranger. For my part, I think the man went off on a spree and smoked too much *kif* somewhere. A minor collapse would explain his disappearance . . ."

*

163

No, that could not have been the explanation for his disappearance, for at lunch in the officers' mess Major Borotra was delighted to be able to announce that he had been informed that very morning by Captain Lartigue, the officer in command of the Mounted Company of the 3rd Regiment in Gourama, that Collani had turned up there, fit and well. Collani claimed he did not know where he had spent the past few months and Lartigue believed him. He would, the captain had said, get the doctor to examine the clair-voyant corporal and then he could look forward to his discharge. He had qualified for a pension anyway.

"Is there no photo of this Collani?"

"I do not think so, Inspector Fouché," said Borotra. "But we can give you a good description of him, can't we, gentlemen?"

Three captains, two lieutenants and six second lieu-tenants replied in chorus, "Yes, sir."

Then it was like a party game in which everyone has to add one feature in turn: "Short." – "Skinny." – "Thirty-inch chest." – "Grey hair." – "Clean-shaven." – "Ears sticking out." – "Flat." – "No lobe." – "Olive complexion." – "Blue eyes."

"Thank you," said Studer, "that will be sufficient. If I have understood correctly, his ears stick out, are flat and have no lobe? . . . Yes? . . . Thank you again. And how tall was Collani?"

A little lieutenant raised his hand.

"Lieutenant?"

"Five foot four."

There didn't seem to be much going on in Géryville in the winter. The officers stayed sitting around until half past three. They refused to let Studer go. As a guest from outside, he was entertained and plied with drink. He thanked God that none of the officers came

164

from Lyons. But if the worst had come to the worst, the detective sergeant from Bern, who had illegally assumed the name of a French minister of police from the First Empire, might well have been able to bluff his way out of it.

Finally Studer managed to get away. He wanted to go and see Achmed, the mulatto Collani used to visit every evening to smoke *kif.*

Achmed, the mulatto, was such a giant he could quite happily have got people to pay to see him in a fairground booth. His complexion was the colour of a block of Swiss chocolate, specially made for a special occasion.

In a red clay pipe with a bowl no bigger than a thimble he was smoking some herb that smelt like cigarettes for asthmatics. He received Studer sitting cross-legged on a carpet, like some oriental king. It made you forget the shabby, empty room and the harsh light sprayed round by an acetylene lamp.

There was no air of suspicion to greet a strange visitor, simply a quiet, reserved serenity.

Corporal Collani? A good friend. Very quiet, didn't talk much. Made no close friends so he came to him, Achmed, every evening. Smoked two pipes of *kif.*

"No, Inspector, that amount is not sufficient to make you lose control of yourself. The very idea!" Achmed spoke standard French and Studer would have liked to ask him where he had got his education. "You sleep well after two pipes," Achmed explained, "and the corporal suffered from insomnia. He used to sigh a lot. Not like a man who has something weighing on his conscience, no, more like a person who has lost a valuable pearl and looks for it everywhere. This summer it was particularly bad. Once he cried, really cried, like a little child whose favourite marble's been stolen."

A mulatto! A simple man, and a poor one at that!

But what understanding, how well he talked about the workings of the human mind!

"I tried to comfort him," Achmed went on. "I asked him to confide in me, but he wouldn't. He kept repeating, 'If I open this letter, this letter here –' he showed it me – 'then I'll be dragged back into the past and he will come to get me.' 'Who will come to get you, Corporal?' I asked. 'The devil, Achmed! The old devil! I killed him, the devil, but the devil's immortal, we never know when he'll wake up again.' So he posted the letter, on 20 July last year.

"The next day he told me he had a copy of the letter, but he didn't know where it was. 'I've searched through all my things,' he said, 'but I can't find it anywhere . . . And it's better that way.'

"Two months later a stranger came to see me, asking about Corporal Collani. He waited, but on that evening the corporal came late. He didn't notice the stranger, he just said to me, 'Now I know where that copy is. I sewed it into the lining of an old woollen waistcoat. I've just seen it quite clearly.' – 'Where have you been until now, Corporal?' I asked. 'With the priest,' he replied. And then he saw the stranger."

Achmed fell silent. With a guileless look in his brown eyes, eyes that were so dark they seemed almost black, he looked up at Studer, who was leaning against the wall beside the hissing acetylene lamp. So there was a copy of the temperature chart! Where was it to be found? And if it had fallen into the hands of the "opposition", to give the mysterious people he had become involved with a name, where should he start looking for it? And if the opposition had the chart, why hire two petty crooks from Bern to steal it from him?

Studer had the feeling something inside his head had suddenly been set in motion. It was a strange sensation: one cogwheel is turning beside another that is still; a lever is switched over, the teeth of the revolving cogwheel mesh with those of the still one, and now they're both turning. The wheels had been set in motion because the sergeant had suddenly seen the first card in the top row of the cards that had been laid out, both in Basel and in Bern: the jack of spades! Spades – the unlucky suit. The jack of spades – death. Strange how memory works sometimes, Studer thought. You store up images, then forget them, until suddenly one rises from the depths and is developed, printed out, in sharp focus.

Achmed sat cross-legged in his corner, puffing on his pipe. Sergeant Studer was so immersed in his thoughts, he did not notice that he had slid down on to the floor himself, though he couldn't manage to squat on his heels in the authentic posture. Too preoccupied with his deductions to fill a pipe for himself, he stretched out his hand, then sucked dreamily at a mouthpiece, drawing the smoke deep into his lungs, then blowing it out again. "Another," he murmured.

"Brother," Achmed told him, "you have to say *amr sbsi*. That is, fill me a pipe."

Obediently Studer repeated, "*Amr sbsi.*"

The smoke tickled his throat slightly, but inside his head it sparked off colours.

"*Amr sbsi . . .*" Achmed smiled. He had broad teeth. In the whitewashed room the light from the acetylene lamp was white. But when Studer looked through his eyelashes, all the colours of the rainbow danced a stately gavotte.

"*Mlech?*" Achmed asked. Studer nodded. He felt he could speak Arabic excellently. *Mlech* meant "good", of course. He nodded vigorously and repeated, "*Mlech, mlech.*"

For a brief moment he sobered up again and tried to recall the date. He wanted to ask in Arabic, but his Swiss dialect got in the way, and even that refused to cross his lips. All his question produced was a mumbling stammer, although Studer was convinced he had spoken particularly clearly.

A smile of astonishment appeared on Achmed's face. And then he made three gestures that shook Studer's West European conception of time to its very foundations. He held out his hands, palms upward, lifted his arms, and let his hands fall back on his knees; next he raised his right hand with the index finger outstretched, his other fingers clenched; finally the outstretched index finger was placed on his lips and then pointed up at the sky.

And these gestures were so expressive, Studer had no trouble translating them: "My brother! How can you hope to hold time in your open hands? You can only despair when you think of eternity. What is time to Him, the Eternally Silent who sits enthroned above, to Him to whom eternity belongs?"

Having seen and understood these gestures, the sergeant had a vague feeling he would never be able to resume his activity in the Bern police force. He saw himself getting up in the morning, shaving . . . There was a smell of coffee in the apartment – half past seven already. He had to be at the police station by eight, in his office . . . But what was that? Two hands stretch out, palms upward, an index finger points to the sky. Go to the office? Why? The station, work, the blessings of Western civilization: keeping busy, working to the clock, being there on time, getting paid at the end of the month, what had happened to all that? What was the point? For the love of Allah, what was the point? You sank into the sea of eternity, you died. What was the use of all that hustle and bustle? Why did you take yourself so seriously? Travelling with false papers, looking for people who had disappeared, trying to find buried treasure. You were just a tiny droplet in the bank of cloud that was humanity, you evaporated . . .

The mulatto was still sitting opposite the sergeant, and his face looked like the eternally young countenance of an alien god . . .

"*Amr sbsi*. Fill my pipe."

The pipe, the tiny clay pipe the size of a thimble, was filled, and beside the sergeant a cup suddenly appeared, giving off the most fragrant odours. Studer was no longer capable of seeing that it was a plain cup of tea with a few mint leaves floating in it. He drank and he drank . . .

Where was that music coming from? There was the wild stamp of a dance right next to his ears and he could see women flinging their toes up far above their heads. Then there was the scent of roses, lots of yellow roses; the sergeant lay down on damp moss, a garden spreading out all round him with a smell of earth after a rainstorm. Once more the pipe was placed in his hand. Now he could see stars, swirling round in huge circles . . . And the music? The music ringing out?

It sounded like the Bern March played by the heavenly host . . .

Later, especially when playing billiards with Münch, the lawyer, Studer would often describe the delights of being high on hashish. Eventually, however, he would run out of adjectives and finish with the most emphatic superlative his Swiss dialect possessed:

"Brilliant!" he said. "Bloody brilliant, so it was!"

*

169

Achmed, the mulatto, smiled. He spread two horse blankets out on the floor, lifted up Studer – the sergeant's fourteen stone was no problem for him – laid him down gently on the warm bed and covered him up. Thus the detective from Bern slept, in a shabby room in some godforsaken place far from the comforts of the Swiss capital, a place that was probably not even on the map. And he slept the best sleep he had ever had; the most vivid, too, brimming over with sounds and scents.

But there was a price to pay, a hangover which made him very grateful for the understanding behaviour of Fridu the mule as he rode back to Bouk-Toub. It placed its tiny hooves as carefully as possible on the frozen ground, as if it were well aware of the dreadful migraine from which its rider was suffering. Yes, there's always a price to pay if you hear the angels playing, "Tum, tum, tum, didahdi . . ."

People talk a lot about the desert, its endlessness, the frisson it gives you. In Colomb-Béchar Studer was seriously disappointed. Yes, there was lots of yellow sand, but growing in it were strange plants: cans that had contained sardines, tuna, corned beef, which, with their jagged lids, suggested improbable cactuses. The horizon was overcast, the date palms with their bilious green leaves recalled garishly coloured postcards – and it was cold, bitterly, outrageously cold. Studer felt cheated. Naturally his room was unheated. They put an uncovered brazier in it, against all health and safety regulations. It's a well-known fact that coal when it burns gives off carbon monoxide, and that's a poisonous gas.

Fortunately the commanding officer in Colomb-Béchar gave *monsieur l'inspecteur* Fouché permission to continue his journey the following day. Or, to be more precise, the following night. Five Saurer trucks were heading for Midelt via Bou-Denib and Gourama. Then the sergeant asked the commandant – he was a major and just as fat as Major Borotra in Géryville – whether a certain Corporal Collani had reported on his way through.

"He did, Inspector, he did," the officer said. "Just imagine, he had the cheek to report here. He'd been absent without leave for three months, you know, so I really ought to have locked him up as a deserter. But the man was ill, very ill, and he begged me so insistently to be allowed to travel on to Gourama that eventually I gave him my permission."

"Was he in uniform?"

"Yes. But after he had left, an Arab told me he had changed beforehand in his house. I demanded to see the civilian clothes, but they had long since been sold."

"What did the corporal look like?"

"Short, Inspector, shorter than you. Tell me, has he been back in Europe during his absence? Has he committed some crime there? Is that why you're looking for him?"

Studer placed his finger on his lips. It was always the best answer.

They left around midnight. He clung on to the image of Marie; it was the only reality left for him to cling on to as, squashed in between armed legionnaires, he was driven along roads that were really nothing more than rivers of yellow mud. It was a clear night; the moon shone until the first light of morning, then the sun appeared and warmed the air a little. The sergeant sat on a wine barrel, his legs going to sleep alternately, smoked his pipe and said nothing. His companions were wearing those pale green greatcoats, which were not picturesque enough for American films about the Foreign Legion, which dressed them

171

up in fantasy uniforms. Their rifles were rusty and he wondered whether they could actually shoot with them. Authentic French incompetence! Sergeant Studer thought of the recruits in the far-off training camp and was glad he could feel annoyed, for that at least partly displaced the image of Achmed, the mulatto, who, with a few simple gestures, had demonstrated the pointlessness of all activity.

On either side of the broad plain bare mountains appeared, and villages surrounded by olive groves, with skeletal hens scratching at the dung heaps. Small children with shaven heads picked their noses; their mothers stood beside them and did not shout, "Don't do that!"

Little donkeys trotted past, nothing more than skin and bone. The women driving them were not veiled, so one could see the blue dots on their foreheads arranged in the shape of a cross.

Then came Gourama.

Captain Lartigue

The fort was square, with a wall round it and three lines of barbed wire. At one corner the barrel of a three-inch gun jutted out over the wall. The entrance was free of barbed wire and a man in a crumpled khaki uniform was leaning against the gate pillar. The faded kepi on his head was squint and his trousers were too short, revealing the grey woollen socks inside his open-toed sandals.

"Is Captain Lartigue available?" Studer asked, while the trucks, already far away, fired salvoes from amid clouds of dust.

The man did not move, just raised his eyes from the ground and stared at the sergeant, subjecting him to an intensive examination. He asked, "Why?" and clicked his tongue. A gazelle appeared from behind the wall, peered at them shyly, then trotted over on its delicate hooves and rubbed its nose against the hip of the man in khaki.

Studer cleared his throat. He was appalled at the reception – no discipline! – and the man was beginning to get on his nerves. Fourteen hours in an army truck do not have the same effect as bromide in your tea. The sergeant showed his French police identity badge. "Police!" he snapped.

The man in khaki shrugged his shoulders and stroked the gazelle's head. Studer took out his passport and pointed to the authorization from the War Ministry. The man's lips twisted in an insolent grin.

"Take me to the captain," Studer barked.

"What if I am the captain?"

"Then you're damn discourteous."

"And you're going to teach me to be courteous?"

"It wouldn't do any harm. You, sir, are a boor."

"And you, sir, are a spy."

"Say that again."

"You are a spy."

"And you are a moron."

"Now that's a word you should only use if you can use your fists as well. Can you box, fatso?"

That touched Studer in a most sensitive spot. His dark overcoat flew through the air. It snagged on the barbed wire, but that didn't bother him in the least. His jacket took the same route. And then Sergeant Studer – alias Inspector Fouché – did something he had not done since he was a boy. He began to roll his sleeves up.

And put up his fists.

He had never done any boxing, he knew, but he had seen off better men than this little French officer, who was not even wearing his insignia of rank.

Suddenly the man laughed. It was a pleasant laugh. "You must excuse me, Inspector, I'm in a bad mood today. You showed me your passport. Inspector Fouché, wasn't it? Of the Sûreté in Lyons? I'm from Lyons myself. I remember the name very well, it was often mentioned during my time there. But you're supposed to be dead, aren't you? Weren't you shot during a police raid? Apparently not, since you're here, alive and kicking. Come on, come on, put your jacket back on. Your coat, too, otherwise you'll catch pneumonia and I've got enough men in the sickbay already. Let's go and have a drink instead."

The effect was like what the French called a Scotch shower: the blood froze in his veins when the man said he was from Lyons, then he went hot all over when he was invited to have a drink. But the expression on his face did not change. "Oh yes?" he said. "From Lyons? I was told you came from the Jura, that you were a fell— er, half Swiss. From Lyons. Aha."

"A bit of both," said Captain Lartigue. "My parents came from St Imier, but my father set up a watch factory in Lyons. I did go to Switzerland quite often, though. And now I'm here . . . But you'll be hungry. Come along."

Barracks squares surrounded by huts . . . Corrugated iron roofs that were so smooth they reflected the sun's rays like gigantic mirrors. Men in blue linen uniforms crept round, casually raising their hands to their foreheads – you didn't know whether it was a military salute or a friendly wave.

One of these men came over, stood in their way and said, without standing to attention, "I've got a fever."

Studer's companion stopped, took hold of the man's wrist, let go after a while, thought for a moment and then patted him on the shoulder. "Go and have a lie down, *mon petit*, I'll send the nurse."

At the word "nurse" Sergeant Studer gave a start. Could . . . could . . . but he brushed the thought aside with a characteristic gesture, as if he were trying to drive away invisible midges from his face.

Captain Lartigue walked on. Studer stared at him from the side. What kind of a man was he? His voice could be gentle, like a mother's voice.

"We have a lot of marsh fever in the fort," the captain said, a note of sadness in his voice. "The area is unhealthy. Sometimes half the company's laid up with it. It's not the usual form of malaria, quinine hardly has any effect. It's heartbreaking. If we didn't have the Red Cross nurse the Resident in Fez sent us . . ."

Studer relaxed. Marie was not a nurse, she was a shorthand typist. But – there was always a "but". If a detective sergeant from Bern could assume the character of a French police inspector, why should Marie not be able to transform herself into a Red Cross nurse?

"Is this nurse," Studer asked, and he could not keep a slight quaver out of his voice, "is this nurse you have engaged competent, Captain?"

The captain looked at Studer – and the look he gave him was discomforting.

"Very competent," he said, his voice devoid of expression. "But tell me, *monsieur l'inspecteur* Fouché, what is it that brings you to this godforsaken outpost?"

"It's a long story," said the sergeant.

"They're not always the best," said the captain. "I prefer short stories."

They walked on in silence. In the middle of the fort was a building that looked like a squat tower. Stuck against the wall was a chicken ladder.

"I'll show you the way, *monsieur l'inspecteur* Fouché. *Monsieur l'inspecteur* Jakob Fouché, isn't it?"

"No. Joseph, Joseph Fouché."

"Of course, Joseph. A little mistake. I'll lead the way, *monsieur l'inspecteur* Joseph Fouché. That's the correct name, isn't it?"

"Yes, that's correct." Quick, while this awkward man's got his back turned, quick, quick, your handkerchief. The leather inside his beret was soaking wet. And his handkerchief! That's what you got for having a good wife, a wife who insisted on sewing in your monogram herself. Clear to see in one corner: J. S. – Jakob Studer . . . One couldn't think of everything.

The steps had no rail, so they made a nasty little climb. At the top they entered a very high, very bright room. Square. Whitewashed. Like that room on Spalen-berg in Basel ... Opposite the entrance was a huge glass door, giving onto a balcony with no railings. The glass door was open and the sunlight flooded into the room. Hung on the walls were Moroccan carpets, red, black, white. And, above the carpets, shelves full of books.

"Do sit down, *monsieur l'inspecteur* Joseph – that is correct, isn't it? – *monsieur l'inspecteur* Joseph Fouché. I'm delighted to welcome a fellow Lyonnais to my apartment. How is Locard?"

Now Dr Locard from Lyons is a leading light of crim-inology, so Studer was able to answer the captain's question. He had spoken to Locard only a year ago.

"Fine, thank you, very well, the same as ever ..." and he started to tell a story he had from Locard.

"You don't have a Lyons accent at all," said Lartigue, without looking up, as he filled two glasses to the brim.

"No, no," the sergeant stammered. "I was posted to Lyons. I come from Bellegarde originally. Yes ..."

"Aha, so you're from the Swiss border too?"

"Yes, of course ..." Studer's agreement came too quickly.

"Good, good. And what is it His Excellency the Min-ister of War wants to know? You must realize I've a very bad record, which is why I've been sent out here. But of course, if I can be of some service ..."

"It's about ..." said Studer, then broke off. The silence that followed was long. Finally Captain Lartigue took pity on his guest. "You must be tired, Inspector," he said, dropping the ironic tone. "I think the best thing would be if you had a little lie-down. My bed is at your service, just until we've found one for you. I have things to do, so you'll be undisturbed. Have a good sleep."

This was a pretty pickle he'd landed himself in and no mistake. He hated the whole business. It went against the grain to have to go under an assumed name; he felt oppressed, constrained, inhibited in all his movements. And he hated having to lie to this Captain Lartigue, who was obviously a decent fellow. Studer's judgement of character was not something he'd learnt from books, it was not based on physical appearance, handwriting analysis, psychological typologies or phrenology. He just allowed people to be themselves and relied on his instinct.

This Lartigue! Just the way he'd spoken to the legionnaire: "*Mon petit*," he'd called him. And challenging him to a boxing match at the entrance to the fort!

He had a round skull with short, blond hair, did this Lartigue, and blue eyes in a broad face. His chin jutted out.

From outside, the long-drawn-out call of a bugle broke the silence. Three low notes, then, a major third above it, four long notes. The last was held and died away in a melancholy diminuendo.

Studer stood up and went out onto the balcony. For a moment he felt dizzy, only too aware of the lack of railings. But then his attention was caught by the scene being played out below.

The company had drawn up in a square. One man with a curly beard, who was standing in the middle of the formation, shouted a command when he saw the captain coming round the corner of one of the huts. The lines of legionnaires were as motionless as walls. Blue linen uniforms with grey flannel cummerbunds. With a wave of the hand Captain Lartigue indicated that they should stand easy and said a few words, which were immediately blown away by the wind coming from the red mountains to the north. The walls shifted, loosened. The gazelle slipped through a gap between them and stood beside the captain, who stroked it. Suddenly the whole company was laughing. A black sausage shape came tearing along at furious speed, sending up clouds of dust. The sausage yapped, jumped up on the captain, sniffed the gazelle and wagged its tail. Then it gave a loud sneeze – a Scotch terrier.

The captain strode along the rows and at first Studer could not understand what he was doing. Every time he stopped in front of a man, the latter opened his mouth and the captain popped a little white pill into it, then went on to the next.

A brief command and once more the walls were motionless. A wave of the hand and they crumbled.

"What were you putting in the men's mouths, Captain?" Studer asked when Lartigue reappeared in the tower. Under his arm he held the terrier, which was desperately scrabbling at him with its feet.

"Quinine. I feed my men quinine, two grams a day. They all have ringing in the ears, but it doesn't help."

"Quinine," Studer repeated. Suddenly he slapped himself on the forehead.

"What's wrong, Inspector?"

"Nothing, nothing," said Studer, his mind elsewhere. In it he could see the temperature chart. What was it that was written opposite 20 July?

Quinine sulphate 2 km.

Since when was quinine administered by the kilometre? But didn't that note come just before, or just after, the letters SSE? That was it! The treasure was buried close to a cork-oak beside a red rock in the shape of a man, two kilometres south-south-east of Gourama.

"Have you got a compass?" Studer asked, not realizing he was excitedly pacing up and down in someone else's room. When he did realize, he looked up and met the captain's eyes. He couldn't quite make out the expression in them. Was it mocking? Pitying?

"You want a compass, Inspector Jakob – sorry, Joseph Fouché?"

Why did the man keep going on about Jakob? Did he know something?

"Yes, please," said Studer, his voice slightly strained.

"There you are. I imagine you're going for a walk. Don't bother about me, go and get something to eat. One of the men will show you the canteen. And this evening you're dining with me. I have to sleep now. *Au revoir.*"

With that Studer was dismissed. He climbed down the chicken ladder, went into the first hut he came to, demanded a spade and asked for directions to the *ksar*.

The spade had a short handle and the metal blade had a leather cover. Very practical.

The *ksar* was the native village, built like a tower out of clay bricks and half a mile or so from the fort. Beyond the *ksar* the sergeant ascertained which direction was south-south-east and set off. His stride measured roughly two feet six inches, which was eighty centimetres, so for the two kilometres that made about 2,500 steps. But Studer found he could give up counting after only 1,000 steps. The cork oak was clearly visible and from the distance a red rock sticking up beside it looked like a man.

But the sergeant found no need for his spade. Next to the rock was a gaping hole, and the hole was empty.

Deduction? Someone had been there before him. The deduction was so obvious all he could do was shrug his shoulders. But who was that someone? For the moment that didn't matter. What did matter was that Captain Lartigue obviously knew everything. He'd indicated it clearly enough with the suggestive way he'd kept on saying, "*Monsieur l'inspecteur* Jakob . . . sorry, Joseph Fouché." OK, Jakob was his name. What was the problem with that? But he was sailing under false colours and that *was* a problem. Still, he'd made his own bed, so now he must lie in it. And if you looked at it another way, it was a completely new situation. In Switzerland he could count on support wherever he went. He had friends in the police and the authorities would cover his back. Here? . . . Here he was all on his own, he had to fend for himself, he couldn't rely on getting help from anywhere. That nice Captain Lartigue, for example, could arrest him on the spot and send him under armed escort to Fez – that is assuming he didn't decide he'd rather get things over and done with and put him before a firing squad. If, on the other hand, he was tried under military law, the prospect was a few years in Cayenne, where things would undoubtedly be made hot for him. The only enjoyable aspect of it was thinking up the articles that would appear in the Swiss newspapers:

We regret to have to report that an experienced police detective, highly regarded in his native canton of Bern, has been found guilty in France of a serious infringement of international law. The French government . . . The steps our ambassador in Paris has taken at the behest of the Federal authorities have, unfortunately, so far yielded no result. In its sitting of 2 February the Federal Council voted to appoint a committee to explore the steps that might be taken in this regrettable affair. The committee will be selected in the next few weeks. Its first task will be to set up a subgroup to commission a report from a leading expert on international law which will examine this sad case from all sides. According to sources close to the government, the committee is expected to delegate the drawing-up of an initial report to a subcommittee. It is hoped that this unfortunate matter will be resolved as early as next year . . .

That's the way things were, a committee was a committee and you couldn't do anything to hurry it up. But perhaps a committee wouldn't be necessary? Perhaps rescue was closer at hand than he thought?

Far away on the horizon a dot appeared, a tiny blob. Studer took out his binoculars. A mule! And on the mule was a patch of white. Perhaps the patch of white was coming to rescue him.

With these thoughts going through his mind, Studer reached the fort. It stood there, silent, in the slanting rays of the early evening sun. Beside the guardroom Studer saw two heavy wooden doors – clearly the two cells. Perhaps a Swiss detective would spend the next night behind one of them?

Studer returned the spade. Then he climbed back up the chicken ladder and knocked. Since there was no answer, he went in. Captain Lartigue was lying on a couch in one corner of the room, asleep. The gazelle and the Scotch terrier were stretched out in peaceful companionship between the captain and the wall. Both blinked sleepily at the sergeant; the dog briefly raised its head, then let it slump back down onto its crossed paws. Studer tiptoed across to an armchair, sat down, picked up a book that lay open on the little table and started to read. It was poetry, French poetry, mellifluous and sad. it suited Studer's mood. Some prisoner had probably written it:

> The sky above the roof,
> So blue, so calm;
> The breeze above the roof,
> Rocking a palm.

Sergeant Studer's eyes filled with tears and he fell asleep . . .

182

The shared repose seemed to form an invisible bond between the four of them. When they woke a couple of hours later they seemed glad to be together.

The captain said, "Had a little nap too, *monsieur l'inspecteur*?" and Studer countered with, "How about a vermouth, *mon capitaine*?" The gazelle and the dog played tag in the room, round and round the sergeant's chair; then they suddenly stopped and looked up at Studer with a friendly gaze. The gazelle had moist eyes, like a girl in love, and the dog was like a grizzled negro. It was very cosy in the tower room.

And outside was an evening as cool and red as strawberry ice. A gentle breeze wafted in through the open balcony door. A few stars, round and white and shining, were scattered like peeled hazelnuts among clouds that looked like lumps of bramble jelly. A little later the moon appeared, putting an end to this confectioner's delight. It was huge and pale, and the light it cast over the huts and yards recalled gigantic white linen sheets that had just come from the bleaching green. A bugle sent out its mournful cry again, a signal, with trills and coloraturas – and, like a great Italian singer, it held the penultimate note for so long, you started to tremble waiting for the return to the tonic. And hardly had the final note died away than a song started up, soft, muted. It went with the evening, with the plain and the clear light of the moon. At times a male voice soared above the choir accompanying it in a rumbling bass.

"The Russians are singing," the captain said in a soft voice. Studer listened, rapt. It was deeply moving, in a way he had never experienced before; there was nothing like this at home . . . So this was the Legion, the Foreign Legion: a song of the great dream, the dream of horses, mountains, plains and the sea . . .

Lartigue was still lying on the couch, his hands

clasped behind his head, breathing in the songs like a strong perfume. Suddenly the singing broke off. The captain leapt up.

"You're looking for Collani, the clairvoyant corporal, Inspector . . . No, don't deny it." Lartigue went over to the little door leading out onto the wooden steps and whistled. From below came the clatter of footsteps. The captain gave a quiet order, then closed the door, went to the fireplace and put a lighted match to the wood that had been laid there. The scent of thyme gradually filled the room.

"Should I put the light on? Or are you happy with the moon?"

Studer nodded. He couldn't speak. The captain seemed to understand how his guest was feeling and filled two glasses with a liquid clear as water. Studer took a sip. It was damned strong and tickled his throat, but it was warming.

"Date brandy," the captain explained. "The Jew who supplies me with sheep bribed me with three bottles. And that was very sensible of him, otherwise I'd have had him making bricks for two months, because he'd tried to pull the wool over my eyes, so to speak, with his sheep. They were only twenty-five pounds live weight, and that's too little . . . But I presume you're not interested in that, *monsieur l'inspecteur* Jakob – sorry, Joseph Fouché."

But he was! He was very interested in that kind of thing. The demands that were made on the commandant of a little outpost like this! He had to be a doctor, livestock dealer, vet, military strategist, judge, commander of a fort, father to his men . . .

"Who is your immediate superior, Captain?" he asked. "Who do you report to?"

"Me?" Captain Lartigue grinned, and it would have

184

been an exaggeration to call it a good-natured grin. "Me?" he repeated. "I'm a little king. No one tells me what to do, apart from the Resident in Fez. Officially, my company is part of the Third Regiment – but it's regarded as a battalion. And the colonel of the Third Regiment is much too far away. In Rabat. Just imagine, 250 miles as the crow flies. So I'm commandant of the fort, of the battalion – and the area all around is subject to me as well. So you see, *mon cher Inspecteur . . .* Fouché, that's it . . . So you see, *mon cher Inspecteur* Joseph Fouché, – remarkable, isn't it, that you have the same name as the great emperor's minister of police? – there's nothing to stop me having you summarily executed."

The grin – good-natured or not – had vanished from the captain's lips. His mouth was narrow, straight, his lips slightly pale.

"If I were to put a man who bears the name – let's assume legally for the moment – of a French imperial minister, if I were simply to put this man before a firing squad, there would be no one to prevent such an act of summary justice. It may be summary, but you must agree that executing a spy is an act of justice. To satisfy the formalities, I might call a little court-martial, say a lieutenant, two sergeants and two corporals. Five men – plus one: me as both prosecutor and judge. You'd be allowed to conduct your own defence. As prosecutor – and judge – I would say, 'Before you stands a man who has entered an occupied zone with a forged passport. I suspect him of being a spy. At the moment there is no one we can spare to escort him to Fez, so the case must be decided here. We do have the necessary powers. Since it is a case of espionage and since – as the interests of France are at stake – I cannot present the evidence in open court, there is only one possible verdict: guilty; and one possible sentence: death.' What would you say to that Inspector Jakob – sorry, Joseph Fouché?"

"Do you mind if I fill my pipe?" Studer asked, unperturbed. Even as he asked, he took out his tobacco pouch and calmly proceeded to fill the bowl, tamping the tobacco down properly with his thumb. Then he got up and stayed standing there for a while, a tall, broad, massive figure, before he strode over to the fireplace with heavy steps, bent down, took out a piece of kindling with a little yellow flame, lit his pipe, went back to his chair and blew clouds of smoke into Lartigue's face.

"Once the court had answered that initial question," he said, "I would go on, 'Gentlemen, it is true that I am travelling on a forged passport. But I have never engaged in espionage. I am a Swiss policeman investigating a double murder, which I have been given the duty of ... of ...'" Studer searched for a suitably impressive word, but, not finding one, he simply ended with, "'... solving.'"

He fell silent and stroked his upper lip, feeling for his moustache; twirling it had always calmed him during awkward discussions. Not finding it, however, he resorted to a thorough clearing of his throat. Then he continued: "Anyway – and I'll be quite open with you, *mon capitaine* – I am not only looking after the interests of my country, but those of a young woman, whose father ... But I don't think that would be of interest for your court-martial. And to return to those proceedings: first of all I would demand to be treated as a representative of my country. Since that request would probably be refused, I would take the liberty of following a highly idiosyncratic interpretation of the law of self-defence. Two Brownings contain sixteen rounds, assuming my arithmetic is correct."

"Bravo!" said Captain Lartigue. "Marie's description hit the mark exactly."

"Mar—" Studer said, but he was interrupted by a woman's voice.

"Evening, Cousin Jakob."

Studer grasped the bottle of date brandy, filled his glass, emptied it and put it back down.

"Hello, Marie." His voice was perfectly steady.

A morning in the fort of Gourama

"Cousin Jakob," Marie asked, "have you got the temperature chart?"

Studer nodded, nodded and nodded, his head wouldn't stop. Marie had sat down on the couch where, not too long ago, the captain, the dog and the gazelle had been fast asleep. And Studer was still sitting in the armchair with the comfortable shape that had allowed him, too, to rest and close his eyes. The book with the lines

> The sky above the roof,
> So blue, so calm . . .

was still lying on the little table. But Marie's arrival had changed the mood in the room. She was wearing a white linen apron, such as nurses wear as part of their uniform, with a thin hairnet held by a linen band tied round her forehead. And proudly in the middle of the linen band stood a red cross. Marie sat on the couch in a modest posture, hands clasped, elbows resting on her knees. Beside her sat Captain Lartigue in his crumpled khaki uniform, leaning so far back that there was only a dark blue cushion between his shoulder-blades and the wall. At his feet sat the dog and the gazelle, like a tangled ball of brown and black wool.

Yes, he had the temperature chart, Studer said, staring at the floor. That is, to be precise, he had one half of the chart; the other half was safely locked up in a lawyer's office in Bern.

Now it was Marie's turn to nod. And she did. Slowly and repeatedly. Finally she asked whether no one had any cigarettes in the room. Cousin Jakob – what she actually said was *l'oncle Jacques* – had his pipe to smoke, what about her? Studer sighed. How many names had he had to put up with in this messy case? For Madelin he was "Studère", for the dance teacher "Styoodah", for Murmann "Köbu", on his passport he was called Joseph Fouché, and for Hedy he was "*Vatti*". Marie had christened him "Cousin Jakob". He was happy with that. But "*Oncle Jacques*"! It was too much. And as Captain Lartigue took a blue packet – similar to the blue packet on the seat beside the then unknown girl in the Paris–Basel express – out of one of his pockets and offered Marie a cigarette, Detective Sergeant Studer gave vent to his protest, a protest expressed in the most vigorous Swiss terms.

His protest died away. Studer had the impression he was talking to two dolls. He felt a pang of sadness. Lartigue was looking at Marie and the girl only had eyes for the captain. There was a French expression *faire le Jacques*, which could perhaps best be translated as "to play the fool". The sergeant could not get the silly pun out of his mind.

What did these two, there on the couch, care about the temperature chart? What did they care about the treasure under the cork-oak beside the red rock that looked like a man? What was the tragedy of two old women, who had both come to a miserable end in their kitchens, to Captain Lartigue, livestock dealer, garrison commander, military strategist, doctor and father to his men? Could two lovers spare a thought for things that quickened the pulse of every detective?

The "Big Case", for example? Studer sighed, and since, at the same time as he sighed, he knocked out his pipe on the rim of a pottery ashtray, the two finally looked across at him. And about time too!

"Let's leave the serious business until the morning," said Captain Lartigue. "You're tired now, Inspector. We'll have some supper, then you can have a good night's sleep and tomorrow we'll see what's the best way to sort out our affairs."

"Our affairs," the young French whippersnapper had said. Our affairs! If he insisted. It was fortunate that "our" affairs included supper. It was lavish, and it turned into a pleasant meal, too. The captain's batman, a Hungarian with a beard like Old Father Time, served it up.

Lamb chops. Risotto garnished with chicken livers. Artichokes with mayonnaise. Salad. Cheese. To wash it all down was a wine called Kébir. *Kebir*, the captain explained, was the Arabic for "great". The wine deserved its name.

The camp-bed had been set up in an empty officer's room. It was narrow, but that made no difference. The sergeant immediately fell into a deep sleep. When he woke up and looked at his watch, ticking on a chair beside his bed, it was five o'clock. He got up and went out of the room. The sky was an immense sheet of wild silk, very bright, with folds here and there; the folds were darker.

At first it seemed as if the fort was as quiet as the grave. The huts grouped round the one-storey tower, which was more or less in the middle of the fort, had no windows. Studer crossed the sandy yard in almost complete silence; he had put on his leather slippers with soft soles, which made his steps nearly inaudible. He tried to orientate himself. Yes, that must be where the way out was. He set off towards it. What he had in mind was to go out of the fort and have another look at the cork-oak, to check again that there really was nothing there.

There was the gate. A legionnaire was sitting on a kerbstone with his rifle, bayonet fixed, leaning against the wall beside him, his head in his hands – he was asleep. To the right of the entrance crouched a hut that didn't look at all like the other huts, even though it was actually built in the same way: whitewashed walls, corrugated iron roof. But in the first place it had two doors, made of massive beams, with heavy iron bolts. The ends of the bolts went into the wall. Then – and that was the really striking thing – that hut had windows. Two windows. And the windows were barred.

The sentry at the gate was asleep. Studer crept up to one of the windows. If he stood on tiptoe, he could see inside.

A cell, roughly six foot by four and a half. A cement block along one side formed a bed. A man was sitting on the block. It was dark in the cell and therefore a bit difficult to see what the man was doing. Studer leant forward, taking care not to cast a shadow in the cell with his head. He couldn't say why he felt it was so important the man didn't notice him, but he did. Now he could see clearly: the man had a pack of grubby cards in his hand. He shuffled them, put the pack down beside him, cut them, then began to lay them out in a row.

He laid out four rows, they were clearly visible, four rows of nine cards each. Then the man shook his head, gathered them up, shuffled them again, cut – with his left hand – and played a different solitary game.

191

He took three cards, picked one out and threw the other two away. He picked three more, looked at them and threw all three away. He took another three, kept one of those three and threw two on the pile of discards. He continued to do this until he had been through all the cards Then he took the discards, shuffled them, cut and started all over again. The cards he had picked out were laid down in an odd arrangement; it looked like a cross.

The sentry sitting by the gate was still asleep. But the fort was no longer silent. There was a distant sound of pans being bashed against each other. Invisible hands pulled the wild-silk curtain away from the sky. Now it was the blue of coloured glass.

The sergeant gave a start. A bugle, not five yards away from Studer, sent its morning song ringing round the fort ... Was it behind that corner? The sergeant crept over. Yes, there was a man in his light-green uniform, the mouth of his instrument aimed at a dull, tired sun, which was wearily inching its way up over the red mountains – and the man was blasting his morning song straight into the weary sun's face.

Then the wall of silence in the huts began to crumble: coughing, cursing, swearing ... Suddenly the air seemed permeated with the smell of coffee. Figures crept past carrying buckets filled with brown liquid. Their faces were covered in dust – covered in dust and thin. A few times the sergeant was unceremoniously shouldered aside, it was as if the coffee-bearers were blind. But Studer did not notice this jostling at all. There was an image he could not get out of his mind: a lonely man in a cell, laying out the cards for himself after what must surely have been a sleepless night on the cement block, in the cold, with no blankets; and now he was taking advantage of the first light of dawn to peep behind the curtain that hid the future from him.

The cards laid out in Basel, the cards laid out in Bern. What part did the clairvoyant corporal have in all this? Who was this Corporal Collani, who had deserted from Géryville on 28 September to rejoin his mounted company, fit and well, on 15 January in Gourama? Was this shadow, who was using the first pale light of a new day to lay out the cards . . . yes, who was the shadow in the cell? An absence without leave of three months would be punished in any army, it was called desertion. The clairvoyant corporal would, of course, be treated as a sick man. There was even a marvellous scientific name for the condition from which the corporal was suffering – suffering? Maybe. It was called amnesia. Even a simple sergeant was not without a certain amount of scientific knowledge.

Amnesia. Fine. But, as he had just established, the clairvoyant corporal was now locked up behind bars. How was it possible, then, for the said Collani, even if he was one and the same as Victor Alois Cleman, alias Koller, the murderer of Ulrike Neumann, to have gone out to the man-shaped rock by the cork-oak to dig up the buried treasure? How was it possible? The answer was simple.

The man had an accomplice.

But the next question was, how did the accomplice, together with his employer, intend to go about realizing the value of the hidden treasure? That is, to put it simply, to turn it into money?

On the one side was the geologist Cleman, whether he was the clairvoyant corporal or not, together with his accomplice . . . Right . . . And on the other were the Canton of Bern and Marie Cleman, represented by Detective Sergeant Jakob Studer. Two parties. All very neat and clear. But the equation didn't work out. To make it work out, there had to be an intermediary. An intermediary! Not a very good word. A third party, that was better, if only to demonstrate the old German proverb that when two people quarrel it's the third party that comes off best.

Who was this third party?

Studer had not noticed that he had already walked round the same hut seven times, often – very often – colliding with men who were not happy about it. Let them swear, swearing had never disturbed the sergeant when he was mulling over a problem.

On his eighth circuit he collided with someone who didn't swear, and that did rouse the sergeant from his ruminations. The someone was dressed in white, with a hairnet. The someone said, "Up so early, Cousin Jakob?"

Studer hated silly questions, so he growled an answer to the effect that if he was walking round on his two legs it was safe to assume he had got up. – Was that a way to address a lady? – Lady, lady? As far as he could see, there was no lady here, only a chit of a girl. And he would like to take the opportunity to point out once and for all that he was not called *Oncle Jacques*. That meant fool in French, and even if *he* sometimes thought he was a fool, he didn't need it confirmed by some slip of a girl . . .

With that the sergeant started to stalk off on the silent soles of his leather slippers, but Marie grasped his sleeve, saying she was sorry, she had only meant it as a joke. Everything had happened differently from the way she'd expected. She'd thought she wouldn't be able to get to Gourama until much later, and she'd expected to find her Uncle Matthias, the White Father, already here. But, with the way things were in this world, Father Matthias had only arrived last night. And very late, at around one o'clock in the morning. That was why she'd asked the captain not to wake Cousin Jakob —

Marie broke off, startled, as Studer grasped her by the upper arms and held them tight, staring her in the face. When, alarmed, she asked what was wrong, she found herself under a hail of questions, questions asked with such quiet urgency that she felt dizzy.

"Just think. Try to remember. How often did Father Matthias come to see your father?"

"Never. Never."

"Why?"

"Because Uncle Matthias had converted to Catholicism."

"That's not a reason."

"It's the only one I know."

"How old were you when the postman brought the registered letter?"

"Eight."

"You're sure?"

"Of course."

"When were you born?"

"In 1909."

"Sure?"

"Yes!"

Silence, if only briefly. In his mind's eye Studer could see the kitchen in Gerechtigkeitsgasse, could see the priest playing with his *sheshia*. He heard himself asking, "When did your brother get his divorce?" And the answer: "In 1908. He got married again the next year. Marie was born in 1910." In 1910! He didn't need Hedy's new ring binder, it was engraved on his mind. In 1910! And what had Marie said – and she really ought to know? Marie said: in 1909. A mistake on the part of the priest? A slip of the tongue. Not the kind of slip of the tongue one usually made.

"OK. In 1909. When was the first time you saw your uncle?"

"After Father's death."

"In the same year?"

"I think so."

"You're not sure?"

"No-o-o."

"Once? Twice? Several times?"

"Once a year."

"Regularly? Until very recently?"

"No. His visits stopped five years ago. But after that we still got letters."

"Did nothing strike your mother about the letters?"

"One thing. She once said you could tell Matthias was getting old, his handwriting was getting very shaky."

The entry in the register at the Hotel zum Wilden Mann wasn't shaky at all. Make a note of it, and move on to the next question . . .

"And you recognized your uncle, recognized him straight away when he came to see you in Paris?"

"I . . . I . . ."

"Out with it, girl."

"I . . . I didn't really recognize him. The Uncle Matthias I remembered was taller. And his face was a little different too . . ."

"Where did your mother keep the letters from your Uncle Matthias?"

"Together with her souvenirs of father."

Studer let go of Marie so suddenly she staggered a little. But then she stood up straight and stared at the sergeant in astonishment. The expression on his face had changed. You try to smile and whistle at the same time; the grimace you'll see in the mirror is the grimace Marie saw, and she started to laugh.

"Go on, laugh. In the police station in Bern they all say Köbu's got a screw loose. But what's all this with the captain? Are you engaged? Yes? And he likes you? A stupid question," said Studer, answering it himself. "Who wouldn't like you, Marie?"

Marie didn't blush, she didn't toy modestly with the corner of her apron, she didn't fiddle with her hairnet. She said, "If you like me, Cousin Jakob, and Louis likes me, what more do I need? The others?" She shrugged her shoulders. And Studer commented dryly that it was nice of her to mention him before her fiancé. Everything would turn out all right, there was no need to worry.

She wasn't worried, Marie said. At least not for herself. But wasn't Cousin Jakob taking a big risk? There he was, alone and in a foreign country. She'd heard something about buried treasure. Wouldn't it be better to forget about it? After all, if she married Louis, his pay would be enough for the two of them. And all that money? It did nothing but harm. It just made people bad, wicked.

Studer was only half listening. When she stopped he said caustically that if it were only a question of her, of Marie, he wouldn't lift a little finger. But there were interests of state at stake. Interests of state! he repeated, wagging his finger under Marie's nose.

Marie went off, but the sergeant stayed rooted to the same spot, his hands clasped behind his back, shaking his head. He shook it long and hard, like a horse plagued by flies.

It was scandalous. And it was scandalous to allow himself to be fooled like that. He did have an excuse. It was the first time he had had to wrestle with such an opponent. And it would have been no contest, if something unforeseeable, one of those imponderables – imponderables! The favourite word of a man from whom he had learnt much – had not happened. Something quite simple, really: the man who commanded the fort at Gourama had fallen in love with a girl . . .

The sergeant would have stayed standing on the same spot if he hadn't been roused by Lartigue's voice.

"What's going on, Inspector? Doing your morning exercises? You think your neck's getting too fat? Is that why you're waggling your head like that?"

Studer looked up – no he didn't look, he stared at the captain with the same empty look in his eyes he had had once before.

"One question, Captain," he said. "Might I ask, if it's not being indiscreet, where you first met Marie?"

"We met in Paris, when I was on leave. Do you know Bullier's?" Studer nodded. He knew the dance hall in the Montparnasse district. "We danced together there. Then in the following days we met several times, until my leave was over."

"OK. But how does Marie come to be in Gourama?"

"I got a telegram from her on 2 January," said Captain Lartigue, producing his wallet and taking out a piece of paper, which he handed to the sergeant. Apart from the address, it contained only four words: *Need five thousand Marie.*

"The little minx!" Studer muttered to himself. When Lartigue looked at him questioningly, he said out loud, "A great girl."

"Yes," Lartigue agreed drily. "And I wouldn't have minded being a fly on the wall when she spoke to the Director of Medical Services for Morocco in Fez. It's certainly true that I've requested a nurse several times, but the director has the rank of general and is a well-known misogynist . . ."

Studer laughed, a long, loud laugh, and slapped his thigh, so that the captain at his side gave him an astonished look. All at once the laugh broke off. Studer turned round and said in a voice the captain would never have believed him capable of, a voice dripping with politeness, like a slice of bread and butter too thickly spread with honey.

"You here, *mon père*? How are you? Have you seen your dear little niece already?"

"Ah, Inspector. Delighted to see you." With only a slight quiver of the straggly goatee. "You must forgive me for disappearing from Bern like that, but I paid my debts, no one was any the worse off for it. I knew I was needed here in Morocco . . . My flock was calling me, Inspector, all my lost sheep. Could I turn a deaf ear to their pleas?"

"But, my dear Father Matthias, who would have expected you to? Did I not make it clear that we in Switzerland have always endeavoured to —"

That was all Studer managed to say. Father Matthias interrupted him with a wave of the hand.

"As I said, I am delighted to find you here. It means we can join forces in enlightening the captain about the role an unfortunate man has played in this affair, a man who joined the Legion to escape punishment. But the Legion is duty bound to hand over *murderers*, is it not, Captain Lartigue?"

It was a triumph for the Swiss sergeant to see the man who had welcomed him with a challenge to a boxing match suddenly unsure of himself.

"A murderer? In my company?" he asked.

Tears welled up in Father Matthias's eyes. "Unfortunately," he said. "Unfortunately that is so. I am sure the reason, the sole reason the Swiss inspector undertook this arduous journey was to shorten the extradition proceedings a little, perhaps even to take the murderer back with him as soon as permission from the ministry in Paris arrives. Is that not correct?"

A sorrowful expression appeared on Studer's face. He nodded.

Captain Lartigue, however, insisted: "But I thought, Inspector, you had come to —"

The rest of what he had to say was drowned in a violent fit of coughing that seemed to be tearing the sergeant's lungs apart. It went on and on, despite the helpful slaps on the back. Eventually he managed to gasp, "You – must – have – some – cough – medi – cine – in your – dispen – sary – Cap – tain."

"But of course, Inspector. Come along with me."

They left a rather surprised Father Matthias standing in the yard. Still coughing, Studer glanced back. The sergeant envied the priest. He still had a beard and moustache, essential for keeping calm in the face of a crisis.

In the sickbay Studer swiftly swallowed the pill the captain had given him. Then he said, speaking quietly and quickly, "Don't say anything about the temperature chart to the priest. Nor about the buried treasure." Studer cast a suspicious look out of the little window, which had a fine wire-mesh covering, and saw Father Matthias hurrying over. In a couple of seconds he would be in the room.

"Yesterday you were talking about a court-martial you could call. Good idea. Do it now, this afternoon, accuse me of spying . . ."

Outside the priest was held up by a man. Studer did not know the man, but he was grateful to him and mentally promised him a bottle of wine.

"Listen, Captain. Come closer." Studer whispered urgently in Lartigue's ear. At first the captain looked astonished, then he nodded, nodded vigorously – the door was flung open and Father Matthias came in.

The sergeant continued to play his part to perfection. He held his breath, forcing the air down into his lungs until he went bright red, then gasped for breath.

"I know an excellent remedy for a chronic cough like that," said Father Matthias. "I remember you having a similarly violent fit in Bern. You must do something about it, Inspector. What did you prescribe for him, Captain?"

"I gave him a Dower's powder," the captain growled, pretending to be in a bad mood. "But now I have things to do. Reports to hear, you know. Lunch is at half eleven in the officers' mess. You're both invited."

With a brief flap of the hand at his kepi, Lartigue went out. Hardly had he left the sickroom than the sergeant, too, felt the need for fresh air.

"*Au revoir, mon père,*" he said. He could feel the priest's eyes on his hunched back and the feeling was just as uncomfortable as when Sergeant Beugnot had been following him . . .

The arrest

It was just the same as the previous day. The company gathered in the barracks square. The huts seemed to enjoy being able to take a rest for once from the noise that was usually raging inside them. They stretched themselves lazily in the sun, which was high in the sky. It beat down on them like a July sun in Switzerland. At least there was something to give you the feeling you were in Africa . . .

Studer went through the empty huts. Either side of a central aisle were rows of mattresses, thin and filled with esparto grass. There was a strong smell of cold tobacco smoke and dirty washing. One hut, two huts . . . There was the kitchen. It smelt of lentils and mutton stew.

Then, unchallenged, he was standing again by the hut that was different from the rest. There was the barred window. Studer stood up on tiptoe . . .

It was light in the hut and the man sitting on the cement block could be clearly seen. So that was the clairvoyant corporal, whose story he had heard right at the start of this tangled case. A broken man, his hair was grey, his features pinched.

Giovanni Collani or Victor Alois Cleman?

Soon, soon he would know for certain.

And once more, as on the previous day, the sergeant gave a start as close by a bugle brayed – "rang out" would not have been the right expression for that sound. Studer looked back into the cell and saw that the man had a pack of cards in his hand again. He shuffled them, cut – with his left hand – took three cards, discarded two, took three more, picked out one . . . With a jolt Studer dropped back onto his heels and quietly slipped away. He went out through the gate. The wide plain was spread out in front of him. To his right it sloped down and there were some trees there. Not palm trees, their leaves had a silvery sheen.

Someone nudged him in the ribs. Again the sergeant gave a start. But it was only the captain's gazelle wanting to play. Studer stroked its tiny head; the animal's muzzle was moist and cool. Why am I so jumpy? he asked himself. I'm not usually. Why now? Because I'm out on my own? Because there's no one I can really trust?

For a moment he thought of leaving the fort without saying goodbye. Let those in there see how they managed to sort things out themselves. He'd done what he could. After all, he wasn't obliged to go round the world on forged passports, assuming the most ridiculous names, just to secure a few million for his home canton. Would they be grateful? Pull the other one! It was the Old Man who would take all the credit. He'd be praised for having recognized the importance of the case and taken the required measures.

Taken the required measures! But that was it. A sergeant just carried out orders. Even if he did everything himself a hundred times over, he remained a subordinate officer carrying out orders. He'd done his duty, that was all. For 600 francs a month – and expenses were checked down to the very last *rappen*. Watch out if you'd put in for too much! Watch out if you could have done it more cheaply and hadn't! It had once happened that Studer had not been paid for his ticket on the Basel–Bern express. "The stopping train would have done just as well," he'd been told. There was that nice series of little books called *No Struggle, No Victory*. It was all right for the authors, they only had to struggle at their desks. And now he had to have lunch in the officers' mess. And afterwards . . .

Captain Lartigue introduced the officers present: Lieutenant Mauriot, Lieutenant Verdier. Marie sat between the captain and Father Matthias, and Inspector Joseph Fouché, as he had been introduced, was placed between the two lieutenants.

The mess was a long room in the same hut where Studer had slept. The soup was eaten in silence. Then there was olives and schnapps. A whole lamb, garnished with peppers and tomatoes, was brought in on a huge platter by the captain's batman. Then the Hungarian with the beard like Old Father Time filled the glasses. Captain Lartigue stood up and proposed a toast to the nurse, whose very presence, he said, was a tonic for the men. They all stood up, there was a soft clink of glasses . . . and the clink was drowned by the stamp of approaching footsteps. A curt order. The door was flung open. A corporal entered, followed by four men. The five men approached, the only sound heavy breathing. Suddenly two shots rang out, there was a scuffle, the table was overturned, three men were rolling round on the floor . . .

Father Matthias had scuttled into a corner and stood there, his face hidden in his hands. Then Marie's voice was heard: "Louis . . . Give me a cigarette."

The three who were thrashing about on the floor stood up. "Take him away," Lartigue commanded.

And Sergeant Studer, his hands tied behind his back, was hustled out of the door. Lieutenant Mauriot bent down and picked up two revolvers. "A dangerous man," he said.

"Indeed," replied Captain Lartigue, flicking his lighter to light Marie's cigarette. "I thought the surprise would work best during lunch, but the man was on his guard. A good thing I chose our best men. No one hurt? You weren't, were you, *mon père?*"

"No! No!" came a voice from the corner.

"You see, I was right, wasn't I, Uncle Matthias?" said Marie when the priest was sitting beside her again. "I always told you you shouldn't trust the man. He's a spy, he's got a forged passport."

"I . . ." the priest replied, "I . . . noticed when the man was first introduced to me. But I didn't like to say anything. I don't like interfering in other people's affairs."

"A good thing I warned Louis. But now you'll sort him out once and for all, won't you, Louis? A court-martial, then the firing squad. I'll be a witness. Uncle Matthias too."

"Yes. Mauriot, you can act as clerk. And we'll have the adjutant, Cattaneo, Sergeant Schützendorf and two corporals . . ."

The trial

The man didn't speak. He sat on the cement block that served as a bed, and shifted over a little towards the rear wall, inviting Studer to sit down with a wave of the hand. Then he had a closer look at the sergeant, pursed his lips, whistled, spat on the floor and said, "A civilian! What are you doing here?"

Studer shrugged his shoulders. The man's French was good, but you could still tell he was a foreigner.

"Where're you from?" Studer asked in Swiss German.

The man raised his eyebrows. His answer was brief: "Bern."

"Me too."

"Aha, you too . . ." Silence. There was a gap between the two heavy planks forming the door through which the sun streamed into the cell. The motes of dust danced in the light. The barred window, however, was in the shadow of the projecting corrugated-iron roof.

The man took a pack of cards out of the side pocket of his uniform jacket and began to lay them out on the small strip of cement between himself and the wall.

"What's that you're doing?"

"Laying out the cards. But I keep getting bad cards. I keep getting the jack of spades."

"Just like in Basel and Bern," Studer remarked casually.

The man showed no surprise. He just nodded, as if in a dream.

"Precisely," he murmured. That was when it had started, he said.

What did the jack of spades signify, then? Death?

The man shook his head wearily. "Death? Rubbish. I'm the jack of spades."

He picked up the cards and shuffled them again. It made a strange noise in the silence of the cell. Then he asked if his new friend could keep his mouth shut.

"Definitely," Studer replied. He was sitting on the cement block in his favourite posture, forearms on his thighs, hands clasped, staring at the ground.

The slap of the cards being laid out, then silence, then the slap of the cards. A few words. Silence. The slap of more cards being laid out ... A few words. Silence. Studer did not look up, even though sitting still like this was agonizing. There was an old man sitting beside him, a man who was in torment. It was immensely difficult to stop himself getting up, putting his hand on the man's shoulder and saying, "You're a poor soul. They've given you a hard time of it, waking you up from your sixteen-year sleep. You'd forgotten, and they forced you to relive the past, just so a big oil company can open up new wells. And now? Will they leave you in peace? No. They'll keep on tormenting you. It's better if I play the dentist and get it over in one go, it'll be less painful."

"Will you lay out the cards for me?" Studer asked.

"Of course," the man said. So far he had had his back to the sergeant, now he turned round. A face covered in wrinkles. The priest's description of him, in the little bistro by Les Halles, hadn't been bad at all. The kind of face you sometimes saw on crippled children, sad and old. Stubble round his chin, a few bristles over his upper lip ... And beneath the care-worn features could be discerned – blurred, like a photograph where the light has got in – another face: the face, an enlarged likeness of which had hung above the bed of Sophie Hornuss in the apartment in Gerechtigkeitsgasse . . .

And the man shuffled the cards. The sounds of the fort coming through the gap between the two planks that made the door were strangely thin, frayed, so to speak: the clatter of mules' hoofs – Studer's thoughts went to his Fridu, with whom he'd had such profound philosophical conversations on the road from Géryville to Bouk-Toub; the crunch of nailed boots on hard ground – Studer saw the White Father lying on the couch in his apartment in Bern and his open sandals with soles that curved up at the front, and he heard his wife saying, "You can see they've been a few miles, can't you, *Vatti*?" From the distance came the sound of gunfire – the company was probably out on patrol – and Studer thought how it was sometimes much more difficult deliberately to miss a target than to shoot someone . . . The shots in the officers' mess had been intended as a ruse, but it hadn't been easy, when the moment came, to fire in the air, when there was someone he would have loved to shoot . . .

Suddenly Studer was startled out of his dreams. The man had spoken! His Swiss German sounded so strangely outmoded, his manner of speaking so child-like, that the sergeant felt like saying, "There, there. Have a rest. If you did commit a crime thirty years ago, you've paid for it, paid dearly for it."

"The nine of clubs," the old man muttered, stroking his stubble with the backs of his fingers. It made an unpleasant rasping noise. "The nine of clubs – money, a lot of money. And the ace of clubs. Money again, even more money. There, the king of diamonds, that's you, and the queen of diamonds is your wife. There's a letter on its way. The letter will get lost. But you will soon see your wife again. She comes immediately after you – in the pack. Cut. The queen of spades, the queen of clubs and the nine of spades. Two women have died. It concerns you in some way, the deaths of the two old women . . . But look, there's money again, the eight of clubs. Luck, a lot of luck. You've got good cards. But I always get bad cards. The jack of spades always comes for me, and the ten of spades next to it. That means death . . ." The old man's hand passed over the cards and they were gathered up in a pack again. He held the cards in his left hand and flicked across the edges with his thumb and middle finger.

"You look clever," the man said in his monotonous voice. "I'll tell you a story. You're not the only one who likes to hear me telling them what the cards say. I used to be married, you know. The first time Sophie kept on asking me, 'Vicki' – she always called me Vicki – 'lay out the cards for me.' Eventually I did because the woman kept going on at me about it. And that was a mistake. You see, when I lay out the cards, I have to tell the truth, that's the way I am. So I told Sophie the story, the story that happened in Fribourg. You see, the girl from Fribourg kept appearing in the cards . . . I can't really remember now exactly what happened all those years ago . . . I was in love, we met, in Bern, in a hotel. We wanted to get married and I kept telling her, 'Ulrike,' I said, 'you'll have to wait. I'm only a student.' 'I don't want to wait,' she said. She was always getting worked up. I was studying chemistry. She was always asking me about poisons. What strong poisons there were. 'Potassium cyanide,' I told her. Could I get her some? At first I didn't want to. But then I let her talk me into it . . ."

Three cards taken off the top of the pack, two

discarded, one laid out. Another three cards, two discarded . . . The monotonous slap of the cards on the cement in the tiny cell!

"Look, there she is again, the girl from Fribourg. The queen of spades . . . and the jack of spades next to her. That's me. We can't get away from each other. We always come out of the pack together. Inseparable . . . And I told Sophie all that. I have to tell you, as well . . . When I lay out the cards, I have to tell the truth. What's your name?"

"Jakob," said Studer succinctly.

"Jakob? Is that so? Strange . . . Like my brother . . . Do you know where my brother is?"

"Yes," said Studer.

A look of immense astonishment spread over the old man's face.

"You know where Jakob is?"

"Yes," Studer repeated.

"How do you know?"

"I know."

The old man shuffled the cards again. There was a smile playing round his lips that presumably no one would have understood. Studer understood it.

Was it really so difficult to understand when one had seen the telegram Captain Lartigue had received from Marie? It had been sent from Bel-Abbès. Why would Marie have needed 5,000 francs in Bel-Abbès? . . . You wouldn't get far with half of the 250-francs pay Despine, alias Jakob Koller, had pocketed. She was a brave girl, was Marie. She'd made proper preparations . . .

"You told Sophie the whole story about Ulrike, didn't you?" Studer said. "And you had to give her money to keep her quiet? Even though you hadn't . . ."

"That's right, Jakob," the old man said. "Ulrike,

that's what she was called, I remember now. And you're right, I didn't kill her. She was a bit crazy, that Ulrike. Once she had the potassium cyanide she left, by the first train . . . To Fribourg. I was worried. I followed her . . . But I was too late. No one saw me go into the house. She was lying on her bed and there was a glass on the bedside table. I picked it up, smelt it . . . Then I knew . . ."

"Show me your thumb."

Pity old Herr Rosenzweig wasn't there, he'd have been pleased to make the acquaintance of the thumb that had produced a unique print.

The door opened. A corporal – he had two tiny stripes on his sleeve – bellowed, "You two – the captain wants you."

The old man stood up. He was small, shorter than the priest. Beside Studer he looked like a dwarf.

The pair were escorted by four men with fixed bayonets, one in front, one behind, one either side. The corporal led the procession. Studer's hands were not bound.

When the old man came out of the cell, he blinked like an owl, dazzled by the harsh afternoon light.

Space had been made in one of the huts. The thin mattresses were piled up outside the door. At the back of the room five men were sitting: Captain Lartigue in the middle, the adjutant on his right, a sergeant on his left; next to the sergeant was a corporal, and little Lieutenant Mauriot was at the end on the right, sitting at a small table with blank sheets of paper in front of him.

It was dark in the room, so that it was some time before Studer noticed Marie, in an armchair next to the captain. And, huddled in a corner, Father Matthias was sitting on a mattress, cross-legged, his hands in the sleeves of his habit.

Studer and the old man had to stand.

The captain opened the proceedings. Turning to the four members of the court-martial, he explained that the man before them had been travelling on a forged passport, posing as a French police inspector. He turned to Studer and demanded the papers from him. Studer made no fuss, but handed over the passport of Inspector Joseph Fouché. It went to each member of the court in turn. There was much shaking of heads.

What did he have to say in his defence? the captain wanted to know.

"A lot," was the sergeant's brief reply.

"Then tell us."

So Studer began. Oddly enough, he began with a question. Turning to the old man beside him, he asked, pointing at the White Father, "Do you know that man there?"

The old man stroked his cheeks, then asked shyly whether it was permitted for him to look at the man from closer to? His request was granted by Captain Lartigue.

So the old man went over to the priest and looked at him for a long time. The priest returned his steady gaze. The old man said, "I know him from Géryville. He took my confession."

"You don't know him from earlier on?" Studer asked.

The old man shook his head.

"Listen," Studer said in friendly tones, "you can tell us the truth now. What is your real name?"

"I've had lots of names. First I was called Koller, then I called myself Cleman. I was rich then. Finally I got bored with being rich, so I bought some papers off a man and enlisted in the Legion as Giovanni Collani. But originally I was called Koller. Victor Alois Koller. That's my real name."

"Right. Now listen," said Studer, "the man before you claims to be your brother, says his name is Max Koller . . ."

The old man shook his head, a long, emphatic shake of the head.

"It's true Max became a papist," he said. "Our parents never forgave him. But that's not Max. I made confession to him in Géryville . . . though that's not quite right, either. He asked me questions and I told him about laying out the cards and how I have to tell the truth when I lay out the cards – what I told you just now, Jakob. Then I had to lay out the cards for him. It was at the beginning of September last year. By then I'd already sent off the letter to Josepha. Fifteen years after my death. I wanted to show Josepha my gratitude and after fifteen years Sophie, the old witch in Bern, couldn't do anything about it. That's what I told this man here. I don't know what he did, but one evening my brother Jakob suddenly appeared and forced me to go with him. I was to get the temperature chart from Josepha, the chart that showed where the treasure was buried —"

Studer interrupted him. "Just a minute," he said. "I would like this gentleman's luggage to be searched." And the sergeant pointed at Father Matthias.

The priest leapt up. He protested long and loud, his voice cracked, sometimes it sounded as if he were about to burst into tears. Studer cast aside politeness.

"You've tried to pull the wool over our eyes often enough with your tears," he snapped. "I demand that your luggage be searched."

Calmly the captain gave the order.

Two suitcases were brought into the hut. Captain Lartigue demanded the keys. Reluctantly the priest handed them over. One suitcase contained vestments and other articles for celebrating mass. In the other, underneath a habit and various items of underwear, an iron box was found. It was rusty. The captain opened it and emptied the contents out on to the table.

Documents, documents . . . Some had seals dangling from them. Others were written in a strange script. The captain picked up one of the latter.

"Deeds of sale," he said as he read through it. "Purchases of land . . . Certified by the Arab Office . . . Definitely valid in law. Sold to a certain Victor Alois Cleman."

"That's me," said the old man. "And I've bequeathed the land to my daughter, Marie, who has my second surname, and to my home canton of Bern . . . Yes . . . He was trying to steal it!" The old man pointed his finger at Father Matthias.

The White Father stepped forward.

"This land," he said, "was purchased with stolen money. The Minister of War has given our order the task of finding the papers. The mission was entrusted to me because I already knew something about the case. Max Koller, who entered our order as a young man, was my friend. He told me a lot. That was why I was given permission to use his papers. I had to find the temperature chart. The genuine one, since this man here," Father Matthias pointed at the old man, "had told me the original chart also contained his will. The one he gave to me was a copy. A copy of the chart without the will."

"Silence!" Studer thundered, as if he, the accused, had suddenly become the prosecutor. "It was not stolen money. The Mannesmann brothers gave the money to their geologist, Cleman." He turned to the old man. "Was it you who betrayed them?"

214

The man who had had so many names shook his head. "They betrayed themselves," he said.

"And I presume the two women killed themselves?" Father Matthias asked maliciously. "And you're not a murderer, Collani?"

Everything happened so quickly, no one had time to intervene. Studer was the only one who had perhaps expected something of the kind, but he didn't lift a finger until it was all over.

The old man, who looked so feeble, had snatched the rifle out of the hand of the legionnaire beside him – a rifle that had a bayonet fixed to the end of the barrel. And one had to admit that the old man remembered what he had learnt in bayonet practice very well. The gun, with just his right hand grasping the butt, shot forward – and back. The blackish iron was covered in a thin film of blood and Father Matthias was lying on the floor. A red stain on the front of his habit slowly grew bigger and bigger.

"Now I *am* a murderer," said the old man. "Now you can do what you like with me."

But Captain Lartigue just shrugged his shoulders. "It's probably the best solution," he said.

And the four members of the court, who had remained as immobile as he had, nodded. Only Marie, in her armchair, was holding her clasped hands in front of her face.

The old man seemed to be waiting for something. Since no one touched him, however, he went – with short, uncertain steps, a real old man's walk – over to the girl. Very gently he placed a hand on her clenched hands.

"You know I didn't kill your mother, Marie?" he said.

Marie's answer was quiet. "I've known that for a long time, Father. You told me before. When we were in the

215

car, driving to Bern with your brother. It wasn't your fault Mother was so afraid of gas . . ."

Studer was standing all by himself in the middle of the room. Not far away was the body of the priest on the floor. In his mind's eye the sergeant could see his apartment in Bern, could see the little man with the goatee lying on the couch, just as motionless as he was now, with a cup of limeflower tea beside him, the tea Hedy had made.

It hadn't been the "Big Case" after all, Studer thought. He'd got it wrong again. It was the cards that were to blame. You shouldn't try to tell the future from the cards. There were lots of things you shouldn't do, he thought. Like pushing yourself forward, for example, trying to play a leading role, to get a fortune back for a girl, to secure millions for your canton . . .

The man who had had all the different names was sitting on the arm of the chair, leaning against Marie's shoulder. He was bent forward, whispering to himself, but the silence in the spacious hut was so profound, every word was audible.

"You know, Marie, I wanted to celebrate New Year with your mother. She asked me to stay up with her until she fell asleep. I held her hand. Then she wanted me to lay out the cards for her. And the jack of spades was the first card to come out. Then we made ourselves a coffee – and she wanted her sedative. I gave it to her. She said she didn't want to go to bed, she wanted to sleep in her armchair and I was to hold her hand until she was asleep. Then I was to turn off the gas at the mains. But to do that I'd have had to get up on a chair. So she said I could tie a string round the lever and take it out through the keyhole. Then all I'd need to do was to pull it and it would shut off the gas. And I wouldn't wake her up.

216

"I'm not used to gas. I tried out the taps – did I forget to shut one off? Outside, on the landing, I pulled the string – and Josepha died. I didn't know . . ."

Silence. The old man was hunched up on the arm of the chair.

"Your mother was so looking forward to seeing you, Marie. Why didn't you come? And Jakob wanted me to get the temperature chart. I looked for it, but I couldn't find it. Your mother wasn't expecting me. She already had her outdoor shoes on, she was going to see the New Year in with a friend. And then I arrived. She laughed and told me she'd lost her keys that very day . . . She wanted to show me all the souvenirs she'd kept, but the drawer was locked. I forced it open . . ."

Studer nodded, kept on nodding. He'd thought he had uncovered a fiendishly cunning murder – and it had all been down to chance. A chance the priest had exploited. Guilty! If you were trying to apportion blame, then it was the priest alone who was to blame, the priest who had put on an act from beginning to end. But wasn't it irresponsible of him to have been taken in by an act like that? A double murder suited the priest perfectly. If the police think there's been a double murder, then they look for a murderer. A cunning ploy to draw suspicion on to yourself when you know very well you've got an alibi. How the man must have laughed at the "Inspector" as he insisted on calling him!

"Do you know, Captain," Studer said, "Marie's aunt, the aunt who lived in Bern, knew that the man she'd divorced wasn't dead? Her sister in Basel wrote to her about the temperature chart." He turned to the old man. "That's right, isn't it?"

The old man nodded. Then he said, "Jakob, my

brother, wanted me to go and see Sophie. He wanted to get the temperature chart . . ."

The old man stood up and came to stand beside Studer, facing the seated officers.

"Gentlemen of the court, I have to answer for what I have done. It is the man I killed who is to blame. He started everything off again. He told my brother in Paris about it. They wanted to find the treasure and that man, the priest, promised my brother half. There's a lot of oil round here and soon, very soon, it's going to be worth a lot. The man lying there went to see the Minister of War, he told me so himself. He wanted to destroy my will, that's why he roused me from my fifteen-year sleep . . . With the cards! He wouldn't leave me in peace in Géryville, he told people I was a clairvoyant . . . You must excuse me, gentlemen, I'm getting everything mixed up. But I'm an old man and I've had a hard life. All I wanted was for my daughter and the land of my birth to inherit my wealth. For myself, I just wanted to sleep on. He started everything up again. He went to see Sophie and told her I was still alive. And he forced Jakob, my brother Jakob, to drive me to Bern. Sophie threatened me, she said she would tell the police everything, have me arrested. But she also cried. I wanted to talk to her, persuade her . . . Sophie was afraid of the gas, too. I remembered how I did it in Basel with the lever on the gas mains and the string. I dragged her armchair into the kitchen and made some coffee. I still had the bottle with Josepha's sedative and I poured some in her coffee – a lot. She didn't notice it because I poured some kirsch in as well. And then – as a joke, I said it was a joke – I climbed up on a chair and tied the string to the lever, just as in Basel. And I killed Sophie. She was an evil woman. She took everything I had. She didn't want

218

Josepha to have anything. She wanted to give me away. Gentlemen, *mon capitaine,* I haven't got much longer to live. I know that you love Marie . . . and you too, Jakob," he turned to Studer, "you're a better Jakob than my brother . . . Both of you make sure Marie gets what is hers by right, and the land of my birth, too. That is all I have to say."

For a long time it was quiet in the room. Then Marie stood up, went over to her father and led him back to the chair she had been sitting in. "Sit down, Father," she said in German. The old man sat down and leant back.

"Inspector Studère," the captain asked, "why did I have to arrest you, anyway?"

"Two reasons. First, the priest would have realized I was suspicious of him and fled, or at least hidden the strongbox. The second is that I wanted to be able to talk to the old man in the cell undisturbed."

"Yes," said the captain, "that makes sense. But you must admit you were fortunate. If I hadn't been engaged to Marie . . ."

"Then I'd have had a hard time of it," said Studer. "But sometimes you have to count on imponderables."

"Imponderables!" the captain exclaimed. "Just listen to him, talking like a professor."

But Marie went to the sergeant. "Thank you, Cousin Jakob," she said.

The little lieutenant, who was still sitting there with his blank sheets of paper, asked, "What shall I write in the report?"

"Whatever you like," said Captain Lartigue. "How about: the priest arrived at the fort seriously wounded and died here. Everyone agreed?"

The four members of the court-martial, the corporal of the guard and his four men all nodded silently.

"Where is he to be buried?" the corporal of the guard asked.

"He's dug his own grave," Sergeant Studer said. "Under the cork-oak. You know, by the red rock that looks like a man."

The captain nodded.

Studer and Lartigue were walking up and down in the space between the huts. The sun was low in the sky and the cold wind from the mountains reminded the two men that it was still winter.

"There's one thing I'd like to know," the captain said. "Where's Marie's uncle? The stockbroker she worked for as a secretary in Paris?"

"I don't know," Studer replied. "All I can do is guess. You should ask your future wife. Didn't you tell me Marie sent a telegram from Bel-Abbès asking for money? The journey from Bel-Abbès to Gourama can't have cost 5,000 francs, even with a detour via Fez."

They turned round and went back into the hut where the remarkable proceedings had taken place. The members of the court-martial had left. The old man was still sitting in the chair and Marie was on the arm, leaning against her father.

"Marie," the captain asked, "where is your uncle?"

"Your question, *chéri*, sounds like that other, weightier one: 'Where is Abel thy brother?' You mustn't be so suspicious, Louis.

"You sent me money at Bel-Abbès. I'd run into Jakob Koller there – but please, I beg you, never call him my uncle again. You know yourself, Cousin Jakob, that Father Matthias left Bern in a hurry. After that we heard nothing more from him. He had the copy of the temperature chart, that was enough for him for the moment. But Jakob Koller was furious because he knew he wasn't going to get any of all that money now. He enlisted in Lyon. I stayed with my father. I stayed with him until we reached Colomb-Béchar, where I took him to the camp commandant, who was to send him on to Gourama. I'd arranged to meet you there too, Cousin Jakob. The three of us would manage to unmask the false priest, I thought —"

"False priest! What kind of a way is that to speak!" said Captain Lartigue reproachfully.

"I'll speak as I see fit," came Marie's rejoinder.

This is not going to be a particularly harmonious marriage to start off with, Studer thought, but with time they'll smooth down each other's rough edges. Perhaps they'll even be a happy couple? Out loud he said, "Let the girl have her say, Lartigue."

"If you insist, Studère. I'd just like to point out that I was making only a minor criticism. My future wife shouldn't talk like a character out of some trashy novel. False priest indeed!" he muttered.

"Do you mean to say," said Marie in irritation, "that he was a true priest? He was a false priest."

"Yes, he was a false priest and a false person," said the old geologist in his bleating voice.

"Of course, Father. You're right and so is she." Lartigue had adopted a conciliatory tone.

He's already calling the old man Father and using the familiar *tu* to him, Studer thought. A remarkable man. No wonder he gets poor marks at the War Ministry. But still . . . he's . . . he's a man.

Marie went on:

"I ran into him in the street in Bel-Abbès when I got back from Colomb-Béchar. I've never known what fear is, you know, but when I saw Jakob Koller, suddenly I did . . . And, anyway, he'd been good to me, he took me with him to Paris when I couldn't stand it with Mother any longer. That's why I felt obliged to help him. I asked him what I could do for him. We were in a little Arab café and I hardly recognized him. His hair had been cropped short, he was nothing but skin and bones, his uniform hung loose – and his eyes! They were darting to and fro ... When I was a child I once saw a hare in a furrow during the hunting season and its eyes were flickering hither and thither just as fearfully as Jakob Koller's.

"He said, 'Give me some money, Marie. So I can get away.' Perhaps it was wrong of me, but I just felt disgusted by him. Still, I said, 'Jakob Koller, you've got a lot on your conscience, but I will help you. How much do you need?' – 'Ten thousand francs.' At that I laughed and told him he'd get 4,000, not a centime more. I arranged to meet him in the café the following day at the same time and give him the money. Then I sent you the telegram, Louis. The next evening he deserted. I got him some civilian clothes as well. Where he's gone off to, I don't know, but I don't think we've anything to fear from him now. I told him I would give you the whole story, Cousin Jakob. After all that he was decent enough to warn me about the false priest. Yes, the false priest," she repeated, looking at her fiancé with a belligerent expression.

"Yes, Marie, the false priest," Lartigue repeated in a gentle voice. He was at the table, starting to gather together the documents that were lying around on it. "I've put in a request for leave today. I imagine we'll be able to set off for Switzerland in a week's time. And once we're there, we can try to turn these papers" – he tapped the documents – "into money."

For a long time no one spoke.

"What about Father?"

"We'll take him with us. Do you think in Switzerland
. . . I mean . . . I wouldn't want . . ."

Studer interrupted his stammering. "I imagine
they'll put him," he whispered to the man who was fort
commandant, doctor, vet, livestock dealer, military
strategist and boxer all in one but could still be shy
and awkward, "I imagine they'll put him in a hospital."

Lartigue nodded. And Studer went on. "I don't sup-
pose you could find a pair of Moroccan mountain
sheepdogs for me, could you?"

"Moroccan . . . mountain . . . sheepdogs?" the captain
looked at the sergeant as if he was beginning to doubt
his sanity.

"Don't they exist?"

"Not . . . no . . . Not so far as I know."

"Then we'll just have to take your Scotch terrier
back for the Old Man."

"The old man? Which old man?"

"Who do you think? Our chief of police, of course,"
said Studer.

After their evening meal the two men were sitting on
the balcony of the tower.

"Don't you think the story's going to come out some
time or other?" Studer asked. "And your part in it?"

Lartigue giggled softly. Then – Studer could hardly
believe his eyes – he stretched out his hands, palms
upwards, raised his arms, his hands turned over and
fell with a slap onto his thighs. The right hand came
up, clenched in a fist, with just the index finger pointing up, straight, alone. The finger touched his lips and
pointed upwards. And Studer could understand the
mumbled words:

"Why concern yourself with what is to come, my

brother? You would only despair if you tried to conceive what the future will bring. What are past, present and future to Him, the Eternally Silent? To Him to whom eternity belongs?"

A small detachment of men was slowly crossing the flat ground between the fort and the *ksar*; the dull thump of drums reached them. Father Matthias, the "false priest" as Marie had called him, was being carried to his final resting place.

A quiet voice could be heard from the room: "Don't think I want to be a burden on you, Marie. You mustn't think that."

"Of course not, Father."

"Come on," the captain's voice was hoarse, "let's go and accompany him down there" – he pointed at the procession on the ground – "to the cork-oak. After all, he didn't want the money for himself."

Studer was happy with that. He claimed he was freezing and asked the captain for a coat. He was given a thick, pale green greatcoat lined with white linen. The lapels bore the emblem of the Foreign Legion: the red grenade with flames flaring up out of it. Putting on the uniform gave Studer great satisfaction. For once before he died he could wear the uniform he had dreamt of so often in Bern when life had seemed pointless . . .

THE MANNEQUIN MAN

Luca Di Fulvio

Shortlisted for the European Crime Writing Prize

"Di Fulvio exposes souls with the skills of a surgeon, It's like turning the pages of something forbidden – seduction, elegant and dangerous." *Alan Rickman*

"Know why she's smiling?" he asked, pointing a small torch at the corpse. "Fish hooks. Two fish hooks at the corners of her mouth, a bit of nylon, pull it round the back of the head and tie a knot. Pretty straightforward, right?" Amaldi noticed the metallic glint at the corners of the taut mouth.

Inspector Amaldi has enough problems. A city choked by a pestilent rubbish strike, a beautiful student harassed by a telephone stalker, a colleague dying of cancer and the mysterious disappearance of arson files concerning the city's orphanage. Then the bodies begin to appear.

This novel of violence and decay, with its vividly portrayed characters, takes place over a few oppressive weeks in an unnamed Italian city that strongly evokes Genoa . . .

The Italian press refers to Di Fulvio as a grittier, Italian Thomas Harris, and *Eyes of Crystal*, the film of the novel was launched at the 2004 Venice Film Festival.

" A novel that caresses and kisses in order to violate the reader with greater ease." *Rolling Stone*

"A wonderful first novel that will seduce the fans of deranged murderers in the style of Hannibal Lecter. And beautifully written to boot." *RTL*

£9.99/$14.95
Crime paperback original, ISBN: 1–904738–13–3
www.bitterlemonpress.com

SOMEONE ELSE

Tonino Benacquista

"A high-wire act that plays hide and seek with appearances. Benacquista is an extraordinary novelist. A book to be celebrated." *Le Point*

Who hasn't wanted to become "someone else"? The person you've always wanted to be . . . the person who won't give up half way to your dreams and desires?

One evening two men who have just met at a Paris tennis club make a bet: they give each other exactly three years to radically alter their lives. Thierry, a picture framer with a steady clientele, has always wanted to be a private investigator. Nicolas is a shy, teetotal executive trying not to fall off the corporate ladder. But becoming someone else is not without risk; at the very least, the risk of finding yourself.

"The author keeps up a breathless pace, touching effortlessly on identity, love, alcohol, old age, the cynicism of the business world, friendship. A wonderful novel that would make a wonderful film." *Les Echoes*

Winner of the RTL-LIRE Prize.

£9.99/$14.95
Crime paperback original, ISBN 1–904738–12–5
www.bitterlemonpress.com

ANGELINA'S CHILDREN

Alice Ferney

"A beautiful, haunting novel that takes the reader into the heart of a community frequently seen only as problematic. Within the gypsy encampment, life is physically hard, and Ferney writes unsentimentally about the getting and nurturing of children and the hostility of and to outsiders. Yet *Angelina's Children* **is a profoundly moving, life-affirming story which outclasses any of those 'Baguettes in Bordeaux' holiday reads so often marketed as true to French life."**
Glasgow Herald

"Few gypsies want to be seen as poor, although many are. Such was the case with old Angelina's sons, who possessed nothing other than their caravan and their gypsy blood. But it was young blood that coursed through their veins, a dark and vital flow that attracted women and fathered numberless children. And, like their mother, who had known the era of horses and caravans, they spat upon the very thought that they might be pitied."

So begins the story of a matriarch and her tribe, ostracized by society and exiled to the outskirts of the city. Esther, a young librarian from the town, comes to the camp to introduce the children to books and stories. She gradually gains their confidence and accompanies them, as observer and participant, through an eventful and tragic year.

Alice Ferney's distinctive style powerfully involves the reader in the family's disasters, its comic moments and its battles against an uncomprehending, hostile world; in the love lives of the five boys, the bravery of the children, and, eventually, in Angelina's final gesture of defiance.

"A wonderful portrait of a woman both imperial and bruised, a greying ravaged mother-wolf that still controls all those around her. A novel of rhythm and grace, a beautiful voyage with the gypsies." *Le Monde*

"A beautifully feminine and fertile book . . . Ferney's prose at its most powerful." *Le Figaro*

**WINNER OF THE LITERARY PRIZE
CULTURE ET BIBLIOTHEQUES POUR TOUS**

£8.99/$13.95
Paperback original, ISBN 1–904738–10–9
www.bitterlemonpress.com

INVOLUNTARY WITNESS

Gianrico Carofiglio

"*Involuntary Witness* raises the standard for crime fiction. Carofiglio's deft touch has given us a story that is both literary and gritty – and one that speeds along like the best legal thrillers. His insights into human nature – good and bad – are breathtaking." *Jeffery Deaver*

A nine-year-old boy is found murdered at the bottom of a well near a popular beach resort in southern Italy. In what looks like a hopeless case for Guido Guerrieri, counsel for the defence, a Senegalese peddler is accused of the crime. Faced with small-town racism fuelled by the recent immigration from Africa, Guido attempts to exploit the esoteric workings of the Italian courts.

More than a perfectly paced legal thriller, this relentless suspense novel transcends the genre. A powerful attack on racism, and a fascinating insight into the Italian judicial process, it is also an affectionate portrait of a deeply humane hero.

Gianrico Carofiglio is an anti-Mafia judge in Bari, a port on the coast of Puglia. He has been involved with trials concerning corruption, organized crime and the traffic in human beings.

"A powerfully redemptive novel beautifully translated from the Italian." *Daily Mail*

"I enjoyed every moment of the book. Bitter Lemon Press have yet another winner on their hands." *Eurocrime*

"A new template for our literature, the mechanics and suspense of the American court procedural made profoundly Italian by its characters, its atmosphere, emotions and concerns." *La Stampa*

A best-seller and a major TV series in Italy, *Involuntary Witness* has won a number of prizes, including the Marisa Rusconi, Rhegium Julii and Fortunato Seminara awards.

£8.99/$13.95
Crime paperback original, ISBN 1–904738–07–9
www.bitterlemonpress.com

HAVANA RED

Leonardo Padura

Winner of the celebrated Café de Gijon Prize, the Novela Negra Prize and the Hammett Prize.

"A scorching novel from a star of Cuban fiction. Lt Conde's quest follows the basic rhythm of the whodunit, but Padura syncopates it with brilliant literary riffs on Cuban sex, society, religion, even food." *Independent*

On August 6th, the day on which the Catholic Church celebrates the Feast of Transfiguration, the body of a strangled transvestite is discovered in the undergrowth of the Havana Woods. He is wearing a beautiful red evening dress and the red ribbon with which he was asphyxiated is still round his neck. To the consternation of Mario Conde, in charge of the investigation, the victim turns out to be Alexis Arayán, the son of a highly respected diplomat. His investigation begins with a visit to the home of the "disgraced" dramatist Alberto Marqués, with whom the murdered youth was living. Marqués, a man of letters and a former giant of the Cuban theatre, helps Conde solve the crime. In the baking heat of the Havana summer, Conde also unveils a dark, turbulent world of Cubans who live without dreaming of exile, grappling with food shortages and wounds from the Angolan war.

Leonardo Padura was born in 1955 in Havana and lives in Cuba. He is a novelist, essayist, journalist and scriptwriter. *Havana Red* has been published in Cuba, Mexico, Spain, Portugal, Italy, Germany and France, and is the first of the Havana quartet featuring Lieutenant Mario Conde, a tropical Marlowe, to be published in English.

"So many enchanting memories, sultry Cuban nights and music in this novel that you let the author take you by the hand, impatient to find out what comes next." *Lire*

"Nothing is what it seems in this case, which has less to do with crime than with the struggle for identity in a corrupt society where outsiders are exiled in their own country.
Daily Mail

£8.99/$13.95
Crime paperback original, ISBN 1–904738–09–5
www.bitterlemonpress.com

IN MATTO'S REALM

Friedrich Glauser

"**Glauser's second novel involving the dour Sergeant Studer, a Swiss Maigret albeit with a strong sense of the absurd. Studer investigates the death of an asylum director following the escape of a child murderer. A despairing plot about the reality of madness and life, leavened at regular intervals with strong doses of bittersweet irony. The idiosyncratic investigation and its laconic detective have not aged one iota. Who said the past never changes.**" *Guardian*

"**Glauser was among the best European crime writers of the inter-war years. This dark mystery set in a lunatic asylum follows a labyrinthine plot where the edges between reality and fantasy are blurred. The detail, place and sinister characters are so intelligently sculpted that the sense of foreboding is palpable.**" *Glasgow Herald*

A child murderer escapes from an insane asylum in Bern. The stakes get higher when Sergeant Studer discovers the director's body, neck broken, in the boiler room of the madhouse. The intuitive Studer is drawn into the workings of an institution that darkly mirrors the world outside. Even he cannot escape the pull of the no-man's-land between reason and madness where Matto, the spirit of insanity, reigns.

Translated into four languages, *In Matto's Realm* was originally published in 1936. This European crime classic, now available for the first time in English, is the second in the Sergeant Studer series from Bitter Lemon Press.

Friedrich Glauser was born in Vienna in 1896. Often referred to as the Swiss Simenon, he died, aged forty-two, a few days before he was due to be married. Diagnosed a schizophrenic, addicted to morphine and opium, he spent the greater part of his life in psychiatric wards, insane asylums and prison. His Sergeant Studer novels have ensured his place as a cult figure in Europe.

"***In Matto's Realm*, written in 1936 when psychoanalysis was a novelty to the layman and forensic science barely recognized, makes gripping reading as Studer questions both staff and patients and tries to make sense of the inscrutable Deputy Director's behaviour.**" *Sunday Telegraph*

£8.99/$13.95
Crime paperback original, ISBN 1–904738–06–0
www.bitterlemonpress.com

BLACK ICE

Hans Werner Kettenbach

"A beautifully translated thriller, not a drop of blood on its pages. The nastiness takes place off-stage which makes it all the more threatening." *BBC 2 "Culture"*

"A natural story teller who, just like Patricia Highsmith, is interested in teasing out the catastrophes that result from the banal coincidences of daily life." *Weltwoche*

Erika, an attractive local heiress, is married to Wallmann, a man with expensive tastes. When she falls to her death near their lakeside villa, the police conclude it was a tragic accident. Scholten, a long-time employee of Erika's, isn't so sure. He knows a thing or two about the true state of her marriage and suspects an almost perfect crime. Scholten's maverick investigation into the odd, inexplicable details of the death scene soon buys him a ticket for a most dangerous ride.

This beautifully crafted thriller set in a European world of small-town hypocrisy was made into a film in 1998. It is written by an essayist, scriptwriter and best-selling novelist whose work is now available in English for the first time.

"*Black Ice* isn't just a class crime novel. It is one of the most beautifully told stories of our years, in which humorous *noir* dialogue and poetry flourish side by side." *Stern*

£8.99/$13.95
Crime paperback original, ISBN 1–904738–08–7
www.bitterlemonpress.com

GOAT SONG

Chantal Pelletier

Winner of the Grand Prix du Roman Noir de Cognac

"More than an intriguing mystery. It reveals a picture of contemporary Paris unseen by tourists, with two fascinating central characters." *The Sunday Telegraph*

The naked bodies of a star male dancer and a beautiful young girl have been found entwined together, murdered in a dressing room of the Moulin Rouge. A junkie is killed in a nearby flat, his throat chewed open, the teeth-marks human. Seemingly unconnected, these deaths form part of a sinister pattern involving crack dealers and addicts, wild sex parties and shady property deals.

In charge of both investigations is Maurice Laice. Depressed by what is happening to his beloved Montmartre and exhausted by the emptiness of his love life, Maurice is plagued by a female boss who bombards him with tales of her sexual exploits. Yet they make a good team, each obsessed for different reasons by the crime at hand. Together, they start to uncover a twisted trail of fear and broken dreams, greed and revenge that reaches from Corsica and Algeria into the very heart of old Paris.

Chantal Pelletier, born in Lyon, began her career as an actor. She founded a theatre company in Paris and is the author of novels, essays, plays and film scripts. It is not unusual to find her engaged simultaneously as author, director and actor in the same project.

"Chantal Pelletier is a wonderful story teller; she captures your heart in three short sentences, and takes you through the gamut of emotions, from laughter to tears. A master of funny, bittersweet dialogue. A classic *roman noir* hero, the world weary inspector, is completely reinvented." *Le Monde*

£8.99/$13.95
Crime paperback original, ISBN 1–904738–03–6
www.bitterlemonpress.com

THE SNOWMAN

Jörg Fauser

"A gritty and slyly funny story. About the life of the underdog, the petty criminal, the fixer, the prostitute and the junkie. With a healthy dose of wit." *Cath Staincliffe, author of the* Sal Kilkenny *series*

"German author Jörg Fauser was the Kafka of crime writing." *Independent*

Blum's found five pounds of top-quality Peruvian cocaine in a suitcase. His adventure started in Malta, where he was trying to sell porn magazines, the latest in a string of dodgy deals that never seem to come off. A left-luggage ticket from the Munich train station leads him to the cocaine. Now his problems begin in earnest. Pursued by the police and drug traffickers, the luckless Blum falls prey to the frenzied paranoia of the cocaine addict and dealer. His desperate and clumsy search for a buyer takes him from Munich to Frankfurt, and finally to Ostend. This is a fast-paced thriller written with acerbic humour, a hardboiled evocation of drug-fuelled existence and a penetrating observation of those at the edge of German society.

"Jörg Fauser was a fascinating train wreck: a fiercely intelligent literary critic who also wrote the occasional nudie-magazine filler; a junkie who got clean in his thirties only to become an alcoholic; a tragic figure who died mysteriously at 43 in a 1987 Autobahn accident. Oh, and along the way he managed to crank out one of the most indelible crime novels in Greman history. Fauser writes with a gimlet eye and a black, acerbic (so, German) wit, creating an unflinchingly brilliant tale of a perspective – the outsider among outsiders – he knew all too well." *Ruminator*

£8.99/$13.95
Crime paperback original, ISBN 1–904738–05–2
www.bitterlemonpress.com

THE RUSSIAN PASSENGER

Günter Ohnemus

"A recommended summer thriller. High-octane odyssey across the new Europe and eventually the United States. All the makings of a new genre – the Russian mafia road movie."
The Times

"Much to enjoy in this sharp pacy *roman noir*. Packs an emotional punch rare in a thriller." *Independent*

At fifty the good Buddhist takes to the road, leaving all his belongings behind. His sole possession is a begging bowl. That's fine. That's how it should be. The problem was, there were four million dollars in my begging bowl and the mafia were after me. It was their money. They wanted it back, and they also wanted the girl, the woman who was with me: Sonia Kovalevskaya.

So begins the story of Harry Willemer, a taxi driver and his passenger, an ex-KGB agent and wife of a Russian Mafioso. In an atmosphere of intense paranoia *The Russian Passenger* follows their flight from the hit-men sent to recover the cash. This is not only a multifaceted thriller about murder, big money and love, but also a powerful evocation of the cruel history that binds Russia and Germany.

Günter Ohnemus, born in 1946, lives in Munich and writes novels, essays and translations. He has written three collections of short stories and a best-seller for teenagers. This is his first novel to be translated into English.

"A road adventure that reads like a movie, ... an alternately dark and sunny journey of redemption, with German cabbie and Russian passenger earnestly trying to resolve their nationalist prejudices and absolve their collective guilt – in colorful settings of course."
New York Times

£9.99/$14.95
Crime paperback original, ISBN 1–904738–02–8
www.bitterlemonpress.com

TEQUILA BLUE

Rolo Diez

"Like a Peckinpah movie: violent, funny, sad, as hot as salsa, as tasty as tacos and twice as enjoyable."
Independent on Sunday

It's not easy being a cop in Mexico City.

Meet Carlos Hernandez, Carlito to his women. He's a police detective with a complicated life. A wife, a mistress, children by both and a paycheck that never seems to arrive. This being Mexico, he resorts to money laundering and arms dealing to finance his police activity. The money for justice must be found somewhere.

The corpse in the hotel room is that of a gringo with a weakness for blue movies. Carlito's maverick investigation leads him into a labyrinth of gang wars, murdered prostitutes and corrupt politicians. A savagely funny, sexy crime adventure that is a biting satire of life in Mexico.

Rolo Diez, born in Argentina in 1940, was imprisoned for two years during the military dictatorship and forced into exile. He now lives in Mexico City, where he works as a novelist, screenwriter and journalist.

Both a scathing an picaresque comedy, a biting and spicy concoction. Just like tequila." *Le Monde*

£8.99/$13.95
Crime paperback original, ISBN 1–904738–04–4
www.bitterlemonpress.com

HOLY SMOKE

Tonino Benacquista

"An iconoclastic chronicle of small-time crooks and desperate capers, with added Gallic and Italian flair. Wonderful fun." *Guardian*

"This prizewinning novel is guaranteed to keep you up late at night, driven to discover the ending. It's exciting, funny and bizarrely even includes tips on cooking Italian food; it makes you glad they decided to translate the novel into English."
Coventry Evening Telegraph

Some favours simply cannot be refused. Tonio agrees to write a love letter for Dario, a low-rent Paris gigolo. When Dario is murdered, a single bullet to the head, Tonio finds his friend has left him a small vineyard somewhere east of Naples. The wine is undrinkable but an elaborate scam has been set up. The smell of easy money attracts the unwanted attentions of the Mafia and the Vatican, and the unbridled hatred of the locals. Mafiosi aren't choir boys, and monsignors can be very much like Mafiosi. A darkly comic, iconoclastic tale told by an author of great verve and humour.

Tonino Benacquista, born in France of Italian immigrants, dropped out of film studies to finance his writing career. After being, in turn, a museum night-watchman, a train guard on the Paris–Rome line and a professional parasite on the Paris cocktail circuit, he is now a highly successful author of fiction and film scripts.

"An entertainingly cynical story. I read it in one sitting."
Observer

"Much to enjoy in the clash of cultures and superstitions, in a stand-off between the Mafia and the Vatican. And a tasty recipe for poisoning your friends with pasta. Detail like this places European crime writing on a par with its American counterpart." *Belfast Telegraph*

£8.99/$13.95
Crime paperback original, ISBN 1–904738–01–X
www.bitterlemonpress.com